I quickly looked at Jack and Gillian, but Jack was looking at the car. He ran trembling fingers over the trim.

Gillian stood apart, keeping well away from the grime, and I could see the shock on her face, her eyes wide, mouth open as if to scream. She saw the ghost, but Jack didn't.

"Do you know what this is?" His voice wavered slightly.

"A gho—car?" I ventured.

"A Packard Roadster." His voice broke. "Look at the running boards. The wooden dash." He rubbed dust off the fender. "Gorgeous gold."

"I take it that's a good thing," I said faintly.

The beautiful ghost shifted her pose, putting her face mere inches from his.

Gillian's hysterical laugh was shaky, but it was better than having her scream. She couldn't take her eyes off the ghost. "Oh, you've done it now, Cass. We'll be lucky to get any work out of him around the house." The hand she held up to her mouth shook.

"We can get this running again," he whispered with reverence, buffing the hood with his shirtsleeve.

The ghost leaned toward him with a smile on her face. She turned toward me and stage-whispered, "Oh, I like him! Abyssinia!" Then she was gone.

The instant she vanished, Gillian let out a burp of a scream, quickly smothered.

Jack turned, stared at us, and stopped babbling. "What are you girls looking at?"

Gillian and I exchanged a glance.

"N-nothing," I said. He hadn't seen her!

Praise for Rena Leith

"Take a haunted cottage on a foggy coast, add a town populated by eccentrics, mix in a flapper-era ghost with plenty of moxie, and you have the first of what I hope will be a long, long series."

Murder Beach

by

Rena Leith

Murder Beach

COPYRIGHT © 2017 by Rena Leith

Cover Art by *Debbie Taylor*

The Wild Rose Press, Inc.
PO Box 708
Adams Basin, NY 14410-0708
Visit us at www.thewildrosepress.com

Publishing History
First Fantasy Rose Edition, 2017
Print ISBN 978-1-5092-1338-2
Digital ISBN 978-1-5092-1339-9

Published in the United States of America

Dedication

For Jason, Amy, Mia, and Luke

Chapter 1

Ghosts can murder property values.

Buying a house on the Northern California coast had seemed like a good investment, but that was before I knew about the ghost. Post-divorce, I'd been determined to hang onto the house in upscale Pleasanton, just 25 miles east of Oakland in the San Francisco Bay Area. Financial reality had other plans. In the end, I threw my life's possessions into a storage unit and stayed with a friend temporarily while Phil's girlfriend moved into my house and my bedroom. At the last moment, I decided not to take "vengeance" possessions, such as Phil's signed first editions or his Van Briggle vase collection. Well, maybe just a few things I could sell for ready cash. No point in paying exorbitant California storage unit payments for things I didn't really want just to cause Phil a little pain.

Contrary to popular opinion, not everyone who gets divorced in California makes out well. At first, realtors laughed at me and my budget, but finally Clarissa, a newbie agent, took pity on me. She followed her training and tried very hard to sell me properties that would require a second mortgage with a balloon payment of hundreds of thousands of dollars due in five years. It's a common practice in the inflated California real estate market that often traps buyers who later find they can't refinance for better terms.

After the third place in San Mateo, I stopped and refused to get into her ancient Camry. "Clarissa, dear, please believe me when I say that I have no idea where my next penny is coming from. The balloon payment could be in five, ten, fifteen, or a hundred years, and I still couldn't pay it."

"But you can remortgage before then!" She smiled brightly and opened my car door, giving me a little shove.

I resisted the shove. "No, I can't. I have a finite amount of money, and I'm prepared to throw all of it—cash—at the right property. That means that it is totally pointless to show me anything that costs more than the cash amount I have in the bank. I won't qualify for that mortgage you want me to get because I don't have a job."

That made her hesitate, but she gave it one more try. "But think of your resale."

"I'm not planning to resell."

"You want the best neighborhood you can afford."

"The operative word being 'afford.'"

She sighed heavily. "But—"

"Is this where we part company?"

Her shoulders slumped. "Well… There are a few places…"

I can't tell you how many crappy condos I looked at on the San Francisco peninsula and all the way south nearly to Gilroy with Clarissa saying things like: "The neighborhood isn't really *that* bad."

Finally, we hit the coast where I discovered something called a land lease. Always in good locations, the "structures" built on the land could usually be knocked over by one good sneeze. Often they were functional one-bedroom workshops where metalworking hippies had built their own houses on land owned by someone else.

At first, that's what I assumed about the little blue bungalow with navy and burgundy trim that was beginning to flake as though it had dandruff. The price was more in line with a land lease where you own the structure but not the land—a bit like living in a lone trailer.

Clarissa was hesitant to show me the place even though it was right on the beach. "I don't know, Cass." Her expression was pained. "It's listed 'as is'. That's never a good sign."

I waved her off.

"It means there's something wrong, Cass."

She hurried to keep up with me as I strode up to the door. "You have to take the whole thing, contents and all. The sale can't be reversed. It's a cash only deal."

I laughed. "Haven't I said all along that all I want is to pay the place off all at once with cash?"

"Just promise me you'll be cautious." Clarissa's famous last words.

But when I saw the place, caution was the last thing on my mind, and I totally lost interest in reading the fine print. The beach sat practically outside my back door—a matter of yards and a gentle slope away. I was already thinking about it as mine as I walked around the outside, checking out the shack at the back of the lot, the overgrown garden, and the trees, including a Meyer lemon tree, brimming with sweet fruit. The vegetable garden was seriously overgrown, but the raised beds were still there. The flowers and weeds had all gone wild. Ivy of some sort grew up the chimney. I hoped the chimney wouldn't require too much repair. A fire on the chilly nights on the coast would be lovely. On those nights when wood burning was still allowed, I reminded myself. The porch ran along the front of the cottage that faced the street. Although the cottage didn't face the ocean, I pictured myself sitting in the repaired porch swing, sipping lemonade made from my tree's fruit, and watching the glorious California sunsets.

Once I'd seen it, I had to have that cottage. I was in agony waiting for Phil to buy me out of my half of the Pleasanton place. With Phil's buyout money and my savings, I barely had enough to get the cottage by the sea. I was elated when my offer was accepted!

I was so concerned that I'd lose the cottage to someone with more money to bid, that I overlooked how long it had been on the market. Only later did I find out the rationale behind the sale not being reversible. Several prior sales had been reversed. Only after the deal was signed, sealed, and delivered did one of my new neighbors tell me the story.

The day after I got the keys, I went to my cottage—my cottage!—and took a longer, more leisurely look. There was a bottle of champagne on the stoop with a note from Clarissa: *Good luck!* I laughed with joy and tucked it into the fridge. I'd turned the electricity, the water, and the Internet on and bought a leaf antenna to hook up to my TiVo. I had the vague thought that I might stay the night instead of waiting for my brother Jack and his wife Gillian to arrive to help me clean and move in tomorrow. However, as I walked from room to room, I became aware that I'd seriously underestimated the accumulated grime and detritus.

I went back out to my Subaru, left the suitcase, but

carried the box of cleaning supplies from the trunk into the kitchen, set them on the trestle table, and got to work. The cobwebs had to go first.

I'd finished a first pass at the kitchen and started on the living room when I heard the weird buzz of the doorbell. I added getting a new doorbell to my 'to do' list, got up, and went to see who was at the door.

The slender pallid woman on the stoop carried a foil-covered plate and navy blue cloth bag. Her long lilac and gray dress swirled around her ankles.

My stomach growled. I didn't care what was under the foil. I was hungry. "Hi." I smiled, opened the door and, taking the foiled plate as a cue, invited her in.

The nervous woman stepped across the threshold. "Hello, I'm your neighbor Wilhelmina Weber. I live two houses over toward town." She gestured vaguely in that general direction.

"Pleased to meet you. Your timing is great! I just cleaned up the kitchen." I took the plate, led her into the kitchen, and set it on the table. "Sorry, but I've only started cleaning. At least this room is clear. I'm Cass." I held out my hand. "Cass Sander—Cass Peake."

She shook it. "Call me Mina."

"I'm glad to meet you, Mina. I'm new to the coast. I'm moving…I've moved here from Pleasanton, so it's nice to know someone local and nearby." I pulled out a chair for her.

"Pleasanton. That's over the hill in the East Bay." She set the navy bag on the table and pulled out a thermos and two cups. "I'd love some tea to go with my cookies, wouldn't you?" She sat down and looked around.

She was right: tea would hit the spot. She still

5

seemed nervous to me, twitchy even, but I put it down to the dirt and mess. I took the foil off the plate to reveal homemade Linzer cookies. My mouth watering, I exerted all my willpower to wait for her to pour the tea before grabbing a cookie. "I'm so sorry everything is such a mess. My brother and sister-in-law will be here tomorrow to help me get my things out of storage and finish cleaning the place up."

"So you haven't spent the night here yet?" Mina's eyes kept darting into the corners of the room as if she were looking for something, but her hands were steady as she poured steaming tea from the thermos. The fragrant scent of jasmine wafted upwards.

I took the cup from her, sat down, and picked up one delicate cookie. It was dusted with powdered sugar and with a circle of what smelled like strawberry jam peeking out of the hole in the top half. Yum. "No. I was thinking about staying tonight. If I do, it will be the first night."

I took a bite before I noticed that she was focusing on something through the archway in the dim corner of the living room. I turned to follow her gaze and could have sworn that I saw someone. I frowned, but when I focused, there was nothing there but a tattered curtain.

Her voice broke. "P-perhaps you should wait for your relatives. We have some lovely B&Bs here in Las Lunas."

"That's not a bad idea. It's pretty dirty and messy in here. I doubt that I'll get to cleaning the bedrooms by tonight." I also wondered at the wisdom of sleeping in an unfamiliar house by myself. Who knew what pests might be sharing the place with me? My thoughts went to the beds and the couch that had been absorbing dust for years. All the cushions and mattresses would have to be aired and examined. I'd rather sleep in my own bed, which would mean moving furniture and getting into my storage unit. In my excitement, I hadn't thought this through. "Do you know why the former owners didn't remove their belongings?" I popped the rest of the cookie into my mouth.

"No one really knows." She pulled her tea bag from the cup and put it into the small bowl I'd set out for it. Then she knitted her fingers together. "This place, well, it has sort of a r-r-reputation."

I didn't like that stutter. A shiver went down my back. "Reputation? What kind of reputation?"

Mina twisted an opal and gold ring around her finger. "Well, I don't like to gossip, but," she looked around as if someone might overhear, "they say your house is haunted."

"Haunted? By whom or what?" Although I didn't believe her, that B&B was looking better all the time. Besides, a nice hot bath tonight and a hearty breakfast in the morning held a lot of appeal.

"Well…" She leaned forward conspiratorially, her hands fluttering. "I should tell you that I'm a writer. I write ghost stories. You can buy my books at Dreams and Dust in town. So I have a particular interest in your house and in the group of women mystery writers who used to meet here in the Sixties."

I looked around for my spiral notebook, located it and my favorite wood-turned ballpoint pen, and jotted a note to myself to find Dreams and Dust tomorrow and get copies of her books. "Mystery writers? That doesn't sound supernatural."

"It's what they used to do here."

My eyebrows rose. All sorts of images of wild bawdiness raced through my head, and I doodled freeform. Doodling was one of those habits I'd picked up in high school social studies, the most boring class in the world. Once I started drawing my thoughts, I'd never been able to put the habit back down.

"As I recall the story, they used to rent your house as a kind of clubhouse from Francie Macalin, one of their members. She was the daughter of Shelagh Macalin, a writer of macabre ghost stories published in magazines in the Twenties and Thirties." Mina's voice dropped to a whisper, and she leaned forward as if she might be overheard. "I have several copies of magazines containing her stories. She was a bit bizarre even for the times. She reveled in her notoriety. They all had keys, all the writers, and one night they held a séance to conjure up Shelagh's ghost as a kind of a muse for their group." She paused for breath and a sip of tea.

A new owner really does not want to hear that the former owners conjured up anything in a house she just paid every dime she had in the world for. "Uh, sounds like fun although I'm not into those sorts of parlor games. And the critical bit, did they succeed?" I drew a key.

Mina winced. "In a way. The séance went a bit awry, and instead of the muse they wanted, another ghost moved in. A bootlegger's daughter. She was a flapper, by all accounts." Then Mina glanced around nervously and said to the air, "I'm sorry. I didn't mean any disrespect."

I followed her darting gaze. "What, you think she's still here?" I scribbled a classic sheet ghost with holes for eyes.

She nodded. "Of course her ghost is still here. Don't you feel her?"

I stopped doodling. "The bootlegger's daughter? Seriously?"

Mina smiled wanly. "Sorry to tell you, but everyone hereabouts knows you have a ghost."

"Great. Today is move-in day." No return, no refund. I've never really believed in ghosts, but I've always used the stories to my advantage. When Jack and I were kids, I used to make up stories about the body buried in our basement and the ghost who hung out down there, earning the ire of my mother because he refused to ever go back into the cellar to help with the laundry.

But now I realized that the house that had seemed so bright and cheery during the day was gathering creepy shadows as the sun dropped lower toward the horizon and cast long shadows in the house.

Mina seemed to have spooked herself. She stood up, walked through the archway into the living room, and with a few more furtive glances into the shadowed corners, prepared to leave.

I stood as well and followed her out. "Thanks for coming by."

Mina stepped out onto the stoop and said cryptically, "Be careful. Women never seem to get their due." A small smile flickered over her face as she bid me adieu and left quickly.

I closed the door behind her and returned to the kitchen to put the foil back on the cookies. "That was strange," I said out loud. Although the electricity was on, the lights flickered ominously, and I knew I'd have to get an electrician in quickly to upgrade my service as well as replace the doorbell. I decided to put the cookies into the fridge just in case there were vermin in residence.

As I closed the fridge door and turned, I saw her, reflected in a silvering mirror. She sat on the arm of the couch. Bobbed hair. Cloche hat. Rayon stockings rolled to her knees.

I turned quickly.

Nothing.

I looked back at the mirror and saw the distorted image of a woman. I tilted my head and realized that it was the reflection of a sepia-toned, framed photo hanging over the couch. The glass was rounded like half a bubble, which gave the picture some dimensionality that I must have mistaken for a physical woman. The words "or a ghost" echoed in my head. My neighbor was getting to me.

"It's time to call it a day," I said to no one in particular. I turned off the lights, made sure that the windows and doors were closed, and headed for my car. I hadn't lived alone in a very long time.

For thirteen years I'd depended on Phil for my sense of safety and wellbeing. I guess I was more shaken than I thought by the prospect of being entirely responsible for myself. I was experiencing new feelings: independence, fear, but also joy and lightness at not being answerable to another person. But I needed to get a grip.

In retrospect, I'm surprised I made it out of there without serious injury. I normally don't believe in ghosts by the light of day, but it was getting on to twilight. I kept telling myself that I hadn't seen anything but an illusion; however, I found myself hurrying to get to the car. I dropped my keys, stepped on my own hand picking them up, but finally got into my car. I locked the door and didn't hit anything as I tore off down the road on instinct until I found the B&B at the end of the road.

Moon Coast Inn. Light streamed from welcoming windows as I pulled into the lot next to the inn. By the time I got there, I'd worked myself up. I must have looked like a madwoman, disheveled and wild-eyed, as I charged through the front door.

A round button of a woman with sea-blue eyes and a bubble of white hair looked up from a computer screen. "Hi."

I opened my mouth, but nothing came out because I felt like a complete idiot. I had allowed an atmospheric tale told by a master storyteller to spook me, and I'd run away like a child. So much for having control of my primal brain. "Uh. Hi."

I looked around at the completely normal, well-lit surroundings. The parlor was decorated in sandy beiges and browns, grassy greens, and watery blues. Perfect for the inn's location just off the beach. Warm, indirect lighting illuminated nature photographs and woven wall hangings in sunset colors.

"May I help you?" She smiled and gave me her full attention.

"This is really nice."

"Thank you. Are you in need of help or a room?"

"Oh, um, a room." I hadn't checked for a vacancy sign. "Do you have any available?"

This time she laughed, and it was a lovely, tinkling sound.

I couldn't help but smile back at her.

"Do you have luggage?"

I remembered my suitcase. "Actually, yes, I do."

She pursed her lips slightly but not unkindly. "Very good. We have two rooms available. The Iris room, which is large with a private bathroom, and the Audubon, which has a lovely whirlpool tub."

Her unspoken words echoed in my head: *which you appear to need.*

She cocked her head. "The Audubon also has a balcony with a lovely view of the ocean, but it's on the second floor."

"I'll take it!"

Again, the laugh. "As we're not full, we have a special running. One night, $125."

"Really?" I couldn't believe it given that this was high season. I'd expected a price that started with a two at the very least.

"It's mid-week, and we're slow. Usually, the price is higher, and there's a two-night mid-week or three-night weekend requirement, but as I said, we're slow right now and I'd rather rent the room."

"Thank you so much."

She pushed a card and a pen across the table toward me. "Would you please fill this out? Do you want to use a credit card? Cash?"

I picked up the pen, filled out the card, and then pulled a Visa out of my pocket and handed it to her.

She ran it and returned it to me. Picking up the card I'd just filled out, she read, "Cassandra Peake."

"Call me Cass."

"Cass. Nice to have you staying with us." She held out her hand. "I'm Natalie Sandoval. Do you need help with your luggage?"

"Oh, no, it's just one suitcase."

She nodded. "Here's the key to your room and one to the front door. Room's at the top of the stairs. The door is labeled. This time of year there're two breakfast seatings: one at 7 and one at 8:30 am. Follow me."

Natalie led me through to a dining room with half a dozen tables and a fireplace. "Although there are only two rooms available, there are four of you here tonight. Two other rooms are undergoing some renovation to be ready for Labor Day when I have a full house." She walked back out to the base of the stairs. "There's a small refrigerator in your room that contains some complimentary bottled water. There's a one-cup coffee maker in the dining room. It makes coffee, tea, hot apple cider, or hot chocolate. I can show you how to use it if you've never used one before. There's an ice machine, and there are also packets of shortbread. Is there anything else you need?"

"I can't think of a thing. I'll, uh…" I pointed over my shoulder. "Just go get my bag."

"I'll see you in the morning." She turned back to her computer.

When I came back in, Natalie wasn't there, so I went up to my room, which smelled of lilacs. I set the suitcase on the luggage rack and walked out onto the balcony. It was freezing, but the view of the ocean was spectacular with the full moon glistening off the waves. I shivered and went back inside to draw a bath and have a good, long soak. I was already feeling foolish. I should have realized that the cottage was filthy and unfit for human habitation and thought ahead to booking a room. Jack and Gillian would arrive before noon, and I could go home.

Home. That sounded so nice.

I slept like a tired child, completely secure and safe. The susurration of the waves had lulled me to sleep quickly. I awoke hungry and a little blurry but rested. As I stretched, I felt as though I belonged here in this room. It was so familiar as though this were the room I grew up in. Rolling over, I started to go back to sleep as a delicious drowsiness settled over me. Then I remembered what the day held and shook off my happy lethargy.

It was a moment's effort to pack and head down to breakfast. Over frittata and fruit, I realized that by the light of day I didn't believe in ghosts. Night might prove to be something else, but I symbolically dusted my hands off as I stood up to go.

Natalie appeared next to me. "Would you like your receipt sent to your phone or an email address or do you prefer paper?"

"Phone's fine. Let's save a tree."

She smiled and nodded. "I'll send you a coupon for 10% off on your second visit."

"I'm hoping to have my house ready to go today."

She patted me on the shoulder. "I know, dear. But I'm familiar with that cottage, and I suspect that it has, well, issues that you haven't thought about yet."

"Thank you." I think. "I appreciate the thought, and I'll keep it in mind. But if you mean the ghost, I've already been warned."

She nodded. "Yes, I imagine you have. This is a very small town."

I wanted to ask her what she meant, but I bit my tongue. I owned that cottage, and although I might be behaving like an ostrich, I couldn't change my mind and there was only so much that I was strong enough to know right now. "This is a lovely B&B."

I carried my suitcase out to the car.

She followed me out. "You come back anytime. We'll have coffee on the veranda, and I'll be happy to tell you what I know about your cottage."

I drove home at a much slower pace, thinking about what she'd implied. I would want to know the history of my cottage eventually, but today I had to focus on getting the place sufficiently cleaned up for Jack and Gillian. I could only deal with so much at one time, and I was still processing the radical turn my life had taken.

On the way home, I stopped off for groceries and a case of bottled water—just in case. I added a mental note to my 'to do' list to test my own water.

When I pulled into the driveway, Jack's car wasn't there yet. Although he hadn't called and I really hadn't expected them to arrive yet, I balked at going back inside alone. Echoes of last night. I shook it off and propped the outside door open as I carried things inside. Then I left it propped open as I began cleaning. Given that we all would have to eat and sit to rest, I kept working on the kitchen to get it as clean as possible. I'd only hit the surface yesterday.

I threw open the windows and the back door that led out onto the beach and let the cross-ventilation air the whole place out. I briefly considered that I was letting bugs in, but then it occurred to me that perhaps some of the small inhabitants of the cottage might take this opportunity to find a new place to live.

Soon the joy of discovery diverted my attention

from squeamish concerns to the thrill of finding half a dozen beautiful china cups with matching saucers and four cut glass goblets. I set them aside for careful hand washing and made a note on my growing list to talk to the plumber about a dishwasher and garbage disposal unit.

Eager to see what other treasures the kitchen might hold, I put the stepladder in the pantry and climbed up to see what was on the top shelves. The single bulb cast a pale orange glow. Note to self: contact electrician today and buy light bulbs. I switched on my flashlight and swept it over the cans, jars, and crockery. Most of the cans and jars would have to go.

The crash from the living room scared the bejeezus out of me. I spun on the top of the stepladder, lost my footing, dropped the flashlight, and fell against the shelving, some of which accompanied me down to the floor where I landed unceremoniously on top of the case of bottled water.

Footsteps echoed across the kitchen and I tried to scramble up to meet the ghost head on.

"Cass?" a familiar voice called.

"Jack! Thank heavens. In here."

He appeared in the door and, for a shocked moment, just stood there.

"Can you give me a hand?" I said in exasperation as I scrabbled for purchase amidst the detritus and tried to get my legs under me.

"Oh, sure." He reached down for my hand and pulled me to my feet.

I stood and dusted myself off, raising quite a little cloud. "Sorry. I was wedged in there."

"Anything broken? Do you need to see a doctor?"

"What? And confess my clumsiness? No way. I'm fine."

"You'll have bruises." Gillian came up behind him. "You should have waited for us."

"Actually, I thought you were someone...something else."

"Huh?" Jack said.

I exhaled. "Nothing." I swear the air vibrated as if my ghost laughed. "It's great that you're here."

"How hard did you hit your head?" Jack reached for me, frowning. "You *were* expecting us, yes?"

I dodged back. "I'm fine."

Gillian swept a finger over a shelf and stared at the results. "You stayed here last night?"

"No, although that was the plan. I stayed at a B&B." I told them about the conversation with the owner offering me a discount as if she were sure I'd be back.

Jack looked around. "We might all want to consider the B&B tonight or a motel. I don't think this place will be livable by then. There's a lot to do before we even get your things out of storage."

"You might want to consider an exterminator," Gillian said, wrinkling her nose.

"The place was inspected. No termites or other noticeable vermin. Nothing alive... That they found, anyway. We do have to wash all the dishes, which is why I bought a bunch of disposable plates, cups, and plastic flatware."

"Does the fridge work?" Jack asked.

"Yes, but it looks cranky to me. I think I need to get a plumber and an electrician in here. The guy who did the inspection rated the place poor in a number of areas but said the foundation was sound, and he thought it was a great buy despite the rumors."

"Rumors?" Jack got a bottle of water out of the fridge. "Keeps things cold at least, but you're in serious need of beer."

We all heard a scratching sound from the second floor.

"Nothing alive?" Jack asked. "Or are those the 'rumors'?"

"Okay, so I have a feeling that there's something here. Mice, maybe. And maybe they're the source of the rumors."

"Maybe you should consider a fumigation tenting?" Gillian asked.

"I think I'd feel better with a dog," I said.

Jack and Gillian exchanged a glance.

Jack asked, "How about a cat? Works better with mice."

I shrugged. "Might work. I don't know much about cats, but I hear they kill pests."

"Have we got a cat for you!"

Chapter 2

"Seriously? You have a cat? I thought your little rent-controlled love shack over in Berkeley didn't allow pets."

"Yeah, well, therein lies the problem." They exchanged a glance. "Cass, it's you or the pound."

"And this suddenly came up because…?"

"Thor started out as the cutest little puffball of black fur and amber eyes. Very small, sweet, easy to conceal. I used to carry him around inside my bomber jacket."

Gillian covered a laugh with a cough.

Jack pursed his lips. "Now there's no hiding a 23-pound part Maine Coon with 'catitude.'"

"It's lose the cat or give up rent control. Guess which we're giving up," Gillian linked her arm in his.

I shook my head. "But 23 pounds! That's bigger than a lot of dogs."

"No rat in its right mind would stick around."

"Good point." Would a ghost?

"Tell you what." Jack looked around. "It's pretty obvious that we won't get far enough along to sleep here tonight. I think we'll need a junk pickup before we can even get part of your stuff out of your storage locker and in here. So Gillian and I will work here all day but go sleep at home and come back with Thor and breakfast tomorrow morning."

"It's a long drive!" I protested, not wanting them to leave.

"But once Thor arrives, you won't have to worry about whatever that noise is," Gillian said.

"Another good point," I added, raising an index finger.

"Seriously, it's not that bad a drive," Jack said. "And I'd rather spend the money on a good breakfast than a motel."

I thought about having a warm, loving, furry kitty to keep me company and chase away the spooky blues that came over me here when the sun went down. Kitty would dash into those dark corners and scare the dust bunnies away. My imagination wouldn't run as wild with a cat for company. I opted for the permanent company. "Works for me. I'll get on the phone now to the plumber and electrician and make a reservation back at the B&B. Guess I'll get to use my coupon after all."

Jack asked, "While you're doing that, do you mind if we poke around before we start cleaning? I'd like to see what the possibilities are."

"Possibilities?" I asked.

"You have two storage units, and this is a relatively small cottage. I thought it was one story, but it looks like a split level or maybe there's a loft or attic. There's also an extension or a building toward the back nearly hidden by bushes."

"It's kind of a shack. I have the plans here somewhere." I rifled through the papers from the closing that I'd stacked on the table and pulled out a floor plan.

Jack bent over, studying it.

Gillian came over to take a look. She pointed at the date on the addition. "Not part of the original building; however, if it's secure and in decent shape, it might be a good place to start. If it's empty, we could sweep it out and then we can just haul the stuff from your storage lockers into that addition, and you can go through it and rearrange things in the house the way you want over time."

"First, we need to find out if there's anything in there," Jack said. "And we still need to go through the house. At the very least, we have to get beds in here."

"And there is a loft or attic," Gillian said. "Here on the plans it's labeled as a loft."

"I haven't climbed up there yet."

"I think we can leave that for later. Gillian and I will scout the place while you make your phone calls."

I doodled a u-bend while talking to the plumber and then called the electrician. As I hung up after scheduling the electrician for tomorrow, I heard a dull, clunking sound, followed by a rap at the back door.

I opened it to a tall, thirty-something, tow-headed stranger, who looked like he'd be more comfortable on a surfboard than standing on my stoop. "Yes?"

"Hi. I'm Dave. Welcome to the neighborhood." He handed me a bottle of wine with a bright red ribbon around its neck. "I live right next door. And by the way, your doorbell doesn't work."

That meant that both the front and back doorbells needed replacing. One more thing to add to the list.

I held out my hand. "I'm Cass Peake. Just moving in as you can see." I glanced around. "And I'm pretty sure there's a lot that doesn't work around here. C'mon in."

"I hope you last longer than the last owners." He stepped over the threshold and looked around.

Someone else with knowledge of the house's history. Cool. "I almost hate to ask, but how long did they live here?"

"It's not so much how long they lived here—that was about two weeks total on and off—it was about five years ago that they bought the place. Couldn't find a buyer until you came along. The last night they tried to spend here I'd been planning to go meet some friends in San Francisco, but there was a terrific lightning storm, so I was home when they came pounding at my door. Nice couple. Charlie called after you signed the papers to say goodbye, thank me, and tell me he was filing for divorce and moving to Kansas."

That was shocking. Two weeks in the cottage? Yikes! "Did he move for business?"

"Don't think so. I think he wanted to move to a location that wasn't known for séances." He coughed. "I saw you here yesterday, but you left before I could catch you."

I was having a little cognitive dissonance. Dave grinned in a slow, easy way—very non-threatening—and yet his comments seemed pointed. "Are you telling me they had séances here five years ago?"

"Oh, yeah." He nodded enthusiastically. "Just wanted to let you know that I'm up for it if you're going to do the same thing."

There was a Golden Retriever quality to Dave that was at odds with his words.

"Not having séances, Dave. I actually want to live here. In fact, I don't have a choice. Every dime I had went into purchasing the place."

He frowned, clearly disappointed. "Oh. Well. If you need to, you can always crash on my couch. Too bad about the…" He waggled his fingers in the air. "They were wild. Charlie always had good food and beer." He turned to walk out the door. Two steps out he stopped and waved goodbye.

"Dave?"

"Yeah?"

"Who attended?"

He thought for a moment. It looked like hard work.

"Me, of course; Charlie; LaVerna, his wife; Alan, who owns a bookstore; Marcy, the vet; and Mina, the ghost writer. Sometimes a gamer would ask to join, but Charlie always said no."

"Gamer?"

"LARP."

"LARP?"

"Sorry. Live action role playing. Kind of like you're the game pieces."

"I've met Mina. I can't imagine her being a live game piece."

"Yeah, she told us all about you." Dave grinned.

"Who's us? The gamers?"

But he headed off to the beach cottage next door. Guess he hadn't heard me. Or didn't want to answer.

"See you later," I called out of habit and closed the door. Now I was seriously confused.

I turned around and jumped. Jack and Gillian were standing in the kitchen doorway.

"Who was that?" Jack said.

"If he's to be believed, he's my neighbor, Dave. Apparently, he used to attend séances here that were held as a sort of a party or maybe a game of some sort by the former owner, who, again, if Dave's to be believed, only spent two weeks in residence. Before I forget, I have something else to add to my list." I tried to draw a doorbell, but it looked too much like a nipple. I settled for an old-fashioned maid's bell. My 'to-do' list looked a lot like a rebus. "There." I looked up.

The air in the corner shimmered.

"Did you see that?" I asked.

Jack frowned. "See what?" He looked around.

"The electricity might still be shaky," I said.

"The attic is filthy, but the antiques stashed up there are amazing," Gillian said.

That diverted me.

Jack added, "It's as though they stashed the good stuff up there and left the junkier stuff down here. Doesn't make sense if they wanted to sell. In fact, they could have sold the Deco stuff for quite a bit on its own. Unless the owners didn't know the stuff was up there."

"That would make sense if they really only lived here two weeks," Gillian said.

I could believe that. "We should leave everything where it is, take an inventory, and then call Goodwill or whoever picks up furniture for charity and get rid of the pieces that I don't want."

"You'll need paint pretty soon. You may want to hold off on bringing the antiques down until you decide what you want to do with the walls."

I was beginning to feel overwhelmed.

"Jack," Gillian said. "We should take pictures of the stuff upstairs. Look up the history of the pieces. Cass, if you want, we could do a little research on wall coverings for the same period." She shrugged. "I guess it depends on how much you like Deco. There are places that sell reproduction papers. Do you want to keep the Deco flavor?"

Good old Gillian. She had such a talent for organization. "Sounds good though I don't really know that much about it."

"You will by the time we're through. For example, look at this." Gillian brushed off the grates in the wall and the fireplace surround.

They were decorated with stunningly beautiful geometric patterns, but the brass was so dull that the patterns were barely visible.

"We'll need a lot of brass polish," I said.

****

My second night at the B&B was as delightful as the first. There was a skin-cooling chill in the air that made the Jacuzzi such a treat. This time I was relaxed, knowing that Jack and Gillian would be there in the morning.

Before bed, I stepped out onto the balcony and yawned into the sharp night air. I hadn't seen much of the "June gloom" the realtor had mentioned. The sea was relatively calm, but it was 57 degrees Fahrenheit. The down duvet was getting more attractive by the minute.

****

True to his word, in the morning Jack and Gillian arrived at my bungalow with a lovely breakfast and their cat, or rather now my new cat.

"Hi." I walked down the steps. "I see you've brought my new roommate."

"Thanks again for taking Thor, Cass," Jack said without preamble.

"My pleasure…I think." I eyed the large black ball of amber-eyed fur jammed into the soft-sided cat carrier strapped into the back seat of their car. Twenty-five pounds if he was an ounce.

Jack unstrapped the seat belt from around the carrier. "Thor moaned for two hours straight."

"Must have seemed like a long drive."

Jack muttered something unintelligible. Then he hoisted the cat carrier. I revised my estimate of Thor's weight upwards.

"I'll get the door." I ran up the steps and held the battered old screen door open and wondered briefly if I should get a security door.

As Jack crossed the threshold, a low grumble issued from the carrier. It wasn't friendly.

"You two are going to get along really well." He set the carrier down on the carpet.

Gillian followed us in and carried the food into the kitchen.

Although Jack and Gillian hadn't lived far from us in the East Bay, somehow they always seemed to come down to our house. We hadn't been to their place since… Well, I'd have to think about when that'd been, and I was pretty darn sure this cat hadn't been around then.

Thor was wedged in the cat carrier so tightly that Jack had to shake him out by turning it upside down. Either that or Thor was digging in. All I could see at first was a mound of black fur slowly distending from the open carrier. Then he fell in slow motion, hind legs first. His amber eyes met mine.

Gravity is amazing. I said, "That's not a cat; that's a dog!"

Jack sighed. "We've heard that one before. His size is the source of our problems with keeping him."

"Here, pretty kitty, kitty," I called.

Thor shot me a dirty look.

I was having second thoughts. "Jack, I don't know. This cat seems…well…angry."

"Cass, if you don't take him, you could be condemning him to death at the pound," Jack pleaded.

Gillian watched me.

Blatant emotional manipulation. But who would adopt him? I could tell by Jack's voice that giving Thor up was hard to do, and Jack was my baby brother, after all.

"All right," I said, giving in.

"Thanks. It'll work. You'll see."

I shook my head, but Jack's relief made me smile. That was Jack all over. Do the deed and ask forgiveness later. His boyish charm had gotten him out of a lot of pickles.

I looked at Thor. Jack had a point about the pound. Thor wasn't the kind of cuddly kitty most people were looking for when they went to adopt. I understood loving a pet this much. When I was younger, I'd had an Irish Setter mix named Rufus who had seemed to understand what I was saying to him. We'd shared many secrets over the years. I sighed.

"We brought you some supplies," Gillian said. "Maine Coons and other breeds with furry paws need grain-based litter so when they clean their paws, what they swallow is digestible and doesn't form a clay bolus in their stomachs that has to be removed surgically."

"Yuck," I said, putting a hand to my stomach.

"I'll go get the rest of the stuff. Cats are obligate

carnivores. There's special food." The door banged shut behind him as he made a quick exit.

"Yeah, you'd better run," I said to his back. What was it about little brothers? Then I turned to Gillian. "Special food?"

She nodded. "Prescription. You can get it from your vet. Thor seems to have a bit of a delicate stomach. He's turned down most of what we've offered him."

Judging by his size, I didn't think Thor had many issues with food. "Yesterday my next door neighbor mentioned a vet who used to attend séances here. I'll get the name, and maybe I can do a little sleuthing and find out some more stuff about the house while I'm at it."

Jack came back in laden down with the last of the supplies and dumped them on the trestle table.

Then he turned to stare at Thor, who was standing in the middle of the living room, hissing. Every bit of fur on his body was standing on end as he arched his back and danced sideways. He struck out with his big paw full of sharp talons…at nothing.

Then he ran off and hid while we all stared after him.

"That was really weird!" Jack said. "He's never done that before."

"It's the house," I said. If he'd met the bootlegger's daughter, it hadn't gone well. There went my plan to be reassured by Thor's presence.

Gillian said, "No, Thor's just annoyed about the trip. Cass, you might expect him to either hide or act out a bit after we leave."

That made a lot more sense than thinking that Thor

had encountered a ghost. "Come into the kitchen and eat. I've got the quiche warming in the oven."

We ate croissants and quiche at the trestle table in the kitchen, silently at first while I added to the list, which had already rolled over to a second page. Then we all started talking over each other but stopped and laughed.

"Go ahead," Gillian said.

"The electrician will be by at two. He'll check the service and bring along what he needs to add another line or two. I want a washer and dryer hooked up soon, but that'll have to wait a day or two."

Jack said, "Are you taking the washer and dryer from your old place?"

"No, those are staying with Phil. I have to buy new appliances. I'm looking for sales, discounts, floor models, anything to save a dime."

"We'll keep an eye out," Jack said.

"Yeah, well. C'mon, slackers. Let's get busy." I wiped my mouth, got up, and chucked the napkin in the garbage. "Everything needs to be cleaned, but I suspect we're going to run into a lot of stuff that's just trash. I've got large trash bags so that we can just move stuff outside. There are two bins, and trash pickup is Tuesday morning, but I suspect we're going to need a junk hauler. I think we should start on the bedrooms. I have a couple of mattress sets in the locker. I'm hoping we can get two rooms done and usable by nightfall."

"Sounds like a plan," Jack said.

Gillian pulled out the architectural drawings again. "The bedroom on the other side of the living room toward the back looks like it might be the master."

"They didn't have dens or family rooms back in the

day, at least not the way we know them. But it looks like there's another bedroom at the back with the bathroom in between the two. Frankly, I'd like a clean bathroom about now."

"Good thought," Jack said. "I volunteer for the bathroom if you two want to scout the bedrooms."

"I've trained him well," Gillian said.

"Good job, Gillian. Works for me," I agreed.

With a flick of the switch, I discovered that the hall light outside the bathroom didn't work. "There's a pad and pen on the trestle table. Let's start a list of what we're going to need. Light bulbs for starters and maybe a couple of LED lanterns. I suspect there's a lot of stuff around here that doesn't work." I turned on the light in the second bedroom and the bathroom and was stunned by the piles.

Gillian came up next to me, carrying Clorox wipes. "I'll do this bedroom. Think of it as a treasure hunt."

Jack joined us, carrying a stepladder. "I'm going to check out light bulbs, toilet paper, paper towels, and so on because I'm going to need to make a beer run here pretty quick."

"Before the bathroom?" Gillian raised an eyebrow.

"Sustenance, Sweet Pea, sustenance."

Gillian just shook her head.

"The fridge works, so we should lay in some cold cuts and drinks while you're at it. Don't use anything in the pantry. I picked up some stuff on my way back this morning." I turned to the master bedroom door, opened it, turned on the bed lamp, and screamed.

There was a dead squirrel in the middle of the bed.

Jack and Gillian were next to me in an instant.

Jack asked, "Do you want that bedspread?"

"No!"

"Good. I'll go get a trash bag."

Gillian put her arm on my shoulder. "The dead can't hurt you."

I shivered. "I like the bedstead, but that mattress is going out."

Gillian chuckled. "Gotcha. We can scrub the wood."

Jack shoveled the bedding into the bag and took it out. Then he and Gillian wrestled the mattress out. Sitting on the slats across a three-quarter frame was a set of exposed metal springs. I could put my mattress on top of the springs plus my bedding and sleep here tonight. I started cleaning up the springs and making sure that the slats weren't broken or weak. The carpet under the bed was a Persian area rug that needed cleaning, but I was willing to settle for vacuuming for the time being. For the first time since opening the door with my own keys, I felt as though this space was mine. I really hoped the other bedroom would be as easy to set up for the night.

"Going now," Jack called down the hall.

"Hang on. Can you pick up some of those little carrots and cherry tomatoes?"

"Yogurt," Gillian called from the other bedroom. "And a bottle of wine. Do you have any idea where you're going?"

"Nice combination, Sweet Pea. And yes. We passed a few stores on the way in. I was paying attention."

"Check my list in the kitchen for any food items. We can go out to dinner tonight," I said. "I just want some munchy food in here for now to keep us going.

It'll be my treat because you all are helping me out."

"Sounds good." Jack was back in a moment, holding my pad. "Is this what you think of my cat?" He waved it an inch from my nose.

"Oops." I had drawn a mean-looking cat with bared teeth and a pile of food next to him. My version of "buy cat food."

"Yeah, oops." He turned and left the room. The front door slammed behind him.

I poked my head into the other bedroom. "How's it look in here?"

"Don't mind Jack. He loves Thor." She pointed to a stack of linens. "I've set aside two quilts that are stunning and look handmade. I get ditching the bedding in your room, but we should keep on the lookout for embroidery with cutwork. Even stained, we can save it. Also, weavings, quilts, doilies, hair jewelry although that would probably have been out of fashion by the time of this house, there still might have been some from ancestors. You might be able to make a little money off some of this stuff. There's a gorgeous secretary in here that's solid oak."

I stuck my head in further. "That's beautiful! I'm keeping that."

"I thought you might. By the way, I think your bedstead is walnut. I don't know what the other owners had problems with, but to me it looks like you got a smoking deal." Gillian pulled open a drawer in the secretary. "Full of papers. Once we get the basics done, it could be a lot of fun to go through some of this."

I nodded. "I'm not going to throw any personal papers away. At least not right away. I want to learn about the history of this house." I looked around. "Have you seen Thor? I'm afraid I forgot about him."

"Come here." Gillian beckoned me further into the bedroom and pulled the open door to the armoire wider. Thor was sound asleep on a pile of quilts that were stacked inside.

"Guess there aren't any mice in there! Do you think you and Jack will be able to sleep here tonight?"

She scanned the room. "Yeah, I think so. It's stuffy. I've got the window open. I think our next trip out—maybe after lunch—should be to your locker for the mattresses, linens, and anything else we can fit in for the first trip."

I sighed heavily.

She put a hand on my shoulder. "Don't worry. We'll take it in stages and won't leave until you have what you need set up to handle daily living. Are you planning to get a job?"

"Yeah, I have to. I don't have any laurels to rest on. I'll take anything I can get. I have a degree in international business from San Jose State, and I was a program manager until I married Phil. But since then I've only volunteered for nonprofits doing their web sites. I don't really want to do a commute again so I'm hoping to use my web skills to start a business I could run out of here creating and maintaining web sites for small businesses."

"It'll take a while to get a business going, establish a reputation. It might be easier to get a regular paycheck that you can count on."

"I know, and I will if I have to. But from the time I saw this house, I've been thinking about new beginnings."

Gillian put a hand on my arm.

"When life as you know it ends…" Unexpectedly, a tear ran down my cheek. "I really really liked my life."

"I know you did, but now you get to try something new."

I knew she didn't understand. She'd never dealt with the fear that sits like a rock in your stomach all the time. I had no idea what to do next. I'd had my whole life planned out, including retirement with Phil. All that was gone now. I had no idea if I could even get a job. I might end up a bag lady on the streets.

But I followed her quietly as we carried the quilts and bedspreads worth salvaging out to my car and put them into the back for a trip to the drycleaners…as soon as I found the local one.

As we went back in, I stopped for a moment on the porch to enjoy the view—my view—again.

Back in the bedroom I'd chosen, I pulled a cloth and several scarves from the mirror on the vanity. For a moment, I thought I was seeing things. The large, round mirror was tinged pale pink.

Gillian followed me in. "That isn't going to give you accuracy when applying your makeup."

"Maybe not," I said, sitting gingerly on the stool. "But it might be nice to see the world through rose-colored glass." I smiled up at her.

"Ha ha. The curtains haven't held up well," she said, turning to the window.

They'd shredded when I ran the upholstery tool over them. "My fault I'm afraid."

Gillian shook her head. "I suspect they were older than we thought and already decaying."

I stood. "I think we have enough floor space for the

basic boxes and suitcases."

"As soon as Jack gets back, we should make a U-Haul run."

"I think he's ditching his bathroom duties."

We continued to clean the nooks and crannies and fill the trash bags until we heard Jack's car pull back in the drive.

The front door banged, and Jack stuck his head around the corner. "Through with the vacuum? I've got to get the bathroom ready enough for tonight, and we need to get a move on if we're sleeping here."

Gillian laughed. "As if we haven't been working for the past hour and a half."

I rolled the vac over to him. "Should we call a junk dealer to get the mattresses?"

"Let's worry about that tomorrow," Gillian said. "Jack's right. We need to finish and get to the locker."

"We can lean them against the side of the house and throw a tarp over them," Jack said.

"They'll get awfully damp from the fog," I said.

"Do you care?"

I shrugged. "Guess not. Let's get them out of here and have some lunch. The electrician will be here soon. Then we can make a locker run." I scanned my list. The electrician was represented by a lightning bolt and the locker by a padlock with an "er" after it.

Hours later as the fog rolled in, Jack and I backed the U-Haul into my drive. The sun was low on the horizon, but there would still be enough light to get the mattresses and boxes unloaded before dark.

I hopped out and gestured to Jack to keep backing up toward the porch. I signaled stop when he got close enough.

He joined me around the back of the truck just as Gillian came out the front door.

"Lots has happened while you were gone. The good news is we can all plug our laptops in now, and your washer/dryer hookups are in. The bad news... You might want to have a look down toward the beach."

My gaze followed the line of her finger. Gathered on the beach in the incoming fog were half a dozen people in costume and what looked like an EMT team.

"There's an ambulance and a cop car parked down on the end of the lane," Jack said.

Chapter 3

"Maybe we should see if we can help."

Gillian walked over to us. "They've been there a while. It looks like an accident or drowning."

"What's with the costumes then?" Jack asked.

I shivered as the temperature dropped. "No idea. But that sea foam green mid-calf afternoon dress is lovely."

Gillian frowned. "Wrong period, though. Everyone else is Victorian. Look at the fascinators and bustles. She's more Twenties or Thirties."

"Costume party run amok?" I asked.

"Maybe," Gillian said.

Jack unlatched the back of the U-Haul. "Are we sure the EMTs are really EMTs? Could be they're in costume, too."

"With an officially marked ambulance?" Gillian asked. "Highly unlikely."

"Should we go down to find out?" I asked. My curiosity was peaked.

"I think we'd just be in the way," Gillian said. "I've got Thor in his carrier, so we can prop the door open and get this stuff inside before the sun goes down completely."

I'd left the king-sized bed in its place back in the master bedroom in Pleasanton. I tamped down the evil thoughts I was having about what my ex and his 'friend' might be doing on it as I helped Jack get the full-sized mattress from my former guest bedroom in place in what was now my room.

"Not a bad fit," Jack said. "If you keep the bare springs that came with the bedstead, which fit perfectly in this frame, the mattress is a little larger than the three-quarter springs. I don't think they make that size anymore, and your covered box springs won't fit inside the three-quarter frame. What do you think, Gillian?" He turned to ask his wife only to discover that she wasn't there.

"She's probably getting a box," I said, "Maybe the linens. I'll go help her."

She wasn't in the house, so I stepped onto the porch. Gillian was down on the beach talking to a man. I let the door slam behind me.They both looked up, and I stopped in shock. Gillian gestured to me to come to her.

I yelled to Jack. "I'll just be a moment." Hesitantly, I headed down to where they stood, feeling suddenly hyperaware.

I saw a young woman with her sleek chestnut hair in a French braid circling the area, taking pictures, placing numbers, kneeling and leaning for different angles. Two others seemed to be moving along the beach, eyes intent on the ground. A white van with a black logo containing a caduceus on the side was parked next to the police car, and a woman in a white Tyvek suit knelt by what had to be a body. I guessed she was the medical examiner and that all this was real. I had a fight or flight moment but continued down toward the body as if I had no will of my own.

"This is my sister-in-law, Cass Peake. She lives

here. Just moving in," Gillian said as I stopped next to her. "Cass, this is Detective—"

"George Ho," I said, my voice shaking slightly. "What are you doing here?"

"You two know each other?" Gillian asked.

A more distant door banged in its wooden frame. I turned my head, distracted again. Mina stood out on her porch, a long, gauzy dress swirled around her legs. She pulled a heavy woolen shawl tighter around her body and stared at us.

"Cass?"

I turned back at the sound of George's well-remembered voice. "Sorry."

"I'm with the Las Lunas police. I investigate dead bodies." His smile was easy, and I had the impression he was teasing me even though we hadn't parted on the best of terms.

I wasn't as sanguine. "I just bought this place, and we're moving stuff in today. We've been in and out. Gillian's my sister-in-law. Jack's here. Up at the house. You remember Jack? We did see some people in costume down here when we got back from the storage locker a little bit ago."

George pointed to a group of five of the people we'd seen earlier, the ones in the Victorian costumes. "That group?"

I frowned. "I think there were six of them. I remember one young woman in a lovely sea foam green dress."

"I remember her," Gillian said. "We commented that her dress was from the wrong period."

George frowned. "There were five when we arrived, and no one in a green dress. Are you sure?"

"Absolutely," I said. "It was a gorgeous dress. Had some beadwork on the bodice."

He made a note on an iPad mini. "Thank you. Anything else?"

I shook my head again, my thoughts racing, wondering how he could be so detached. "Not that I can think of."

He handed me a card. "Please call me if you think of anything else." And he winked at me.

"Sure." I took the card, nearly dropped it, stuck it in my jeans, and looked up to see the EMTs load the body on a gurney and take it to the ambulance. The woman in the white suit was packing up a case. "Was it an accident?"

But George was walking away. Just like that. I turned to walk back to the house. Looking up, I saw Mina go back inside her place.

"Neighbor?" Gillian asked.

"Yeah. She writes ghost stories."

"A corpse is right up her alley then."

Jack greeted us at the door. "What was that all about?"

Gillian said, "Looks like someone may have drowned. The detective wasn't giving much away. Seems like you and Cass know him."

"Really?" Jack raised an eyebrow.

"George Ho," I said, my voice breaking.

Jack looked down toward the beach but George was gone. "Wow. Talk about coincidence."

"Somebody want to fill me in?" Gillian said, arms crossed.

"It's nothing really," I said. "I used to date him. I had no idea he was here."

"You sure of that?" Jack asked.

I gave him a dirty look. "A little freaky that it happened on my beach."

"Not technically your beach, Cass, but I get what you mean," Jack said. "Let's get the rest of the stuff in and lock up for the night. Maybe we should order pizza. We have beer." He winked.

"Someone just died, Jack. Have a little respect. According to the police, he was a local bookstore owner."

"Hardly likely to be the victim of murder then," Jack said. "More likely a tragic accident."

The fog was coming in, but that's not why I shivered.

We unloaded the rest of the U-Haul, let an indignant Thor out of the cat carrier again, and returned the U-Haul to the lot. It was pretty dark by the time we got back. I was so tired that I nearly rolled into bed after I'd made it, but I joined Jack and Gillian in the kitchen.

Jack was ending a call. "Dominos won't deliver here. They hung up on me. Thought I was a kid playing a joke. They said they don't deliver to ghosts." He looked up. "Something you want to tell us?"

I sighed. Time to come clean. "It's the reason I got this place and everything in it so cheap. It has a reputation for being haunted."

Gillian nodded. "So buying a haunted house means it's cheap but also means you can't have pizza anymore."

Jack laughed.

"Not funny, Jack."

Gillian snickered. "Actually, it is pretty funny. I

grew up in Indiana in Tornado Alley. Dominos delivered to Purdue in the middle of a tornado." She snorted. "And they won't deliver here to a haunted house!"

"Glad I could provide you two with so much entertainment."

"No, no. You don't get off that easy. You bought it knowing it was haunted?" Jack asked.

"No, I didn't know when I bought it."

"You weren't suspicious of the low price?"

"I didn't think about it too much although I figured I'd find some sort of serious problem. I just didn't think it would be a supernatural one."

"We could bring in an exorcist or have a séance."

I shivered. "Don't go there, Jack. They used to have séances here."

"Seriously?" Jack said.

"You have to tell us the whole story," Gillian said.

"Over dinner," I said. "I guess we're going to have to go out if we want to eat." I picked up my car keys.

****

We slept like the dead that night. I awoke a bit muzzy headed. The whole house would need a good airing. We'd kicked up a lot of dust yesterday, and my allergies had started. I grabbed my brocade kimono, found my Crocs, and headed for the electric kettle in the kitchen. As I plugged it in, I looked out the window.

There was a couple on the beach standing about where the body had been yesterday. They were only about fifteen yards away, but I couldn't see details because of the fog. They looked up, saw me looking at them through the window, and then turned away. It looked as though the young woman was drying her eyes. As I pulled my kimono closer around me, they started up to the house. The young woman was a blonde dressed all in black.

I opened the back door as they approached. "Hi, I'm Cassandra Peake. Cass. I've just moved in."

Up close I could see that the tall young man was about college age with long dark hair pulled back in a ponytail at the nape of his neck.

The young man smiled a warm and welcoming smile. "Welcome to La Bahia de las Lunas or Las Lunas for short. I'm Ricardo Santiago. This is Mia Jamison."

"I'm pleased to meet you. Do you live around here?"

Ricardo nodded his head. "My family lives in town."

"Are you aware of what happened yesterday right about where you were standing?"

The girl with the platinum blonde hair that Ricardo had introduced as Mia looked as though she were going to cry.

Ricardo spoke quickly. "All we know is that Alan Howland drowned yesterday. Did you know him?"

I shook my head. "No, but I hardly know anyone here. This is my first night sleeping in my new place. I moved over here from Pleasanton."

Mia looked miserable, and that made me curious.

"We're students at Clouston College on the other side of the bay." He hesitated. "Do you know about your house? I mean, the rumors?"

"That it's haunted, you mean?"

He relaxed visibly. "Yes. He's not the first to die here," Ricardo said. "We know about the murders."

"Murders?" Suddenly my stomach hurt.

"Yeah, we kinda call it Murder Beach."

Mia shivered. "We think there's something here. Evil ley line. Evil presence."

"Given that I've just bought the place, I'm not thrilled with your repeated use of the word 'evil.'" But Mia's move from murder to the supernatural helped me regain perspective.

Ricardo stepped in. "We're part of a steampunk cosplay group, and the reputation of this place enhances our game. I'm sure you must have told ghost stories when you were young."

I wasn't sure I liked his implication that I was old, but I knew where he was going. "Sure, and apparently I now live next to a ghost story writer."

Ricardo smiled. "That would be Mad Mina."

"Mad Mina?" Despite my attempts to be stern, I smiled. It was a pretty apt description.

Ricardo smiled back. "Look, we don't want to upset you. There was a murder on this beach in the Twenties. A notorious bootlegger's daughter. Then my boss at Crystalline got engaged, and shortly afterward, her fiancé was murdered here. Now Alan…dying."

A sob escaped Mia.

"Is she all right?" I asked.

Ricardo put an arm around her. "Mia used to work for Alan."

She buried her face in his shoulder and cried softly.

"I'm sorry," I said.

"Not your fault," he said.

"I'm fine with your continuing to use the beach for…gaming, you said? What kind of game? It'll be nice to know someone around here."

"Have you heard of steampunk?"

I must have looked blank again.

Ricardo grinned. "It's related to Victorian. We'll show you our costumes sometime. We have to go now. We just came by this early to pay our respects to Alan, but I'd be happy to fill you in some other time. You might even want to join us one evening." He winked.

From the way he said it I knew he was teasing. I watched as they returned to the beach. I was snapped back to reality when I heard a meow-howl and realized that I'd been standing in the doorway while I talked to them and Thor had simply walked out between my ankles. I was so not used to having a cat.

The meow-howl sounded again, and I looked around for Thor. He wasn't on the beach, so I looked up toward the dark windows of Mina's house. He was nowhere to be seen.

Dave, my next-door neighbor, stood on his deck, waving at me. I waved back, torn as to whether to look for Thor or go over and say hi. The conundrum was resolved when Thor appeared at Dave's feet, winding his longhaired body around Dave's ankles. I smiled and walked over.

"I see you've met my cat."

Dave smiled. "I wondered who he belonged to." He bent and scratched Thor's head.

Thor purred. I gaped in amazement.

"He's really friendly." Dave ran his fingers down Thor's back and up his tail.

Thor, you traitor. "Did you see the cops yesterday on the beach, Dave?"

Dave frowned. "No, I was up in the City with friends. Just got back after sleeping off a pub crawl."

"A body washed up on the beach right in front of my place. I'm told it was someone named Alan Howland. Did you know him?"

"No shit! Alan?" He shook his head. "He used to come to the séances. Did I mention? I went to his shop a couple of times. I liked it. Neat, orderly place. I picked up a great book on the history of surfboards. C'mon up."

Dave stepped back, and I walked up the two steps. His deck was primarily designed to give him a relatively sand-free place to sit and sun.

"I can't believe it. What happened?"

"Don't know. I'm hoping an accident." Alan had been in my house. At a séance. I needed to process that.

"Guess so." He shook his head again and conversation died.

Looking for something to talk about, I pointed to his grill with all of the utensils hanging from hooks on both sides. "Do you like cooking outside?"

He glanced around. "Yeah. Alan and I were always saying we were going to have a barbeque, but it never happened."

"Where's Thor?" I looked around for the beast, who, of course, had already vanished again. "Great."

"Don't worry about him. He seems pretty self-sufficient."

"I'm more of a dog person. I think that cat hates me."

"The thing about cats is you can't control them. You have to just take them the way God made them."

"He's originally a pound kitty. My brother can't keep him any longer, so he's mine now. If he went back to the pound, I doubt he'd be adopted at his age."

The wind picked up, blowing my hair around my face.

"You're right about that. During kitten season, many pounds won't even take older cats. I used to volunteer when I was in high school. I thought about being a vet." Dave laughed as if dismissing the idea as absurd. "My cousin's studying to be a doctor. I barely see him; he's too busy." He said it as if it were a bad thing.

"Why didn't you become a vet?"

He shrugged. "My cousin has all the medical brains in the family. When my grandmother died, she left me this place and enough invested in stock that, if I stay single and am careful, I don't have to work. It's not enough to support a wife and kids on, though. So it's the single life for me." He grinned, not looking too unhappy at the prospect.

"Have you ever thought that maybe your wife would be making more than you?" From his expression, clearly this had never occurred to him. "I certainly plan to be supporting myself as soon as possible."

Instead of answering, Dave pointed down the beach. Thor was stalking the seagulls.

I groaned. "If anything happens to that cat, my brother will never speak to me again. He got out accidentally, and I have a sinking feeling I'll never be able to get him back in the house again."

"Oh, he'll come back when he's hungry."

As we watched, the seagulls took revenge, swooping and pecking at Thor, who howled and ran back toward the cottage, every long black hair standing on end.

"Wow! Nice diameter! He looks like a furry black

beach ball."

"He has the personality of a beach ball."

"A little grumpy this morning, are we? He's probably mad that he's been cast off. All he needs is love." Dave half-sang this last bit of an old Beatles song.

I glared at Dave, who grinned at me. "You want him? He's yours."

He held his hands up in mock surrender. "I'm the last one who should have a pet. Never home, you see." He nodded toward my bungalow. "By the way, the cat came back."

"Dave, didn't you mention that you knew a vet?"

"Sure. Marcy. I'll get you her number." He disappeared into his house and was back a moment later with a Post-It. "Here you go. Tell her I sent you."

"Thanks." I walked back over to my place to let Thor in.

He shot past me and sat down in the middle of the kitchen floor. Lifting a paw, he began to groom his ruffled fur back into place.

Then I saw the blood on the floor and bent over to examine Thor's head. As he licked his paw and rubbed his head, he smeared the blood in glistening burgundy streaks across the crown of his head. When he switched paws, he left a bloody footprint on my floor.

"Oh, you poor thing." I felt guilty for maligning him to Dave. I knew I should have him checked out, particularly that paw. "You're going to the vet."

I stripped the top sheet off my telephone pad, crumpled my doodles, and tossed the sheet into the trash. Then I quickly wrote a note, including the vet's phone number. If Jack and Gillian were really worried, they had my cell number and could call.

When I got through to the vet's office, she was sympathetic. "Look, the morning's slow. Why don't you just go ahead and bring him on in?"

"Thanks. We'll be right there."

Jack and Gillian walked in just as I was hanging up.

"Thor got out and was attacked and pecked by seagulls." I pointed at the blood. "The vet can see him right away. I was just leaving you a note. Can you watch him while I throw on some clothes?" I headed for the bedroom.

Jack crouched next to Thor. "This looks bad."

Thor hissed.

Jack stood. "I'll go with you."

"It's okay," I called over my shoulder. "I don't want to spoil your day."

I dressed quickly, no makeup, and returned to the kitchen. "I need to get used to being Thor's owner. I'll just get the carrier."

At the word "carrier," Thor bolted, leaving little red droplets in his wake.

Gillian sighed and said, "We spell that word. Apparently, cats can learn a small vocabulary. About eighty words. That's one of his least favorite."

"I'll bet." Cats could learn language? That was a new one on me. I pulled the cat carrier out of the bottom of the coat closet, set it in the middle of the big oak table, and went to help Jack look for Thor.

"He's gone," Gillian said.

"Why am I not surprised? Look, Cat," I said into the air. "You're hurt, and you need to go to the vet."

Thor ran from under the table to my bedroom with

Jack in hot pursuit.

"Got you now." I followed him into the bedroom and shut the door. A couple of beats later I realized that I didn't have the cat carrier with me. "I'm going back out for the c-a-r-r-i-e-r," I said to the half of Jack that was protruding from under the bed.

When I returned, Jack was sucking on his bleeding thumb joint.

I held the carrier open, and Jack shoved Thor, who moaned piteously, inside.

"Close the door behind me," I said as I carried Thor to my green Subaru, setting him gently in the passenger seat.

Thor moaned again.

A dead body, a haunted house, and a deranged cat. Things could hardly get worse.

Chapter 4

The vet's office was the first floor of an old Craftman style house complete with a covered wraparound porch, low pitched roof, and dormer windows. I hit the bell on the counter just inside the door of the vet's office and called out, "Hello!" I set the carrier on the counter .

Marcy Chesley, DVM, or so the sign on the counter claimed, descended the dark wood stairs from the second floor, and I guessed that she lived up there. The garden was well kept, and the furniture was comfortable. The waiting area looked like a living room complete with a beamed ceiling, two stained glass windows, a TV. It gave new meaning to the phrase "taking your work home with you."

"You must be Cass." She smiled and held out a hand. "Is this my patient?"

"This is Thor."

She moved behind the counter, peered in through the netting of the Sherpa bag, and said to Thor, "Well, hello, Thor. How're you doing?"

"Thor had a serious run in with a few seagulls. Thor lost." I looked around. "Are you here alone?"

"My intern Angela's mom is sick, so I gave her the day off. Here, let's go into an examining room and have a look at your new friend." She picked up the carrier and led me to a small, sterile room. She set her bundle on a stainless steel examination table, unzipped it, and lifted Thor out, talking to him. "Nice kitty. Good kitty." As the case cleared his ruffled black fur, she said, "Well, hello there."

Thor meowed in protest at her. Even I could hear the complaint in his voice.

"Oh, so you feel mistreated, do you? Let's have a look." She set him down gently and started feeling along his sides.

The vet gave him a thorough exam that included taking his temperature and checking his glands. Thor was an angel for her, even licking her fingers at one point.

Marcy appeared to collect animal kitsch. Her examining rooms were loaded with pictures of adorable baby animals of all species. One wall of the waiting room contained a large corkboard full of pictures of her patients.

I caught a glimpse of a large tabby wandering up the stairs. "Do you have cats wandering lose in here?"

"Only two right now: Mister Peepers and Fuzzybutt. And no, I didn't name them. Peepers belonged to an elderly woman who passed. He'd been a patient of mine for years. He's an elderly white Persian, probably sleeping somewhere. Fuzzybutt is a younger tabby with diabetes and other health problems. His owner wanted him put down, but there was something about him, so I agreed to keep him. Both are highly socialized. And speaking of lovely cats, Thor's a real sweetie."

"I just acquired him. He's my brother's cat, but the landlord objected. He's a big boy."

"I'm surprised your brother was willing to give

him up. You really lucked out." She cooed and scratched Thor's ears while he purred.

Then her gaze shifted to me. "I hear you bought the old bootlegger's cottage?"

"Yes. Yes, I did." I braced myself.

"You know it's haunted?"

"So I've been told. Repeatedly. Everyone in town seems to know about it, and I can't get a pizza delivered."

She laughed. "We have a local pizza place that'll deliver once you convince them that you're solid and pay with real money. Clem's Clam Shack."

"Clam Shack?"

"Not so much anymore. But he will put anything on pizza, including clams, if you ask."

My turn to laugh. "I'll remember that."

"Seriously, drop by in person. Tell Clem I sent you. He and I used to…to attend parties at your place."

The séances. "I'll do that."

"I'm going to give you some ointment for his right eye and some antibiotics. One of the cuts on his head is quite deep. You'll need to watch him. He doesn't appear to have a concussion, but if he has trouble with motor skills or seems unduly sleepy—more than just the usual catnaps, call me immediately. Also, let me know if he vomits anything other than a hairball. If he does throw up hairballs regularly, I've got some stuff you can dab on his nose. He'll lick it off, and it'll make it easier for him to pass the hair. But you'll be doing both of you a big favor if you brush him at least once a day. It'll help you bond." She smiled.

"Shouldn't you keep him here? Just in case he does have a concussion?"

She shook her head gently. "I could, but he really needs to be watched. He'd be in a cage down here all by himself in the dark at night. At your place, he'll be with you, cage-free, and interacting with you. If anything happens, you'll know right away and can call me." She wrote a number on her business card and handed it to me. "This is my cell. Also, ask your brother to have his vet send me Thor's records. My address is on the card."

I took the card and stuffed it in my jeans pocket. "Thanks."

She looked away. "I understand you had a bit of excitement near your house yesterday."

"Yes. There was some sort of accident on the beach. It looked like a drowning. A man."

"Alan Howland."

"Did you know him?"

"Oh, yes, I knew him," she said so quietly I almost didn't hear her answer. Then she was silent but recovered quickly. "Small town." She cleared her throat and patted Thor. "You two will get used to each other. It just takes time. He hasn't adjusted yet, but he will. You have to treat him with kindness and speak gently to him. He's having his own traumatic experience."

I must have looked guilty because Marcy said, "You've let his attitude get to you. Have you been yelling at him?"

"Sort of," I said guiltily. "But as I said, there's been a lot going on lately what with the…the body and all. Things haven't been exactly normal since he arrived."

Marcy tried unsuccessfully to suppress a smile. "No kidding, but try commiserating with him. Speak gently and touch him often. Give him treats while he's adjusting. You'll have plenty of opportunity to bond with him while you're caring for him and his wound."

This wasn't going to be easy. I had visions of myself crawling around under the furniture to find Thor. That cottage had a million nooks and crannies.

She lifted Thor into the carrier. "We still need to weigh him. He may need to go on a diet."

"Oh, that'll be fun. He seems to be motivated by his stomach. So far, it's the only sure way I've found to lure him out of hiding. As far as a diet for Thor, you and I need to talk, anyway. He needs some sort of special food that you can only get from vets."

"No problem about the food. Just let me know what kind. If I don't have it, I can order it. But you poor thing! Alan died on your beach? Ghastly." She looked away. "Have you met his wife?"

"No. The only people on the beach were the police, EMTs, medical examiner, and some cosplayers."

"Cosplayers. That's intriguing." She seemed to mull that over before continuing. "I'm sure you'll meet his wife Sara at some point. She's an interesting case, always a bit distracted. I remember the night Sara and I last talked at any length. It started with a knock at the back door that distracted me from making tea. I flipped on the porch light and spotlighted a shivering Sara. You'll find that it gets cold along the Northern California coast at Christmastime, and she wasn't dressed for the weather. I invited her in for a cup of tea. She and I sat down at the table in the back." Marcy pointed toward the back of the house. "I know you haven't met her, but she has a fragile, china doll look. She's a slightly built blonde with a round face and large blue eyes. She sipped her tea and said, 'If I denounce someone as a witch, would they still burn her at the stake?'"

"Seriously?" I said, a little put off and yet fascinated by Marcy's confidences. "What did you say?"

"Yes, dead serious. You'll see when you meet her." Marcy laughed lightly. "I'm used to Sara's odd comments and went with the flow. I told her that went out a few centuries ago. Turns out that Sara was referring to a group of vampire gamers. I wonder if they were the ones you saw on the beach? She was concerned about one female player in particular."

"Vampires," I said. "I was expecting surfers when I moved in."

"Hey, California is home to the Comic-Con known for cosplay. The cosplayers at Clouston College include a lot of steampunkers, but also others into anime and manga. I have to admit, though, that I sometimes have a bit of trouble telling the vamps from the steampunks—both groups wear a lot of lace and velvet and blood red lipstick and nails. Sometimes the gears give it away. Occasionally, one of the vamps wears his dental appliances, smiles, and startles a shopkeeper with his pointy teeth."

"Interesting town," I said, beginning to understand what Ricardo had been talking about.

"Oh, it gets better. Sara asked me if I knew that 'chit Mia Jamison?' I said, 'Chit? Have you been reading Regency romances again?' Then Sara said, 'I think she's having an affair with my husband.'"

That stopped me cold. A cheating husband meant a wife with a motive to kill him, and I'd just met Mia

Jamison. I shook myself. Who said anything about murder? I'd been reading too many mysteries, and Marcy's story had my imagination racing.

"And now Alan's dead," Marcy said. "I wonder if Sara finally had enough?"

I must have looked shocked at the confluence of our thoughts because she laughed.

"Don't mind me. Wild imagination." She waved a hand at me as if to say forget what I said.

She set the carrier and cat on the large scale pad and peered at the readout. "Twenty-five pounds. He needs to go on a diet. He also needs exercise. I wonder if he'd take to a harness? I felt some fatty pads on his belly. He looks like he has some Maine Coon heritage—the bushy tail, fur between the paws, and the hair at the tips of his ears like a bobcat, but he could still stand to lose some. Nice musculature though. I think he's just been overfed. No plaque on the teeth." She lifted the carrier off the scale. "I wouldn't be surprised if you were a bit upset. I've seen dead bodies in class. Not pleasant." She added up my bill and showed me the total. "Cash or check? I don't take credit cards yet."

"Check then. I barely write any these days." I took out my checkbook.

"Sorry about that. I'm slowly moving into the twenty-first century. I've ordered the Square. You know."

I shook my head.

"It's that little square thing that reads credit cards. It's free. Plugs into smart phones, tablets. You pay a percentage like other credit card payment companies, but it's a lot easier to use, and individuals can use it.

That's why I decided to finally start taking credit cards."

The light dawned. "I did see vendors using them at the craft fairs."

She waved a hand at the files behind her. "You'll notice that my records aren't computerized, either. Look at it this way. Your records aren't online, so at least one part of your life isn't accessible to hacking."

I had noticed all the files in the wall-to-wall cubbies. "Good point." I wrote the check.

In the lull, Marcy continued. "Alan's death has been on the news with a nice photo of the beach with your house in the background."

"I didn't see any reporters."

"You will," she said matter-of-factly. The late afternoon sun slanted in through the skylight above her, highlighting her shiny, dark hair. Marcy clipped the check to my bill, dumped it on a desk, and handed me a receipt.

I absentmindedly stuck my fingers through the holes in the side of the carrier and jumped when Thor licked them. I wiggled my fingers again, but he didn't come back. Uncomfortable now, I picked up the carrier in a hurry to get out of there.

"I'll walk you to your car." Marcy held the door for me and walked me down to the curb. "Take care of that sweet little ball of fur."

I unlocked my car. "I really do appreciate your seeing Thor without an appointment."

"No problem. He really is a neat cat. You'll find out. Give him time and space." She handed me the bag containing Thor's medicine.

I put the carrier in the back seat, strapped it in, and

got in.

"Come by anytime."

I waved as I pulled away from the curb. Not anytime soon.

Thor's low moan spurred me on toward home. I parked close to the front door, shortening the distance I had to lug the furball. He protested every time his carrier hit my leg, but finally I got it into the living room, locked the door, and set him free. He vanished under the table.

"Hi, guys. He's going to be hard to catch when we have to medicate him." I zipped up the cat carrier and stowed it in the front closet.

Jack said, "He'll come out when he's ready. What'd the vet say?"

I joined them in the living room. "We have to watch him in case he throws up or acts strange, but he'll be fine. She gave me some ointment for his eye and antibiotics in case of infection. It may take two of us to dose him." I set the bag with the meds on the coffee table. "Oh, and she wants you to have his vet records sent to her." I dug the card out of my pocket and handed it to him.

Jack took the card, glanced at it, and pocketed it. "Sure thing." Then he pulled the ointment out and read the label. He picked up the bottle. "This says the antibiotics need to be stored in the fridge." He got up off the couch and took the bottle out to the kitchen.

When he came back, I said, "The vet—Marcy—was very forthcoming about Alan Howland's wife. Maybe a little too forthcoming."

"Oh?" Jack closed the fridge. "In what way?"

"I got the distinct impression that she was feeding

me negative information about the woman, maybe spreading rumors about her, giving her a motive for murder. At first I was fascinated, but," I paused, thinking about it. "Now I wonder if I was being manipulated. But why? I'm new in town. It was weird. Did you hear anything on the news?"

Gillian paused the TiVo. "I've set up several news shows to record."

I looked at the TV. The picture was paused on my house. "That's my front porch on live TV. I just came in. There was no one out there."

Gillian said, "Apparently, there is now." She pointed toward the front door.

I turned and saw lights shining through the curtains and heard voices and shuffling on the front porch. "Okay, now that's just creepy."

There was a knock at the door. Jack went to the window and pulled the curtain aside. The lights were blinding. He dropped the curtains.

"Don't answer the door," I said, turning to look at the TV. "Gillian, let's get a live picture."

She hit play and fast forward. Sure enough, the reporters were setting up for an interview shot with me. We listened for a few minutes and learned about the background of the house, the murders on the beach, and more about Alan's death, including the presence of two puncture marks on his neck. A lot of speculation followed from that revelation. The last comment was something about trading in a ghost for a vampire.

Then the phone rang.

"Let me guess," Jack said. "You got a landline but didn't think about an unlisted number."

"I actually wanted people to find me. I was

thinking about starting a business, not being hounded by the press."

The knocking on the door continued.

I stood up and moved the bowl of pistachios closer to Jack. "Eat and leave me alone."

He took a couple and cracked the shells open. "They aren't going away."

"I know. I'll talk to them." I had no idea what I was going to say. They knew more than I did.

"Are you sure you should?" Gillian asked.

"No, but I don't see them going away if I don't." I went to the door, and opened it a crack. "Yes?"

"Cassandra Peake? I'm with—" The rest was a blur of microphones, lights, and shouted questions.

"How does it feel to live in a haunted house?"

"Did you see the murder?"

"Was it a vampire?"

"Did you see the body?"

I stepped out onto the porch and pulled the door shut behind me. "I don't know anything. I just moved here." A staccato of lights. "Yes, I saw the body. No, I didn't know him. No, I don't know what happened. No, I haven't...seen...a ghost. No, I'm not a Satanist. What vampires?" Why was I here? A million thoughts. The ocean. As far west as I could go without being in Hawaii. The weather. "That's all I know." I threw my hands up in front of my face and pushed back through the door. I stood on the other side, leaning against it until I heard the noise outside die down.

Gillian peered out the window. "They're going away."

"Good." I walked over and sat on the couch, a little weak in the knees. "We need to watch that. I didn't hear all the questions. The reporters know more about my house than I do."

Gillian hit play, and we all watched as I walked out onto the porch and into incoherency.

Jack laughed. "That was pretty funny!"

"Thanks so much." I said sarcastically. "You've always been a brat." I hoped Phil wasn't watching. That would be all I'd need. "Gillian, can you run it again and pause for each question?"

Gillian did as I asked, and I grabbed my notebook and took notes on the questions.

Gillian paused the tape. "They know more than we do."

Jack said, "I think the background of your house is well known around here. I can't believe so many people buy into this occult crap."

"You seem to be enjoying it," I said.

"I find it all highly entertaining."

"You'd better tell us the story of the house. You told them more than you've told us so far," Gillian said. "How was the girl killed? The one who's supposed to be haunting this place. Jack may not believe in the supernatural, but I'm not so sure."

"Axe murderer?" Jack sounded hopeful.

"Close. But not quite. Probably men her dad owed money to."

"Now she tells us." Jack rolled his eyes.

"I can stop here if you like," I teased.

"No, tell us; otherwise, I'll keep wondering." Gillian grabbed a couple of pistachios and paused the TiVo again.

I cleared my throat. "It's a nice little bedtime story. Realtors were reluctant to show me this place. I found it on my own. When I finally got someone to tell me the story, I learned that legend has it that a group of women mystery writers in the Sixties used to rent this house from one of their members for their meetings. The woman who owned the house at the time was the daughter of Shelagh Macalin, who wrote spooky stories published in women's magazines in the Twenties or Thirties. They held a séance to conjure up her ghost as a kind of a muse for the group. The séance went awry, and instead of Shelagh, they got Doris, the ghost of the illegitimate daughter of a notorious Twenties bootlegger. Judging by my neighbor Mina's reactions while she was in my house, the ghost has a bit of a temper."

"What happened then?" Gillian leaned closer.

"No one knows for sure. The group broke up shortly thereafter, and none of them ever published another story."

Jack shrugged. "If not publishing is the curse, I can live with that."

"Speak for yourself." Gillian poked him in the ribs. "I plan to publish quite a bit in the future. It is odd that it's such a feminist story—all women writers—that ended with the loss of their creativity or receptivity to their creativity."

"What a minute," Jack said. "How did they know they ended up with a ghost? Did they see one? What's their proof? Did they continue to meet here? Did the owner live here? How well known was the story? Did she sell the house?"

I raised a hand. "Hang on. If you want answers, you'll have to run over it again with a smaller truck."

Jack sighed. "How'd they know they got a ghost?

And which ghost they got?"

"I'm not entirely sure. I've only found out about this in the last couple of days. I'm sure there's more to the story given that the cottage seems to have been abandoned with a lot of stuff left behind. Apparently, no one wanted to clean the place out, so I got it lock, stock, and barrel."

Before I could answer, Gillian said, "So who paid the taxes?"

"Pardon?" I asked.

"If that writer abandoned the house, someone must have continued to pay the taxes. Actually, unless the house was in really bad shape when you bought it, someone must have done upkeep from time to time. Leaves in gutters need to be removed. I guess you don't have to worry about frozen pipes out here."

"There have been owners," I said. "Dave said the last owners owned it for five years even though they only stayed here for a total of two weeks."

"Who was on the deed when you bought the house?" Jack asked.

"Now you're going to make me find the paperwork, aren't you?"

Jack nodded.

"We can do that tonight." Gillian extended her long, slim legs and stretched. Her slacks had retained their crease and her pearls were perfectly centered. "Let's do the outside work during the daylight. We still have to find space for the rest of Cass' belongings from the storage units."

"Wasn't there an out building in the floor plans?" Jack asked.

"Yeah," I said. "I think that's the old garage. I

poked my head in when I first looked at the property. There's something out there under a tarp."

Jack perked up. "There's a car out there?"

"Maybe."

"It would be in terrible shape after all these years," Gillian said.

"Not necessarily," he said. "If it's a classic, it could be worth some bucks."

That got my attention. "We should check it out, see if there's a car and if it's salvageable, saleable, or towable."

"Great idea." Gillian's short, blonde hair was tousled, and her peanut-butter-brown eyes twinkled with the excitement of exploration. "In the meantime, we can see what's in the loft."

"We brought a lot more supplies, such as lanterns and Maglites, and some homemade cleaning solution from Gillian's grandmother's formula. It works like a charm."

"Fine with me. We need all the help we can get." I looked Jack over. His loose shirt and baggy jeans hung on his six-foot-two frame. "You're not eating enough."

"Told you." Gillian said, a small smile playing around the corners of her mouth. "He's on a fitness jag. But he does need new clothes to show off his new toned look."

His brown hair was cut shorter than the last time I'd seen him, and I could have sworn his hazel eyes were greener, but that often happened when he was overtired or upset.

I couldn't stop myself from thinking that they were very different. She was so Nordstrom's; he was so Land's End.

I must have been staring because Jack snapped his fingers in my face and said, "Hey! Wake up. Let's go exploring." He looked at Gillian's slacks. "Honey, do you want to change?"

She shook her head. "I don't plan to do any heavy lifting." She winked at me and kissed him on the cheek.

"I have the keys to all the doors around here. It's got to be one of these."

"If not, I don't think it'll be too hard to knock the door in," Jack said. "I'm more worried about the vegetation."

That stopped me. "I didn't think about that. Phil and I had a gardener for years. I don't own anything that would cut away heavy plant growth."

Jack shrugged. "Let's find out."

We trooped out the front door and around back. It was slow going as we picked our way through thick weeds and wild flowers, but it wasn't quite the jungle it might have been because of the sand that had blown up from the beach over the years. The garage was a very small, separate building at the far end of the lot away from the beach. Looking at it, I couldn't believe a car could fit in it. I'd gotten used to the three-car garage we'd had in Pleasanton with a whole bay for tools and storage.

The wood was badly weathered, and the little building hadn't been painted nearly as often as the main house. I couldn't find the key to the padlock, but that didn't slow us down for long. Jack forced the door open and nearly knocked it off its hinges.

At first we couldn't see a thing. Jack swung the big Maglite up and illuminated an ancient car. He gave a low whistle.

"What? It's a pile of—" I inhaled sharply. There was no denying that I had a ghost now, and I think that was her point. A chill shot down my spine.

The woman in the green dress from the beach leaned back across the front seat of the boxy convertible as if the leather weren't stained and torn. She was dressed in a beautifully beaded sea foam green gown, a white fox stole draped across her shoulders. Her body language screamed "mine!"

I quickly looked at Jack and Gillian, but Jack was looking at the car. He ran trembling fingers over the trim.

Gillian stood apart, keeping well away from the grime, and I could see the shock on her face, her eyes wide, mouth open as if to scream. She saw the ghost, but Jack didn't.

"Do you know what this is?" His voice wavered slightly.

"A gho—car?" I ventured.

"A Packard Roadster." His voice broke. "Look at the running boards. The wooden dash." He rubbed dust off the fender. "Gorgeous gold."

"I take it that's a good thing," I said faintly.

The beautiful ghost shifted her pose, putting her face mere inches from his.

Gillian's hysterical laugh was shaky, but it was better than having her scream. She couldn't take her eyes off the ghost. "Oh, you've done it now, Cass. We'll be lucky to get any work out of him around the house." The hand she held up to her mouth shook.

"We can get this running again," he whispered with reverence, buffing the hood with his shirtsleeve.

The ghost leaned toward him with a smile on her

face. She turned toward me and stage-whispered, "Oh, I like him! Abyssinia!" Then she was gone.

The instant she vanished, Gillian let out a burp of a scream, quickly smothered.

Jack turned, stared at us, and stopped babbling. "What are you girls looking at?"

Gillian and I exchanged a glance.

"N-nothing," I said. He hadn't seen her!

It was clear from Gillian's expression that she'd had the same realization. Then I had another.

Holy shit! I really did have a ghost!

Chapter 5

I staggered and my back hit the old, splintered wood, which gave way. I turned and pushed my way out, taking a deep breath of sea air.

Gillian followed me out, whispering, "Ghost. That was a ghost, right? I don't believe it. I don't believe in ghosts. Did you see *Ghost Story*? Can she hurt us? Why didn't Jack see her? Did she say Abyssinia?"

I held a hand up to stop her.

Jack trailed Gillian, looking back over his shoulder, reluctant to leave the roadster and apparently completely oblivious to my spectral guest. "I'll have to get some tarps and check the roof for leaks. I can reinforce that door. Put a better lock on it."

I just nodded at him. He didn't even look at me. Gillian headed for the front door. She opened it and stopped dead. A little shriek escaped from her. I ran into her tense body.

"We can't go in."

I looked over her shoulder into the house. The ghost waggled its fingers at me. I turned quickly to see where Jack was. He'd stopped on the path and was still contemplating the garage.

"Inside." I shoved Gillian ruthlessly into the house and let the screen door bang behind me. I turned to face the ghost. "Who the hell are you and what are you doing here?" It would have been a more effective confrontation if my voice hadn't been shaking.

The ghost arched her eyebrows, leaned toward me, and said, "Boo!"

I nearly peed my pants. She tilted her chin up and laughed. Guess we all knew who had the upper hand.

Her dark hair was cut in a bob with thick, shiny bangs, and she was made up with red red lips and very thin eyebrows. How does a ghost keep her makeup looking good?

"I live here," she said.

"No, you don't. This is my house. I bought it."

"I was here first."

Jack came in and headed for the kitchen. "I'm starving." He walked through her, and she broke apart and faded away.

Gillian giggled nervously. I clamped my hand over my mouth before I could scream. Gillian gained control of herself.

His head stuck in the fridge, Jack muttered, "Man, I'm hungry. Do you mind if I try to weatherproof the garage today? I don't think the salt air is good for her."

"Her?" I asked. Had he seen the ghost?

"The car," Gillian said to me *sotto voce*, gripping my hand. "No, we don't mind, Jack. Knock yourself out."

Someone honked outside, and I jumped before turning toward the screen door. More reporters? A blood red Jeep with a dog crate in the back pulled up, and Marcy hopped out. I took a deep breath and opened the door.

"Hi, Cass. I was down this way and thought I'd come by, find out the name of the food, and check on the patient."

I spoke slowly, making sure I had regained some control. "Hi, Marcy. C'mon in." I held the door for her, looking around to see if the ghost was back. "Meet Jack and Gillian, my brother and sister-in-law."

She shifted her bag to her left hand and held out her right. "Cute names. Did you decide to get married for the joke?"

Awkward silence. Jack set his sandwich down and shook her hand.

I stepped into the breach. "I've tried for years to get her to go by Jill, but for some strange reason she refuses. C'mon in and see the patient." I led everyone into the house.

Thor trotted forward immediately when Jack called him and head-butted his leg. Jack picked him up, and Thor licked his cheek. Jack held him while Marcy conducted a quick examination.

"Hmm. I'm going to debride the area a bit and remove the hair that's sticking to the scab. Do you have a towel we can put on the table?"

"Be right back." I grabbed one from an open box in the hall, looking around for the ghost and wondering if Jack had dissipated her permanently. I spread the towel on the trestle table.

Marcy opened her bag and set to work on Thor's head.

Gillian's eyes met mine, and I knew she was also wondering where the ghost went.

I needed something to do. "Coffee? Tea? I'll just plug the kettle in." I pulled some cups down from the cabinets.

Gillian mouthed, "Where'd she go?"

I shrugged.

"Such a good kitty!" Marcy cooed as she finished up.

"Want him? He's yours," I said only half kidding.

She laughed. "Trust me. You'll grow to love him."

"Sure I will."

Jack downed the last of his sandwich and punched my shoulder lightly.

Marcy stripped off her gloves and dropped them into her bag, before setting Thor on the ground and taking the cup I offered her. "Thanks. By the way, any more news on the drowning accident?"

"Not really," Jack said. "Although my sister had to fend off the press."

Marcy laughed. "I saw that on TV. Nice, Cass."

"I'm never going to live that down. Deer in the headlights."

"I also saw a brief interview with Sara, Alan's widow. Did you see it?"

"No, but we may have gotten it on TiVo. I've been taping the news," Gillian said. "What did she say?"

Marcy said, "You never really know what she's going to say. Once I told her, 'I need to be in two places at once.' Sara said, 'Einstein said everything happens at the same time, so you probably are.' When I said, 'Excuse me?' She said, 'It's that relativity thingy.'"

Gillian laughed. I heard the nervousness in her laughter. I also realized that Marcy hadn't answered the question about what Sara said when she was interviewed. She was like a magician, misdirecting our attention.

"Oh, that's good," Jack said. "You have a friend like that, don't you, Gillian?"

Gillian stopped laughing and glared at him.

Marcy said, "Sara always thought that Alan looked like William Thacker. You know, from "Notting Hill". Hugh Grant."

I had a flash memory of the body on the beach.

"It probably helped that he was a bookstore owner in the movie. Sara's nothing if not earnest. And dramatic." She took a sip of her coffee. "You'll see." Then she looked as though an idea had just struck her. "Why don't you come over to the clinic for coffee tomorrow morning? I'll also invite her and introduce you!"

"I really shouldn't. Jack and Gillian are here to help me move in." I looked at Gillian and Jack for rescue. "And Sara must be in mourning for her husband."

"I'm sure she could use the distraction," Marcy said.

Gillian looked pointedly at me. "You need to have friends here when we leave. Go ahead. We'll keep working on the place, won't we, Jack?"

I got that she meant someone I could talk to about the ghost.

Jack grunted.

"In that case, sure."

"Great! I'll set it up and get back to you." She got up, picked up her bag, and prepared to go. "Oh, before I forget, what cat food do you need?"

Jack handed her a can they'd brought.

Marcy took a look. "Oh, sure. This is a good one. I'll order it and let you know when it's in."

We all stood, and I showed her out to her car.

She got in and leaned out the window. "Don't hesitate to bring him back in if there's any sign of infection."

"Will do."

She waved as she drove off. I walked back in, sat down, and finished my coffee.

"That was a little strange," Gillian ventured.

She could have been talking about Marcy or the ghost. "No kidding."

"Be back in a few minutes," Jack said.

"He's headed back to the car. Can we talk?" Gillian asked as she picked up after Jack and shot a meaningful look at me.

"I'm not really sure what to say." I looked around. "I'm guessing that was the bootlegger's daughter. What was her name?"

"Doris. No idea what her last name is. She looked like a flapper so the right time period. Do we believe in ghosts?"

"Do we have a choice?"

"Oh, Cass. What are you going to do?"

I started to cry. Gillian held me until I got it under control.

"I have no idea what I'm going to do. This is unreal." I wiped my eyes. "I have no place to go. No one will buy this place."

"It'll be okay. We can figure this out. Don't ghosts usually have unfinished business? Maybe we can ask it what it wants."

The front door banged, and Jack came in. "I checked the building. There's really no extra room out there and no other place on the property to stash your stuff. It'll have to go in here." He seemed to notice that I'd been crying. "Are you all right? I hope you don't take my teasing seriously."

"I'm just feeling a bit overwhelmed. Maybe I made a mistake."

"Oh, no." He sat down. "This is a great place. I'm sure there's a lot of stuff here you can get rid of to fit your stuff in."

Gillian added, "Before you make any irreversible decisions, let's check out the attic. I've sold some stuff on eBay in the past. You can always do that. Make it a condition of sale on the larger stuff that the buyer picks it up, though. There should be a local listing site. And there's always freecycling. Post stuff to your local freecycle email list, and people will pick it up from your porch. But it has to be a free giveaway. Better to try selling first."

Jack said, "We're getting ahead of ourselves. We haven't examined the attic thoroughly."

I got up. "Let's find out," I said, moving to the living room and heading up the small circular stair.

"It may be a bit hard to get large items up here," Jack said, following me.

Gillian stopped and knelt on a tread. "This is amazing. Look, each riser has been hand cut. The scrollwork is divine. This staircase is a little gem."

"I hope you still feel that way after we haul a bunch of stuff up here." My head cleared the floor, and I looked around. At first glance, the attic looked like a little harem tent. I hadn't realized that I'd stopped cold until I heard a muffled yell from below. "Oh, sorry." I moved on up into the space, grabbing the railing that extended above the stairs.

Gillian followed me up into the room with Jack on her heels.

"Could this be where they held the séances?" I

lifted some of the scarves and lace off lamps and tables. "Modern lamps in addition to the candles."

Turned wooden candle stands stood around the room with partially burned candles on them. Some were as tall as four feet.

"I'll bet you're right." Gillian put the shades up. "What a view! You might want to rethink your bedroom strategy. How fantastic to wake up with a view of the ocean every morning. You could use the bedroom downstairs as storage."

Gillian's words sparked my imagination. This could be an aerie. I pulled down the extra fabric from the windows facing the ocean, kicked up a cloud of dust, and sneezed three times in a row.

"Bless you!" Gillian said. "Oh, three times. That's supposed to mean good luck or something good is about to happen to you. I can never remember."

"Probably means either you're catching cold or allergic to dust," Jack added.

"Everyone's allergic to dust. I was trying to clear the view. There's no need to block it this high up and facing the ocean. No one can see in."

"Such rich colors. The afternoon sun gilds everything." Jack leaned on the window frame and looked out.

"Only when it isn't rainy or foggy," Gillian added.

"Spoilsport." He kissed her.

"I like your idea, Gillian, but I don't know if we can get the bed up here."

"Sure we can," Jack said confidently.

"Good. This room feels right." And oddly I meant it. I felt more positive even knowing that this was the likely location for the séances.

The large room was peaceful. It was insulated and finished. Under the eaves, someone had built in storage cabinets. It felt more like a loft than an attic because the windows were large, and the room was spacious. With the circular staircase, the entry was always open.

We spent the rest of the afternoon cleaning the loft and hauling my belongings up. This is where I wanted to wake up in the morning.

Exhausted by evening, we ate in front of the TV and scanned the news recordings Gillian had set up. Most were pretty standard and repetitive. Alan Howland had been an attractive man in a slim, intellectual way. His wife was pretty with big blue eyes and a bubble of blonde hair.

"I don't think she's going to be ready to have coffee with me in the morning. I should cancel out."

"I agree," Gillian said. "What was your vet thinking?"

"No idea. Marcy doesn't seem terribly broken up by her friend's husband's death. Maybe she didn't know him that well."

Jack leaned back on the couch after we watched the last newscast. "I'm switching to live feed."

"Vampires have made a second appearance on the California coast." The young female reporter smiled.

Jack sat up straight. "What? Vampires?" He rewound the live news report.

We listened in rapt silence while the reporter discussed a cult movie that had been made years ago about vampires in a small coastal town not far from here.

"I think the reporters ran out of new material," Gillian said. "So now they're creating their own."

I shook my head. "According to the reporter we saw earlier, there were two holes in Alan's neck and his body was exsanguinated." I hit record.

"Sounds like a vampire, but it also sounds like they're trying to blame the local gamers to me," Jack said.

"Didn't you used to play "Vampire: The Masquerade?"" I asked.

"That was a long time ago. College days." Jack carried his plate to the kitchen and got a beer from the fridge. "I just don't like to see blame shifted onto people because they're a little different."

I had a flashback to Jack in college: shy, withdrawn, always reading or gaming. I nodded. "I agree with you."

Gillian added, "They didn't actually say that it was murder, just a suspicious death. I'm going to set up some national news. See if it's a big enough story to get picked up by the networks and CNN."

"With the quirky vampire twist, it wouldn't surprise me," Jack said.

"I hope not. I don't need everyone I know seeing this story." I was thinking about Phil as I wiped the table. "Maybe I should invite Mina to come for a visit now that things are cleaned up a bit." And, I thought, now that I have plenty of lights and company. "Mia mentioned an evil ley line."

"Ley lines?" Gillian asked. "As in Harmonic Convergence? I was a little kid in Arizona when people descended on Sedona because its converging ley lines gave the place great power."

Jack raised his eyebrows.

"Supposedly. Supposedly gave the place great

power."

"You went to the Harmonic Convergence?"

Gillian blushed. "My mother dragged me along with her. At dawn."

"You're full of surprises." Jack laughed and then turned toward me. "Ghost stories and ley lines? Does Mina really know anything about the history of this house?"

"To be honest, I'm not sure. She talks as if she does. She writes those poorly published short collections of ghost stories that you see sold in shops in tourist towns. Line drawing illustrations. Garish single color perfect-bound covers. *Ghost Stories of Las Lunas. More Ghost Stories of Las Lunas*."

"Let's invite her over," Gillian said excitedly. "We should go buy the books."

It wasn't a bad idea. "Would you guys mind picking them up in the morning, and then I'll run over and ask her to lunch. I need to make some friends."

"From what you've said, I'm not sure the two of you will be BFFs," Jack said.

I shrugged. "Maybe not, but she's a neighbor. If I ever need help, she's the closest." And the most likely to be able to shed some light on what I'd seen in the garage.

"Good point."

"I need a bio break." I headed for the bathroom, shut the door, and settled onto the seat when Doris walked through the door.

"I need your help," she said in a high, breathy voice.

"Shit!" I yelled. After I caught my breath, I said, "You're a ghost. What on earth would you need help with?"

"Nice choice of words. 'On earth' I need help finding out who killed me."

"Surely they've been dead for years. Besides, why do you care? Aren't you supposed to go into the light or something?"

"Or something."

"Did you see a light?" Did I really just ask a ghost if she'd "seen the light"?

"For a second and then it winked out, leaving me behind." Her voice was petulant like a disappointed child.

"Bummer. So that wasn't a permanent 'go into the light?'" I felt a little sorry for her. In a well-lit bathroom, Doris was not a frightening ghost.

"Yeah, not so much. Hollywood. What do they know. And don't go inviting that lunatic from next door in here. She gives me the heebie jeebies."

"She gives *you* the heebie jeebies? And anyway I don't see how I can help you." She was so not what I was expecting.

"Hello! No body?" She pushed her hand through my face. "I can't do anything. I need you."

Shockwaves ran through me. It was as if icy water with the consistency of air washed through my insides without a drop touching my skin. I shivered. "Don't do that again."

"Do what? This?" She did it again.

"Cut it out or I won't help you!" I tried to be emphatic while keeping my voice low.

"Does that mean you will?"

"We're going to need rules."

"Like what?"

"Leave me along while I'm showering, dressing, peeing."

"Seriously?" She tilted her head to one side.

"Oh, I'm serious. You're giving me pee fright."

"Agreed."

And she vanished.

Chapter 6

With a sigh of relief, I relaxed and finished up.

As I left the bathroom, Gillian called out, "What happened?"

I had a full body shiver. "I had the *ghost* of an idea." I met Gillian's startled gaze and nodded my head, hoping she'd get the hint.

"No!" she whispered. Clearly, she did.

I nodded. "But now we have a deal. I help her, and she won't do that to me again."

Gillian choked. "Help her? How?"

"Beats me. She said she wants to find out who killed her. Guess we'll find out. I'll need to look for letters, notes, a diary. Any background material. I need clues to guide a search." I looked up and spoke into the air. "Someone should tell me where to look if they want my help." Suddenly, I realized that I was talking to the ghost the same way Mina had. Not good. "Say goodnight to Jack for me. Can you lock up down here?"

"Sure thing, but you know, you and I need to talk about this."

I turned to look at her. Her eyes were pleading, and she looked scared.

"I know. Really I do. I just can't do it now. I'm exhausted." I paused. "I don't think she'll hurt any of us. She asked for my help. Don't worry. Please." I had an odd feeling of certainty about my ghost but no idea why. I thought it had something to do with our bathroom conversation. Doris needed my help, and for the first time since she'd glimmered in my peripheral vision, I felt in control. I didn't know if I could help her, but I did know that I was going to try.

Gillian smiled. "Okay. Tomorrow."

"'Night." I climbed the circular stairs to the loft. I looked out the window at the moonlit ocean for a bit and then turned on the light by the bed and looked around for something to read, my habit before sleeping.

Poking around in the cupboards in the eaves, I found a leather-bound volume. Carrying it to the bed, I propped up some pillows and started to read the lovely script.

****

I woke up late the next morning, wondering how I could get answers. Whether it was the atmosphere up in the loft, the diary I'd been reading, or a dream visitation by the ghost, I didn't know, but I dressed quickly and came downstairs with Mina on my mind. She might have some answers for me.

Gillian stood at the kitchen window, looking at something beachward.

"We could pay a visit to Mad Mina," I said, moving toward the coffee smell that filled the room. Mina had told me when I'd first moved in that my house had a reputation for being haunted, she'd implied knowledge of the house's history, and now a ghost asked for my help finding out who killed her. I looked around. "Where's Jack?"

Gillian, still looking out the window, pointed vaguely toward the beach. "He's chatting with the surfer dude."

"Huh. Maybe he can get us a local perspective on the situation. I need more information. I feel as though everyone knows what's going on but me."

That finally got Gillian's attention, and she turned around. "Have you thought about looking through some of the old papers and letters we've seen?"

"I did, and I found a diary last night. Back in a sec." I climbed to the loft, opened the bedside table drawer where I'd stashed it, and pulled it out. I flipped through it as I returned to the living room. "Here's a June entry. 'Dear Diary, Daddykins bought me a Packard roadster today in a luscious gold with a cream leather interior. I simply must go shopping to find something that matches. I was reading *Time* magazine today and was horrified to read that Mrs. Livermore said that women become incoherent on the public platform because they are so accustomed to talking to husbands and brothers that they can't seem to get used to talking to anyone else. I'm a New Woman and have no difficulty at all speaking whenever and wherever I feel like it. I cut my hair and hemmed my skirts. Of course, Daddykins didn't approve, but I'm his little kitten.'"

The diary slammed shut as if of its own will, and the familiar clammy cold wind pushed through me.

Doris materialized half an inch from my nose. "Who said you could read my diary?"

Gillian let out a small scream.

My blood ran cold as my earlier confidence in Doris' intentions evaporated. "Don't do that! We have a deal." My voice was too shaky to be effective. So much for being in control.

"You aren't using the commode. You don't have

permission to read my diary. That's private!"

"You're dead...Doris." I put a hand through her to demonstrate my point.

She dematerialized and reformed, still glaring.

"Do you still want my help? Then you'll have to cut me some slack. I have to know your story so that I can help you find your murderer. There are things you don't know or don't remember, but your diary... That's a window into your head right at the time things were happening. There are clues in there, Doris. I repeat. Do you still want my help?"

She looked mulish for a few more seconds, and then her body language telegraphed her compliance. "Yes. Go ahead and read it, but if you make fun—"

"We won't. I promise. We may smile and even laugh, but it will be from the sheer enjoyment of your prose."

That made her mouth quirk up slightly.

Gillian had kept a low profile during Doris' hijinks. "Why can't Jack see you?"

Doris shrugged. "I don't want him to. I don't trust men."

"But you loved your father."

Doris shrugged one shoulder.

Something occurred to me. "Doris, did you ever live here?"

"Why?" She crossed her arms over her chest.

"Why's your car in the shed?"

Gillian had started pouring a cup of coffee and spilled it all over the counter.

Doris averted her gaze. "I don't know. We stayed here sometimes. I really liked the place."

"From what I've heard, you were murdered on the

beach."

"I don't remember my death."

"I think whoever killed you hid your car in the shed."

Gillian mopped up her mess. "But wouldn't the owners of the cottage have noticed?"

"You'd think. Maybe they were in on it, or maybe the place has been so rarely inhabited that it never registered with anyone. Maybe no one has looked before. Doris, do you have any idea why you returned during that séance in the Sixties? Why not before? Did you make the decision to come back?"

"I don't think so. I don't know."

"Has anyone lived here very long after your return?" I had an idea. "Or have you made sure that they moved out quickly?"

She actually looked sheepish. "I was in a bit of a snit for quite a while and put the kibosh on some folks' plans."

"That answers that," Gillian said.

"We need some answers. I'm going over to ask Mina to lunch." I handed the diary to Gillian.

Doris made a face.

I looked straight at her, determined. "It's her vocation to collect ghost lore. She can help us."

"She seems a little reclusive," Gillian said.

"Weird," Doris said.

"So okay. She might not win any social awards, but do you want answers or don't you?"

"What's it like being dead?" Gillian asked.

"Not as much fun as you'd like it to be. Pretty boring actually," Doris said with a resigned air.

"*You* seem to be getting a kick out of it or out of

what you can do to us," I said.

"Sorry, but being murdered makes one a bit cranky."

"Apology accepted." Since I seemed to have the upper hand, I decided to push my luck. "And don't mess with us over lunch. We need intel from Mina."

Doris raised her right hand, waggled her fingertips in goodbye, and then faded away, her fringe being the last thing to go.

"I'm going next door to talk to Mina. Do we have enough stuff here to pull together lunch?"

"Cass?" Gillian's voice was very quiet.

"Yeah?" I stopped on my way to the door.

"She's a ghost. I mean, really a ghost. She spoke to us."

"You aren't going nuts. That was a ghost although I wouldn't tell many people."

"Why not?"

"You'd either end up on some reality show or in a loony bin."

"Oh. Good point." She hesitated. "I don't believe in ghosts."

"You said that before. But seriously? You've seen her. Don't you believe what you see?"

"Aren't you scared?" Her eyes were huge. "I mean, I think it would be normal to be scared."

"Surprisingly, no. I don't know why I'm not. I'm just not. I guess you never know how you'll react until you do. I'm curious. I want to know more. I want to know if everyone becomes a ghost. I want to know what she experienced when she died."

Gillian took a deep breath. "Okay. Don't worry about lunch. I'll handle it." Her eyes were fixed on the diary. She didn't notice as I went out the door.

The fog had burned off early today and the sun shone. A gentle breeze blew offshore as I walked up toward Mina's house, which was painted in shades of gray and gray-blue, much like the lady herself. As I watched, she came out onto a widow's walk at the top of the house, saw me coming toward her, and went back in. A moment later, her front door opened, and she stepped out onto her porch.

I waved. "Hi, Mina." I climbed the five steps to her front porch. The railings of the wraparound porch were steel gray and the balustrades were white with star cutouts. "I…we were wondering if you'd like to come over for lunch today. I've nearly moved in, and the place is much more livable now."

She cocked her head to the right, looking like a quizzical bird. "Yes, thank you. I'd like that." Then she just looked at me. She didn't invite me in or ask any questions.

"Uh, shall we go over now?"

She nodded and took a step forward.

"Okay." I turned around, grabbed the railing, and stepped down the stairs.

Mina silently glided behind me. She didn't go back for a purse or to lock her door. Trusting, I guessed.

She didn't say anything as we walked back down to my place. I held the door for her as she stepped inside. She looked around like an observant heron.

"Through here." I led the way to the big trestle table.

Gillian was setting out fixings for sandwiches and boiling water for tea and coffee.

"Mina, Gillian. Gillian, Mina."

Gillian nodded.

Mina said, "Pleased to meet you." Then she turned to me. "Your sister-in-law."

"Yes. Have a seat." I gestured to a chair, and Mina sat. "Gillian, where's Jack?"

"Not back yet."

"His loss." I turned to Mina. "I remember you like tea. I have hot tea, iced tea, water, beer, a variety of sodas. What would you like?"

Mina smiled. "I still like hot tea."

I realized that I'd started to think of her as the Grey Lady. Not gray but grey. The English spelling. There was something proper and faded about her like a rose that's lost its color pressed between the pages of a leather-bound book with thick pages.

"Tea it is." I set the tea caddy in front of her with a creamer and sugar bowl. "I found some exquisite silver tea spoons tucked away in a drawer." I set out the delicate spoons. "I've learned a lot since you were last here. I even bought a couple of your books." I set two thin volumes in front of her, one with a green cover, one with yellow. "Will you sign them for me?"

She hesitated only briefly. "Sure. Happy to. Do you want them personalized?"

"Please. To Cass."

Her handwriting was spidery. She used a fountain pen with peacock blue ink. Not a color I was expecting. I couldn't see her using a ballpoint, but the splash of color made me smile. She was a woman of subtle dichotomies. She pushed them toward me when she was through. "Have you read them?"

"I've read through some of the stories. Not at night, though. You're a very evocative writer. Not what I was expecting in books that sell in tourist centers."

"It's very hard to find markets for ghost stories these days. That is," she amended, "for ghost stories that aren't romance novels."

"Nothing romantic about those stories." I filled her teacup with hot water.

Gillian slipped into a chair and opened a Heineken.

I poured myself a cup and sat down across from Mina. "I've learned more about my house and its former inhabitants since the last time we talked. I've decided to make the loft my bedroom." I put together a provolone and turkey sandwich.

Mina started. "Are you sure that's wise?"

"I'm aware that you were part of the séance group that met here. Can you tell me anything about them?"

She shook her head. "I told you about the one séance, the one that raised the ghost of Doris, who, by the way, still lives here."

Her gaze was penetrating, more than I expected from her. I'd come to regard her as harmless; now I wasn't so sure.

"Do you know who killed her?" Gillian asked.

"No. They found her raped and murdered—throat slit—on the beach in front of your place."

"Murder Beach," I interjected.

"That's right." She met my eyes. "I'm surprised you've already heard the local nickname for the place. You've only been here what…five days?"

"Something like that. Bodies seem to be piling up, though."

Gillian gasped next to me. I hadn't intended to be shocking, but something about Mina was pulling it out of me. I'd already judged her as a flake and half written her off, but now I wasn't so sure.

Mina nodded. "Yes. Alan. Funny that he was murdered on your beach. He had no call to be out here. He's a townie. I've never seen him at the beach."

"And you watch the beach a lot."

She nodded again. "Yes, I do."

"What are you looking for?"

"I don't know yet, but I will when I see it." She half smiled.

Following where she was leading, I asked, "So, is there a tie in between Doris and Alan?"

She frowned. "Hard to tell just yet." She put mayo on a couple of slices of bread and poked through the cold cuts. "I expect that all the pieces will fall into place once you've answered that question."

Odd that she was expecting me to answer it.

She took a bite and closed her eyes for a moment. "I write ghost stories, Cass. I'm fascinated by everything that goes on in this little town. Read all my stories. Let me know if you see a pattern."

I was tempted to tell her that I was also reading Doris' diary, but something made me hold back. "What do you know about Alan? Why would someone murder him?" I pulled a notepad over.

She shrugged. "Why does anyone murder anyone? Love. Money. Vengeance. I bought books from him. The gamers—you've seen them on the beach—use his shop because he has a section on vampires, steampunk, and Victoriana."

"Does he? I mean, did he?" I doodled a pair of fangs on the pad.

"He was in a rivalry with our other bookseller Brendan, who owns Dreams and Dust. I've heard about

91

their contentions over collections and rare books. Alan is…was very private, and it's not as though we ran in the same crowds. He didn't have any enemies I was aware of. If anything, he seemed to go out of his way to be cordial. Cold, in my opinion, but cordial. Now let me ask you something. I've heard he might have fallen from the cliff."

That was a surprise. "I haven't heard that, but then I haven't lived here very long. No one's really letting me in on the local gossip."

"Have you asked your ghost?"

"What?" That startled me. How much did she know?

"I mean, have you tried to have a séance?"

Ah. Got it. "No, no, I don't really want to do that. Certainly not while I'm sleeping in the séance room."

Gillian got up and set her dish in the sink. "I'm going to see if I can find Jack." She went out the back door.

"I don't think your sister-in-law likes me."

"I think all this murder and ghost business is more than she wants to deal with. She only came to help me clean up and move in."

Mina nodded. "But you believe." She squinted at me. "You've seen. You know."

I swallowed. "Yes."

She seemed satisfied. "I will help you in any way I can. You have permission to enter my house any time whether I'm there or not. You may find it a sanctuary when you need it." She wiped her mouth. "I have some old papers and research. I'll look for them. You might be interested." She tapped the green book. "Doris' story is in here. The bones of it, anyway. I couldn't use all

the information I have. Not for public consumption."
She stood just as Jack and Gillian came in the back
door. "There is the story of one of the séances." She
glanced at Jack, "Truncated, of course, and with Doris'
identity masked."

She looked into my eyes. "And, Cass, be careful on
the beach at night." She nodded at me again and swiftly
left.

Chapter 7

Jack came in the back door followed by Gillian as Mina went out the front. "Who was that?"

"My ghost writing neighbor. According to Mina, there're a couple of stories we need to read about my house in her little green book."

Mina was beginning to grow on me as I settled down and stopped acting like one big, raw nerve. Funny thing about me, but when I get scared or nervous, I move emotionally toward center and lop off things along the edges of my life that are strange, unusual, or different. Since I'd moved, I'd been reacting like that. Talking to Mina today reminded me that I needed to be open to the new possibilities afforded by this radical change in my life. Doris had already blown my preconceptions into glittering fragments. I breathed deeply. I had everything to gain.

"Is that *Ghost Stories* or *More Ghost Stories*?" Jack walked to the table and frowned down at the two books.

"No point in using the titles. They're meaningless. Green book and yellow book are sufficient. It's *More*, the green book."

Jack walked over to the table, picked the book up, and skimmed it. "This one looks interesting: 'The YesYes Board.'" He looked up. "Sounds like a séance to me."

I shrugged. "She didn't give me titles, and I didn't

think to ask. But she did mention a story about a séance that was a disguised version of one that occurred here."

"She's an author. She probably wants us to read all her work." Gillian took the book out of his hands. "Jack, I know you're easily diverted, but don't randomly start reading ghost stories. We need to look for the one about Doris."

"We should read ghost stories by the fire tonight." Jack tried to grab the book back.

Gillian swatted him with it but surrendered the book. He thumbed through the book. "Here it is. *Death on Murder Beach.*"

I shivered. "I'm not sure I'm up for this."

Gillian said, "Jack, this had better be—"

Jack raised a hand. "This isn't really a story, probably not even scary. This book is more like an anthology, and this story or article has a different tone, less story, more narrative. 'A small section of beach near the state park in Las Lunas is known to the locals as Murder Beach. No one knows when this appellation started, but the most notorious murder to occur here was that of a beautiful young flapper in the mid-1920s. Her murder was never solved, and her father died a broken man.'"

Someone snorted, and I looked around.

"Was that a comment on my reading?"

"No, Jack. Sorry." I looked at Gillian.

She shrugged, and I knew it had been Doris.

Jack read, "He died shortly after her death." He looked up.

Gillian folded a bath towel. "This investigation is going to take a while at this rate."

"Her throat was slit from ear to ear—"

"Stop!" It was my turn to whip the book out of his hands. "This is daytime reading."

"Okay, that was creepy. Not sure I want you to read more, either. Especially by firelight." Gillian took the book from me, closed it, and set it on top of the yellow book on the table. "Let's change the subject."

"Okay. Hey, Cass, I enjoyed talking to your other neighbor."

"Really?"

"Um hum."

"And?"

"He's really happy that you're in this house."

"And?"

"And he's really curious about what's going on over here. He seems very 'live and let live,' but I don't think he likes to be left out if there's any fun going on."

"And he thinks ghosts are fun?" Gillian chimed in, shivering.

"There's something elfin about him." Jack waved his hands in an indistinct gesture.

"Seriously, Jack?" I said. "He's over six feet tall, shaggy blond, with over-sized feet and a love of falling off wood in the water. Just about as far from elf as you can get."

Jack seemed reluctant to give his idea up. "Okay, but there's something—I don't know—twinkly about him."

"Twinkly?" I sputtered.

Gillian just laughed. "Cass? Please. We have to tell him. I can't take it anymore. He's scampering around the edges of the truth."

"Tell me what?"

"Sit down, Jack." I gestured toward a chair. "What

do you think, Gillian? A beer?"

She got one out of the fridge and twisted the top off, setting the cold one down in front of him. "Drink."

He did as he was told. After a long pull, he set the bottle down. "Okay?"

Gillian sat down next to him and put her hand on his forearm. "I know you don't believe in the supernatural, despite your 'Dave's an elf' riff."

His expression changed from confusion to cynicism. "If this is a practical joke because I was reading ghost stories…"

Gillian plowed ahead. "You were intrigued by Doris' car. Did you see her sitting in the car?"

He rolled his eyes. "Hon…puh-leeze."

"I did."

"Sure."

I closed my eyes and shook my head. "Jack, I've seen her, too. We asked her why you couldn't see her, and she said she didn't want you to because she doesn't trust men."

"Riiiiiiiiiiiight." He drew the word out. "Okay, I'll lay off the spooky stuff…for a while."

"But you were intrigued by the séances! You seem to love the ghost stories."

"Give it up. I'm not falling for it." He stood. "Going for a walk along the beach. Want to come, Gillian?"

With a look over her shoulder at me, Gillian grabbed her jacket and followed him out the door.

"That went well," I said to no one in particular.

"Men." Doris materialized at the table with her chin resting on her hands. "And you wonder why I don't trust them."

I sat down opposite her. "Doris, you could have just appeared to him. Now he's mad at me. Thinks I'm lying to him."

She looked at me slyly. "Will you help me?"

"And you'll appear to him?"

"In Technicolor."

"Deal."

"Thank you. I'll be good. There are things I can do to help you. Things you don't know about yet. I have ways of getting information."

"I'm sure you do, but I'll start with Google. I also need to spend some time looking for a job or I won't be here very long to help you."

She leaned back. "You should talk to Ricardo and Mia."

"Why?" I thought about the two who'd come to my door. "Is he hiring?"

"When they play on the beach, they talk about their plans. He has some ideas for a company he and Mia are trying to start. He's a little…um…unfocused. He's looking for someone who can execute on his business plan while he handles the graphics and Mia handles the techy side."

"Doris, the 'techy' side? I thought you were from the Twenties."

"Get a grip. I've been dead since then, but I've been paying attention. At first I tried to hang on, but things went from bad to worse. The Thirties were beautiful and fragile. The Forties frightening. The Fifties boring. The Sixties rocked my world."

I bit my tongue hard but didn't interrupt her. This was so not what I was expecting.

"I loved the demonstrations over at the college.

Ban the bomb. Civil rights. Women's Studies Program. Lately, it's been against the tuition hikes. I miss disco."

"That makes sense." As much as anything she was saying did. "I can really see a flapper getting into disco."

"The point is that I'm not stuck in time even though my time was the best, most stylish time ever. Bix Beiderbecke. Best jazz cornet ever." She closed her eyes and shimmied.

"I apologize. I was stereotyping you. I guess I thought I knew what a ghost was. You know. All woo woo. Stuck in the past. Moaning. Doomed to haunt the place they died."

"That last bit is true."

"Ah. That's unfortunate."

"Tell me about it." She rolled her eyes. "But I'm working on ways around it. Since you moved in with the mangy beast, I've had a few ideas."

"You aren't going to hurt Thor, are you?"

"Oh, please. I love animals…mostly."

"What does that mean?"

"It means there are downsides to possessing them. Desire to eat mice. Lick between my toes. Yuck."

"*Possessing* them?"

"When I'm possessing someone or something, I can go anywhere they can. At least, I think so. I'm still testing that theory."

"You can possess us?"

"I haven't tried a human yet, but there are a lot of stories about it, so it should be possible."

"Don't even think about it," I said, scowling.

"Oh, I'm already thinking about it. If you won't help me, I'll have to do some poking around on my own."

"I already said I'd help. You're not as forthcoming, though. I'd like to know more about Ricardo and Mia."

"He's an art major. She's a computer science major. He wants to make a go of the company now while he's in school to help with his expenses and tuition. They're piling up student loan debt. He's tried to sell their services as a web site design company, but they're kids and only a few places have taken them seriously. He needs someone older, someone more professional to sell the web sites and designs and handle the business end of things. The two of them will handle the back end, coding, graphics, and stuff. I've watched you on your laptop. You need a job; he needs a front man."

"Front woman. Keep up."

She grinned at me.

I couldn't help the smile that was spreading across my face. "Thanks, Doris. I will follow up on your tip and then get to work on your little problem."

Planning to try to catch up to Jack and Gillian to lure them back so that Doris could dazzle my brother, I pulled on my old dark green sweater and my black nylon windbreaker to offset the wind chill and started for the door. Thor beat me to it.

"Uh uh. No. No way. You'll run away, and Jack will kill me." A shiver shot down my spine. "Sorry. Didn't mean that," I said to the universe. Enough death on this beach.

I started to push the door open. Thor stuck his nose in the crack.

I sighed. "Look, Thor, you can't go with me. Cats stay indoors. There are things out there that want to munch you. Haven't you already had enough of the seagulls?" I looked at Thor's menacing frame. "Then again maybe not."

Grabbing him before he could get his teeth fully loaded, I tossed him on the couch and dashed out the door. I got twenty feet before I heard a sound like a boxer rhythmically drumming a punching bag with his gloves. I turned and saw Thor, standing on his hind legs, beat against the glass pane with his front paws.

"You're going to break the glass," I said. "Okay, you asked for it. I'm going to lock you in the bedroom." I walked back and opened the door a crack, preparing to ease in and grab him. "I'm beginning to understand why Jack and Gillian got rid of you."

Thor threw himself against the door. Startled, I relaxed my grip for a second. He bolted past me and out the door.

"No!" I yelled after him. "There's something creepy about you, hairball."

He chose that moment to meow-howl.

No, he couldn't be answering me. Then again weirder things had been happening. I stuck my hands in my pockets and walked across my sandy lawn toward the rocks that kept the beach at bay. I looked down the beach to see if I could spot them.

With the tide in, the water was wild. The wide flat boulder that marked the border of my property was the best starting point to walk down the beach. I half-jumped onto it, not wanting to get too frisky since the rocks got slippery quickly, and, given the water temperature, I didn't want to go swimming. Not when that might have been what killed Alan Howland.

The sea was gray today, the palette of colors

ranging from pearl gray spray that fanned around the rocks to slate gray in the thickest part of the waves. The patchy surf swirled and then was sucked back into the sea. It was quickly becoming too dangerous to continue walking that close to the water. I found a small trail that led away from the beach and started up the steep incline, using my hands to steady myself. Perhaps it would lead to the road, and I could make my way back home. Tendrils of fog crept up the hillside. I looked up to gauge the distance I still had to go when I saw a large black cat with amber eyes watching me.

"Thor?" I called out, not sure.

The fog swirled around the cat, and it was gone. I headed in the direction I'd last seen the cat, picking my way carefully through the fog and over the uneven ground. I felt cut off from the world, almost as though I'd traveled to another dimension. Sounds were muffled, and it seemed to be growing dark even though it was still afternoon.

Then the fog cleared, and I was standing on my road above Mina's house. Traffic sounds were back although distant, and I could see my own front door. I hurried down and discovered Thor sitting on the front porch, grooming himself. I bit my tongue before I said something that would make him scurry off again. Gently, I turned the doorknob and let us both in. Only then did I breathe a sigh of relief.

"Cass!"

I jumped a mile. "Jack! Don't do that."

He got up from the couch. "We were worried about you."

Defensively, I said, "I went after you. I was only gone a few minutes."

He frowned at me. "Are you all right? Hit your head? We've been back an hour."

That startled me. "You must have come in the front door when I went out the back, but I can't have been gone an hour." No point in arguing. Besides, I was anxious to have Doris show herself to Jack. "Doris said she'd show herself to you," I blurted out. I don't know what I expected, but it certainly wasn't the concern that washed over his face.

"Why don't you sit down?" He tried to take me by the arm, but I pulled away.

"I'm not feeble," I said angrily.

"I'm going to have a glass of pinot. Want one?" Gillian caught my eye with a warning look.

"Yes."

"Jack?"

"Grab me a Heineken."

I watched him warily as I took my windbreaker and jacket off and hung them on the Arts and Crafts hall tree. Gillian returned from the kitchen and handed me a glass of wine, which I took gratefully before saying quietly to her, "Doris?"

"Drink first," she whispered. "Before I forget," she said at normal volume, "Ricardo from the beach called." She looked down at some notes. "He works at the Comic Shack in town and also at a place called Crystalline. Busy boy. He left his cell number and said that, if he didn't answer right away, he might be with a customer."

I wondered how he'd gotten my phone number. I didn't remember giving it to him, but then again this was a small town. "I'll track him down later, but now... Doris!"

She materialized five feet in front of Jack.

"Shit!" He dropped his beer.

Gillian ran for paper towels.

"See?" I was all hands on hips.

To Doris' credit, she didn't disappear when Jack lunged at her, waving his hands in front of him. Encountering her slippery coldness, he jerked back and wiped his hands on his jeans.

"I think I'm offended," Doris said and went hands on hips, too.

He jumped again when she spoke. Then he looked around wildly as if looking for the source of a projection.

"Seriously, Jack, you lunged at a ghost?" I said.

"She's real, Jack." Gillian finished mopping up.

"We tried to tell you," I said. "Believe us now?"

"Where's the projector?" he asked.

I closed my eyes and sighed heavily. "Jack, you felt the clammy coldness, right? How could we have simulated that even if I could have afforded state-of-the-art holographic projectors?"

Doris walked over to face him with an exaggerated sway to her hips that caused the beaded fringes on her dress to swing back and forth. "Hello, handsome." She batted her eyes at him.

"Cass, what the hell?" He backed away in the face of her advance.

"Jack, hold on. Doris, I'm really going to have trouble helping you if you scare my brother and sister-in-law away. Can you take it down a peg?"

She pouted, but she backed away, flouncing down into a chair.

"She's so real." Jack walked over to her and poked

a finger through the top of her head.

"Hey!" Doris frowned and ran a hand over the top of her head as if smoothing her hair.

"Jack, you're not helping. She's a real ghost. The sooner you make peace with that, the better. She lives here. With us."

"Actually," Gillian said, "you live here. We're just visiting."

"Chicken," I said.

"Yeah? So?" She smirked at me.

Doris stood up. "I'm still here, and I can hear you. If you'd care to notice, I haven't hurt any of you. I've asked for your help. What does that tell you? Maybe you're more powerful than I am? Hello?"

"Jack?" I asked.

"Sweet Pea?" Jack turned to Gillian.

"My original vote was for running screaming into the night. However..."

"However?" I asked.

"However, she's growing on me."

For the first time since she'd appeared, Jack spoke to Doris as if she actually existed. "You said you asked for help. What kind of help?"

"I'll get you another beer," Gillian said, heading for the fridge.

I sighed, knowing the first battle was won.

"I want to find out who killed me and why." Doris crossed her arms.

"Talk about a cold case," Jack said, taking the proffered beer from Gillian and taking a long pull. "Cold *and* clammy. Brrr."

I stifled a laugh. "What time is it?"

Gillian checked her cell. "It's getting on for dinner

time."

"Doris, would you be horribly offended if we went out to dinner? I think we need to talk about everything that's happened by ourselves."

She shrugged, trying to look as though it didn't matter to her. "I guess I've waited this long."

"Sounds good to me." Jack finished his beer, grabbed his brown leather jacket, and headed for the door.

I got the impression he was trying hard not to run. "Thanks, Doris. I think that did the trick," I said. "See you later."

We left a light on for Thor—I wasn't really sure that a cat would need a night light but hey—and went out to the car.

We drove down the road a few miles in silence and noticed a quaint old restaurant by the sea with a few parking spots available. I pulled in and turned off the car. Once inside, we only had to wait a few minutes to be seated.

I pulled off my leather gloves, unwrapped the red knit scarf from around my neck, and took the captain's chair by the window. "Great choice, guys." I looked up at the waitress. "Hi. Anything special?"

The waitress, whose nametag read Nita, rattled off the specials.

None really appealed to me. "I'll just have a Greek salad and hot tea. Earl Grey. Thanks."

Gillian ordered blackened salmon, and Jack went for the prime rib.

When Nita left, Jack leaned forward, elbows on the white, linen-draped table. "So, that was a ghost? You really didn't rig something up?" He looked around.

"Are you sure she can't follow us?"

"Jack, seriously?" I said.

He looked down. "I guess not."

Gillian put her hand on his forearm. "Kind of shakes up your world, doesn't it?"

He shook his head. "You have no idea."

Gillian and I exchanged glances. "I think we do."

Gillian and Jack hugged and kissed. I looked out the window, but the dark only threw back a muted reflection of the old restaurant with its brass chandeliers glowing against the carved ceiling beams.

"Cognitive dissonance," Gillian said.

"Rocked my world," Jack said.

"Freaky," I said.

"Your house is haunted," he said.

"No shit."

He laughed shakily. "Are you going to stay there?"

"I am, but are you guys? She's growing on me. She startles me, but I don't feel afraid of her. In fact, the whole town is growing on me. Don't know why, but it's true. It's taking my mind off the divorce."

"I'll bet. You could call in an exorcist."

"Ah, no. I've struck a bargain with Doris. We're partners of sorts."

Jack looked incredulous.

"Yeah. Strange, I know, but look at it practically. I've sunk everything I have into this place. This is my home now. I'll figure it out." I took a deep breath. "You two don't have to stay."

They looked at each other.

It was so easy to read Jack's face, had been since we were kids. I could see the fear, the wonder, the uncertainty, and finally the stalwart support of one sibling for another.

"Don't be silly. Of course we're staying." But there was a slight tremor in his voice.

I'm sure I was grinning ear to ear. "Thanks, guys. I really appreciate it."

Chapter 8

"Dessert?" Nita stood above us, pen poised to jot down our choices.

"No, thanks." I looked up at her. "I think I've just gotten my treat. My brother and sister-in-law are sticking around for a while." I looked at them. "Do you two want anything?"

"Nothing for us," Jack said, smiling up at her. "Just the bill."

As she walked away, Ricardo and Mia walked up to our table. Ricardo was in jeans, boots, and a black Henley, his dark hair pulled back. Mia, by contrast, was tip-to-toe in gold and white.

"Ms. Peake."

"Hi, Ricardo. Mia. Are you having dinner? We're just leaving or I'd invite you to join us."

"We just finished. We were leaving when I saw you." Ricardo hesitated and looked at Mia. "We were wondering if you'd have some time tomorrow to talk?"

"Sure. I have to pick up some cat food from Marcy, but I'm free after that. Want to come by for lunch?"

"Sounds good. See you then." Ricardo put an arm around Mia's waist, and they left.

Jack raised his eyebrows. "What was that about?"

I leaned back as our waitress brought the bill. "Thanks." I waited until she was out of hearing. "It probably has to do with Alan Howland's death on my beach. Mia cried on the beach the other day, so I'm guessing they want access or have questions. Guess we'll find out tomorrow."

"Seems odd."

Gillian poked him.

"Doris told me some stuff about them, so I'm guessing they're on the beach where she can mingle with them fairly often."

He shivered. "You're pretty matter-of-fact about her. I'm expecting her to go all Beetlejuice."

"Great. I really didn't need that image in my head," Gillian said.

"Relax. She won't." I reached for my credit card, but Jack beat me to it. "Thanks."

"If she murders us in our sleep, I won't have to pay the bill," he said grimly.

"Jack." Gillian's tone was chiding. "Don't be so macabre."

****

To everyone's relief, Doris didn't do us in overnight, so the next morning after breakfast I grabbed the car keys and headed for the door. "I'm going by the vet for more cat food. I can stop by the store on my way back to pick up stuff for lunch with Ricardo and Mia. Did anyone start a list?"

Gillian ripped the top sheet off a pad and handed it to me.

"Beer," Jack said.

We both stared at him.

"What? It's not like I didn't drop one when your 'friend' popped in. I'm running low."

He sounded so indignant that I had to laugh. "All right. This time." I grabbed the keys and headed out the door.

I backed out of the driveway and drove toward town. In a few minutes I was bouncing along the coast road, already distracted by the glorious scenery. No one was coming in the opposite direction, so I stared out at the ocean through my side window. Breathing in deeply, I couldn't get enough of it. The water pulsed a neon turquoise in the sunlight close to the shore. All those years living in Pleasanton, and I had rarely driven to the coast. We usually went to Tahoe. I wouldn't be going that direction for a while.

I pulled up outside Marcy's, climbed the steps, and went in. Marcy leaned on her counter talking to a short woman with a mop of blonde hair and big, round blue eyes that were ringed with red from crying. Marcy looked up, saw me, and motioned me in.

"Cass! Come here! It's high time you two met. This is Sara Howland." She indicated the woman. "Sara, this is Cass Peake. She bought the beach house."

Sara's eyes widened. Then she sniffed, hiccoughed, and said, "Really?"

"I know." Marcy's mouth twitched.

I didn't care for the shorthand between the two of them. "Yes, really. I take it you've heard about the ghost, too."

She shrugged and wiped her nose. "Who hasn't?" Then she completely altered the negative impression I was forming of her by walking over to me and hugging me warmly and spontaneously. "I'm so sorry. I'm so sorry that Alan died on your beach." And she burst into tears.

In a natural reversal, I hugged her while she cried. "I'm so sorry about the loss of your husband."

Marcy said, "I knew the two of you should meet. Come. Sit down. Have a cup of coffee."

The front door banged, making me jump, and a bouncy young Asian woman with long, swinging black hair came in bearing a couple of white food bags and a cardboard drink tray with four tall drinks in it.

"Angela, I hope you got some extra. Cass is joining us for breakfast," Marcy said.

Angela set the food down. "Hi! I'm in vet school, doing an internship with Marcy." She held out a hand.

I shook her proffered hand. "I didn't mean to interrupt, and I've already eaten. I wanted to pick up some of this." I dug in my purse and held up a can of prescription cat food.

"No problem." Marcy bent down and hoisted a case of the same kind of cans up onto the counter. "You can write me a check."

"I remember. No credit cards," I said and took out my checkbook.

"Not yet. Soon," Marcy said. "It's getting so easy now I have no excuse."

Angela walked over to a round table by the window and started laying food out. "I actually did get plenty. I couldn't make up my mind between the turkey sausage breakfast sandwich and the cheese danish. I think I'd prefer the sandwich if a danish would do for you." She held out a small bag to me.

"My favorite." I put my checkbook back in my purse and took the bag from her.

"And I also have an extra coffee. Couldn't decide between a mocha and a latte." Angela sat down.

"I'll take either."

Marcy and Sara joined her. Marcy looked up at me.

I hesitated but then pulled out a chair, sat, and sipped the mocha that Angela set in front of me. It wouldn't hurt to hang out for a few minutes even though I'd forgotten that Marcy had said something about getting Sara and myself together. And I was curious about her. We were silent for a few minutes as we tucked in.

Marcy said, "Sara was talking about Alan's store and his personal collections."

"It was a book shop, right?" I asked, sipping the mocha.

Sara nodded agreement as she took the lid off an iced tea and added Stevia. "There's so much stuff. You should see our house. Alan has…had the really expensive stuff in glass cases in one of the bedrooms. There are more numbered, labeled boxes in the garage and the basement. Signed author posters. Pulps are stored in plastic bags. He even saved vintage comics. Remember Errol Flynn? Alan collected all the books he wrote and even had one that Flynn had autographed."

"I'm impressed. I didn't even know Flynn wrote books." I pulled the danish out of the bag.

Sara said, "He wrote books, sailed around the islands, and threw wild parties in his house on Mulholland Drive."

"Sounds like he admired Flynn." I took a bite and decided to ask for the name of the shop where Angela had bought it.

"That was our Alan," Marcy said. "Sort of a local Walter Mitty. Always dreaming."

Sara finished her sandwich. "I think he styled himself after Flynn as much as he could. He fancied that when he had enough money, he'd buy a boat and sail to Tahiti."

"How could he have hoped to put together that kind of money running a bookstore?" I asked.

Sara wiped her mouth. "Oh, Alan had connections. He used to work for a company in Silicon Valley. He talked about cashing in stock or something. Anyway, the house and store are paid for, and we have no debt."

"Have you told your family about Alan yet?" Marcy asked.

"I talked to them last night. They want me to move back in with them and finish my degree as though my... Alan had never existed. I dropped out of college when...when I got married."

I could hear the hesitation in her voice and wondered what she'd left unsaid.

"And what about Alan's family?" Marcy pushed on.

Sara looked up and then dropped her eyes again. "They've been notified. Alan never really got along with his family, but they're apparently mentioned in his will. The lawyer notified them when he notified me and the others."

I felt myself being drawn in by this engaging group of women willing to share the details of their lives. This camaraderie was what I was looking for in my new life here on the coast. My first few days had been full of strange, world-view shattering experiences. Now this felt normal, and I basked in it, feeling energized.

"When's the reading of the will?" Marcy turned in her seat and tossed her now empty coffee cup into the trash basket.

"Tomorrow, actually. Then all will be revealed." Sara made an outward gesture with her hands such as a magician might make.

"Do you know what you're going to do yet? If you stay, are you going to reopen the store?" Angela asked. "It would be a real loss to the community if you closed it."

Sara set the remains of her sandwich down and wiped her mouth with a napkin. "I'm thinking about it. I don't really want to go home to my parents, but I don't have a head for business, and there's a lot of stuff I'd sell that Alan would have kept. Once the will is read, I'm going to go through the store and all the stock. Do an inventory. Have the books checked by the accountant for the final taxes. There's so much to do."

"Sara, would you like us to help you with the inventory? Many hands make light work," Marcy said.

Sara smiled. "Would you guys mind helping me? The will is being read at nine in the morning. We could meet at ten o'clock at the store."

I took a final sip of my mocha, put the cup carefully into the trash, and rose. "It was a pleasure meeting you, Sara." I held out my hand, which she shook gently. "Marcy, thanks for breakfast. I'm off."

Sara looked up at me as she released my hand. "You're invited, too, Cass; that is, if you'd like to come." There was an appealing shyness in her voice, and I felt myself warming to her.

"I don't want to intrude."

Marcy stood up. "You wouldn't be, right, Sara? I suspect all help will be welcome." She winked at me.

I looked at Sara, who nodded.

"Do you have to leave so soon?" Marcy said.

"I'm on my way to the store and then home. I can't let my company do all the cleaning." I picked up my purse and the case of cat food. "Nice to meet you, too,

Angela. Bye."

I chose a local market to learn a bit more about the town and the farms in the area instead of the two chain stores in town, whose general stock I was familiar with already. I wasn't disappointed. There were piles of succulent local produce, and I wondered if a chat with the guy in the produce section might yield a list of local farms and farmers' markets.

I breathed in the earthy smell and stepped back to avoid the misters. The radishes bloomed with rich, red fecundity. The kale and lettuces rustled like freshly starched crinolines. I stopped at the peas. "Peas?"

"That's right," said a deep voice behind me. "Clearly you're not from the coast."

"I moved here recently." I turned back to the bin and ran my fingers through the squeaking pods. "Isn't it late in the season for peas?"

"Our season is much longer on the coast due to the cool coastal fog. This will be the last of it, though, so enjoy it while you can."

"I will," I said, popping a couple of pounds worth into a brown paper bag.

"Welcome to our little community here on the coast. I think you'll find it unique. We hope to see you back here again. I'm Tom, and this is a family run grocery, one of the few left in the area." His smile was warm and neighborly.

"Oh, you will. I hope you won't mind all the questions I'll have."

"Not at all. Any time."

"I'm just grabbing a few things for lunch today, but are there farmer's markets or produce stands you can recommend?"

He laughed. "I buy from the local farmers." He indicated the produce with a wave of his hand. "But there are some who specialize in things we don't carry. I can give you some names and draw you a map." He pulled off his gloves and sketched out a rough map on a notepad that was smudged with dirt."

"Thanks." I took it from him. "I look forward to checking them out."

"No problem." He turned back to loading cucumbers into the wooden bin.

I finished my shopping and headed home to prepare for Ricardo and Mia's arrival, curiosity hastening my steps.

****

Jack and Gillian had cleaned as much as possible given the amount of stuff still in the cottage and laid out place settings on the trestle table for lunch. I set my reusable Audubon Society bags full of my purchases down on the kitchen counter.

"Wow! Thanks, guys." Pulling things out of the bags, I thought about my menu.

"How can I help?" Gillian took the bread and cucumbers from me. "Cucumber sandwiches?"

"I'm thinking soup and a variety of sandwiches." I handed her the cream cheese. "What do you think of cucumber and cream cheese on buttermilk bread?"

Jack made a face.

"I also bought a seed and whole grain wheat bread and some deli ham, turkey, and cheese."

Jack smiled.

"Consommé?"

Jack frowned.

"Tomato?"

Jack nodded.

Jack was my barometer. I'd successfully anticipated both ends of the menu scale. "I've got crudités." I pulled veggies, mixed olives, and Tzatziki out of the last bag.

"Chips?" Jack peered into the now-empty bag.

Gillian patted him on the shoulder, walked to the pantry, pulled out a bag of chips, and dangled it in front of him, bringing the biggest grin yet.

He grabbed the bag on both sides of the top and yanked, opening the top seam. He pulled a Sam Adams out of the fridge and, beer and chips in hand, headed for the living room.

Gillian answered my raised eyebrows. "Marriage."

Half an hour later Ricardo and Mia knocked at the frame of the screen door in the kitchen.

"C'mon in. It's not locked," I called.

Gillian set the last plate of sandwiches on the table.

Jack came into the kitchen, took out a bowl, and dumped the remaining chips into it. "Hey."

"Thanks for having us for lunch," Ricardo said.

"I'm delighted you could join us. I'm still settling in as you can see, but I enjoy having company anyway. Jack and Gillian are helping me out for a few more days before they have to go home."

"Let me know if you need anything after they leave. I'm pretty handy."

"Thanks, Ricardo. I may take you up on that. Once everything here is functional and I clear out my storage locker, I have to concentrate on looking for a job."

"What kind of job are you looking for?" Mia asked.

"I have a degree in international business from San

Jose State, and I was a program manager for a while, but those skills are a bit out of date now. Most recently I volunteered for nonprofits creating web sites and optimizing the sites for search engines. I thought maybe the university might have an opening."

Ricardo said, "The listings should be online, but Mia and I can check the job board for you."

"Thanks."

Mia and Ricardo exchanged a glance. "Lunch looks lovely. Thank you so much."

I liked her manners. "Have a seat. Bathroom is down the hall."

Mia excused herself and went to wash.

"Want a beer?" Jack got himself a second and offered one to Ricardo, who took it.

When Mia returned, we all sat down.

I passed the sandwich plate around. "How'd you two meet? Classes?"

Mia picked up her spoon. "We're in very different programs. We met in Victorian London." She glanced at Ricardo. A sweet smile and slight blush.

He held up a hand. "We're time travelers of sorts. We belong to a steampunk club."

"Where do you buy steampunk costumes? Online?"

"Made it myself."

I nearly dropped my sandwich in my soup. "You sew?"

"Watch out." Jack swigged his beer. "She'll have projects for you."

"I design costumes, sew, and create the appliances."

I offered Mia a sandwich. "Appliances?"

Mia took a ham and cheese. "Not toasters. Gears, eyepieces, mechanical devices. Victorians were obsessed with inventions."

"I'm afraid my knowledge of Victorians is limited to bad corsets and a lack of equal rights for women," I said.

"Personally, I like corsets." Ricardo winked at Mia.

She smirked at him and then turned to me. "I understand where you're coming from, but the Women's Suffrage movement got its start in the late Victorian Age. I won't tolerate unequal treatment… from anybody." Her voice changed, became harsh and raw. Defiant.

Gillian said, "I completely agree with you."

I took a sip, uncertain, but then I decided to share. "I'm here because I recently divorced my cheating husband." I swallowed hard. "Now I have some hard choices. I put everything into this house, and I have to find a job quickly."

"You will," Gillian said.

Ricardo took Mia's hand and rubbed her knuckles gently, looking down. Then he looked me in the eyes. "Mia's had a rough time of it, too."

Mia patted his hand with her free one. "We might as well get it out in the open if we're going to share." After reassuring him, she turned to us.

At the look on her face, I braced myself for something really terrible.

"I was fostered by a couple that weren't very nice. They were paid to take me. There was no love involved. I got booted when my 'dad' started making moves on me." She shuddered, and I felt myself react viscerally. "Alan was helping me out. I got into programming through hacking, which I got into trying to find my real parents."

"That's horrible! What did your foster mother do?" To me this was the worst kind of child abuse. It violated the child's trust as well as her body.

"My 'mother' accused me of seducing her husband and threw me out of the house. I took off and wound up here."

Ricardo's struggle to contain his anger played across his face. "She's had a rough time scraping by, always strapped for cash. I think she got into vampires because vampires don't have to be afraid of anything."

"It's hard not to feel abandoned when your biological parents aren't there when you needed them to protect you from your 'guardians.'" Mia spat the last word. "But then I met Ricardo, and together we found Alan." She burst into tears.

Jack, Gillian, and I just sat there, not knowing what to do while Ricardo held her until her sobs subsided.

"Sorry." Mia hiccoughed. "And then someone killed him just as we were reconnecting. He was helping me with school expenses. He wouldn't tell me who my mother is. I asked if it was his wife, but he said no. He said they married after I was born, and she doesn't even know I exist."

"Wait a minute," Gillian said. "I think I missed something. The man who was killed on the beach was your real father?"

Chapter 9

Ricardo nodded. "We only figured it out recently, but Alan agreed to a DNA test."

"I'm very sorry for your loss. How will you handle your school expenses without his help?"

Mia exhaled slowly. "Ricardo and I have started a business that we hoped would pay for school, but because we're so young, we haven't been very successful at getting clients. Two of the people Ricardo and I work for have indicated interest. But that's it."

"What kind of business?" Jack asked.

They both looked at me. "Designing and maintaining web sites."

I almost choked on my cucumber sandwich.

Jack whacked me on the back, nearly making me choke again. "Seriously?"

Mia smiled. "Yes. Seriously."

"You don't suppose…" I said.

Ricardo said, "I, for one, believe in fate. We have some of our work with us." Ricardo pulled a flash drive out of his pocket. "If you'd like to see it."

Gillian stood and started to clean up. I set my laptop up on the table. Jack got the beer.

****

At ten o'clock the next morning a thin mist still crept around the streets of town. I stood in front of Alan's dark Book Shoppe, having second thoughts.

Although I was on a quest to make local friends, I felt very much the outsider, and I wasn't sure that abandoning my brother to help inventory a bookstore was going to advance me toward my goal.

Besides, my mind was brimming with ideas for my new venture with Mia and Ricardo. Their business plan was well conceived, and I was again struck by the thoroughness of the entrepreneurial course they'd taken at Clouston College. I'd become cynical over the efficacy of most college classes, finding them out of touch with the real world of business. Yet here, students were encouraged to write and execute a business plan that would fly in the real world.

What Mia and Ricardo had presented to us was realistic and practical. They'd done their research to determine how feasible creating a web design business was in the current market, how much competition there was locally and in the broader community, and the talent they'd need to pull it off.

I hoped I could muster the gravitas needed to sell their service to established business customers. We'd start with the two shops who'd already agreed to let them create web sites for them. Ricardo and Mia had given them a substantial discount, so we'd have to bring in more business soon. I'd need to take a salary before long although it could be small at first. It wasn't a sexy enough proposal to get funding as a start up, so we were facing three to eight years of lean times just to get it off the ground. Or was I being old-fashioned? Mia and Ricardo seemed to think that costs would be low with little overhead. But they were college kids with parents supporting them. Scratch that, I thought, remembering Mia's story. She was a scholarship kid, supporting herself. With Alan's death, she had no parental support at all.

I shivered. The chill made me glad I'd worn my old green sweater. Where was everyone? I perked up a bit when Marcy and Angela arrived together. Marcy was in earth-tone practical gear: boots, heavy socks, jeans, sweatshirt, fleece vest. Angela, on the other hand, a vision in shades of red and black, wore heels, leggings, an over-sized sweater, and truly amazing crystal chandelier earrings that glittered against her long, straight, black hair. If she could do inventory in those heels, I'd be stunned.

"Cold morning." I stamped my feet.

Angela nodded. "The June gloom."

Sara arrived a few minutes later, but she wore a friendly smile, bore a pile of paperwork, and brought Starbucks so we all forgave her for being late.

"Do you mind holding these?" She handed Marcy a stack of paperwork and me a cardboard drinks holder with what looked like four coffees and a large pastry bag. She unlocked the glass-paneled door and pushed it open.

"I smell breakfast," Marcy said.

I smelled dust and wondered how soon I could duck out.

Once inside, Sara straightened the 'Closed' sign so that it was clearly visible from the sidewalk. "I bought you a mocha, Cass, because you seemed to like that yesterday."

"Great choice," I said, taking it and finding that it was still hot. A sip warmed my chilled innards.

"And cheese danish?" she queried.

"That would be lovely." It was thoughtful that she

remembered what I'd had with everything that was going on in her life.

"Is this the will?" Marcy asked, holding up the pile of papers.

"Good guess," Sara said. "Set it on the desk, will you?"

Angela took her coffee from Sara. "So how did the reading go?"

Sara took a moment to answer, seemingly fighting a battle inside. "It went pretty much as expected. I inherited the bulk of the estate: the house, the store, his investments in both our names, and a few in his only. I'm doing the inventory because my lawyer needs it to settle everything." She hesitated. "But there were other things I didn't know about that he left to some of his friends and family, most of whom I don't know." Her eyes looked haunted.

This was a change. I had been puzzled by her nearly flat affect despite what I would consider great loss—her husband's death. Although I barely knew her, she smiled and seemed polite all the time. Her face was like a placid lake into which the occasional seedpod or leaf fell. The surface only disturbed minutely. This change puzzled me. What was she really feeling under that still façade? Pain hid beneath that placid surface. Thinking of Phil, I wondered if everyone wore a mask.

"Did they inherit anything important?" Marcy asked.

Odd question, I thought. Why would Marcy care? But perhaps she was just concerned for her friend.

"Thanks for asking, Marcy, but not that I can tell." Sara shrugged, and her face was back to its placid surface. "I have to say that there were things and people

I didn't know about named in the will."

"Seriously?" Angela asked eagerly. "Like what?"

"He left a sailboat up in Tiburon to his cousin Al. I didn't know he had a sailboat or a cousin Al or a slip in Tiburon." Sara's expression didn't change.

Angela nearly choked. "A sailboat? Sara, do you know how much those things cost? That's huge!"

"He always said he wanted one; I just didn't know he already had one."

"Are you going to fight his bequests?" Marcy crumpled up the bag that had held her morning bun and pitched it with the accuracy of an athlete into the wicker basket near the counter.

I realized I was leaning forward, waiting for her answer, my own fight response triggered.

"No, I wouldn't go against his final wishes."

In spite of my desire to watch and learn and not intrude, I blurted, "But why? He's dead." I hadn't intended to be so blunt.

She turned huge blue eyes on me. "We have to respect the wishes of the dead."

My mind flashed on Doris. Not sure why. But there she was, forbidding me to read her diary, telling me I was in her house. I was the first to turn away. Instead, I looked around the store. Books were piled haphazardly on the floor. Large literary posters and signed pictures of authors leaned against the walls under their hangers.

Sara must have followed my gaze because she said, "Alan had started to make some changes. He took the pictures off the walls and was looking for studs. I think he wanted to remodel in here." She looked me straight in the eye again. "But he didn't share those plans with me."

Must have been a very interesting marriage. "Sara, I have Marcy's cell in my phone. Can I get yours?"

"Sure, and I'd like yours." We exchanged numbers and addresses although she laughed when I gave her mine. I realized that everyone in this small town would know my address. Now I was infamous.

"Where would you like us to start?" Marcy asked.

"I have forms." Sara attached them to clipboards and handed each of us a clipboard and a pencil.

I had a passing thought, wondering if there were inventory forms you could use on an iPad and just upload. "Sara, aren't inventories taken electronically? Seems like it would be easier for you."

"We're reconciling with the running electronic inventory. Bigger stores do it electronically. We're too small, and we have too many specialty items that don't have barcodes or ISBNs on them." She raised her voice slightly and said, "You'll see at the top of each page the location and book type you're inventorying. These are the forms Alan used."

I looked over the pages on my clipboard. I was doing mystery, horror, and romance. I glanced around the store. While the categories seemed huge, I saw signs for many more categories. I located my areas toward the back left of the store near a huge walnut desk. It looked simple but time consuming.

Sara handed out all the clipboards, and we moved around, looking for our areas.

I set my mocha and clipboard on the desk as I passed, deciding to have a look around first. I'd read recently that independent bookstores were coming back after a near extinction. This was the sort of business that required startup funding and had some serious overhead and a small profit margin. Ricardo's expense calculations made a bit more sense to me now, as I realized that all three of us would be absorbing some of the business expenses of our new venture by working from home.

Opening the door to the right of the desk, I walked into a large storage room with a red metal door on the far side that had a lit exit sign above it and two smaller, wooden doors to the right. I assumed the red door exited onto the alley that ran down the middle of the block to give ingress to shop owners.

Opening the first door, I stepped into a primitive "studio" with glass-fronted bookcases, an unmade cot, and a plain table littered with plastic book covers and dust jackets on one side of the room and an easel, canvases, paints, and drapes on the other. Alan the artist. Who knew? Somehow, it was not how I'd pictured him from the little I'd heard or seen on the news. That would teach me not to jump to conclusions. I backed out and looked around.

The second door was marked 'Employees Only'. My hand was on the doorknob when I heard a toilet inside flush. I moved quickly back to my post by the desk and picked up my clipboard.

Three hours later, I finished my three sections, set my clipboard down, stretched, and looked around. Sara stood by the large picture window in the front by the door. I walked up behind her to see how she was doing when I noticed that she was watching someone across the street. The June gloom hung in the streets. Mist still curled in low-hanging wisps although it was nearly noon. The figure looked almost Victorian under the iron streetlight. I assumed it was a woman because she wore a long, hooded cape that swept the sidewalk, but this was California, so who knew? While I watched, the woman turned and walked away. As she did so, she walked through a clear patch, and I could see quite plainly that it was Mia.

I started to say something to Sara, but Marcy beat me to it. "Isn't that the girl who was hanging around Alan?"

Sara's body jerked next to me. I was glad I hadn't spoken. Apparently, they didn't know Mia's story. Alan must have kept most of his life to himself.

"I wonder what *she* wants?" There was a nasty tone in Marcy's voice.

I turned to look at Marcy. "What do you mean?" While I regarded Marcy as the most normal person I'd yet met, I thought her comments were crass under the circumstances, and my own challenge slipped out without conscious thought.

Marcy shrugged. "Nothing really. It just came out. Sara doesn't need any more grief right now, but I can't imagine why that girl would be hanging out across the street now that Alan is dead."

I wanted to find out what Marcy knew about Mia. I needed to do due diligence before signing on with my potential new partners, but this was neither the time nor place, so I turned away.

On the way back to the desk at the rear to get my clipboard, I noticed a section labeled in blood-red letters at the end of one bookcase: Vampires. A drop of blood hung off the bottom of the V. This is part of horror, I thought, and I missed it. I picked up the clipboard again. I'd been doodling on the form. Bad habit when it was someone else's paperwork.

Pulling out some of the books, I noticed that many had lurid covers although some had geometric patterns, indicating that the writer was so well known that no money had to be spent on the cover to entice people to buy them. Alan also had carried paraphernalia, such as a few braids of garlic, a bottle of holy water, and some wooden stakes. Interesting. How deep was he into this stuff? I remembered the reporter talking about a vampire attack because of the two holes on his neck. Surely the police had ruled the death as accidental if they weren't here going over things with a fine-toothed comb.

I finished up with the vampire books and called out, "Hey, Sara, I assume we're inventorying everything, not just books, if it's for the estate. There're no entries on these sheets for garlic and stakes."

Angela burst into giggles. I thought I saw a flicker of annoyance wash over Sara's face as she walked over to hand me an inventory sheet with no categories.

"Just enter the junk on this sheet." She sighed. "He has a lot of odds and ends. Now I have to make a decision about whether to sell this shop as a business, sell the stock and the building separately, or run the place myself. I have no head for business. I don't even know who the accountant is. I hope I find it on Alan's computer. His cell is missing, and he had everything on that. I have to find insurance papers, file final taxes, request an audit—"

Marcy interrupted her. "Who in their right mind requests an audit?"

Sara shrugged. "The lawyer says it's normal to request an audit just to close things out when someone dies and a business is involved."

"I'd rethink that," Marcy warned. "Can I have a sheet for the posters and furniture in my section?"

Sara handed her another sheet.

Angela asked, "Do I have to finish the entire storeroom? There's a lot back there."

"No, I don't think this is a one-day job. I appreciate your help, though. Speaking of which, I owe you guys lunch. I can run over to Soupçon and get something, and we can eat back in Alan's reading area. Comfy chairs and tables. It's afternoon."

"Sounds good to me," Marcy said. "Just get me whatever the soup of the day is and a half turkey and provolone on sourdough with mayo."

I pulled a twenty out of my jeans pocket and tried to hand it to Sara, but she refused.

"You're helping me, so I'm getting lunch. What would you like?"

"I haven't been to Soupçon yet, so I'll get what Marcy's having. Can you bring a take-out menu back for me if they have one? I'm just getting to know the area."

"Sure. And you, Angela?"

"Nothing for me. Andy's picking me up here, and we're going out."

Now her outfit made sense. "Is he a student at Clouston?"

She nodded.

"Be right back." Sara picked up her purse and left.

Angela looked over her shoulder until Sara entered the shop across the way. Then she perched on the edge of the desk, instead of returning to taking inventory. "What do you think of Sara?"

"What do *I* think?" I touched my chest with my

fingertips, wondering how I was going to answer her, not knowing her motivation for asking.

Angela nodded.

"Uh, she seems very nice."

She leaned toward me, swinging her leg, the back of her shoe slipping off her heel. "Not the brightest bulb in the chandelier, if you ask me."

I hadn't, and I struggled to find a response.

Marcy joined us, sitting in the desk chair. "Angela, Cass doesn't know about Alan's affairs."

I repeated, "Affairs?" like an idiot. What do you say to a comment like that?

"I told you a little bit about Sara and her, ah, mental processes when I stopped by your house," Marcy continued. "For whatever reason, she turned a blind eye to his affairs."

"Sometimes she talked like she really loved him," Angela said.

"But then she'd say the marriage was arranged," Marcy added.

I opened my mouth and shut it again.

Marcy opened the laptop on the desk. She turned it on. "Damn. Password protected."

"Sara may know the password," I said, thinking a lot of lines were being crossed rapidly.

Marcy continued to snoop around while Angela called her boyfriend. I went back to inventorying garlic braids and wooden stakes.

"Goofing off the minute my back is turned?" Sara came in a little while later, carrying our lunch.

I jumped, startled. "That was fast. No one in line?"

"Had the place to myself. Several people worked on the order." She set the packages on the desk.

"You wouldn't happen to know the password, would you?" Marcy pointed to the computer.

Sara frowned, pausing with her hand on a sandwich. "The password for the old computer was my name: Sara. He was still setting that laptop up when he…he…" A tear rolled down her cheek.

"Oh, Sara. I'm so sorry," Marcy said.

She shook her head, sniffling. "No, it's me. This keeps happening. Not your fault." She waved toward the laptop. "Give 'Sara' a try. See if it works." She carried the bags to the back of the store and began setting out our lunch.

I watched as Marcy typed in Sara. Nothing. Then Marcy typed in 'Mia'. She was in. She gave me a significant look.

I knew why Alan would use Mia's name as a password; he'd only recently found his daughter. But why would Marcy think he would use it? I thought back to her snarky remarks about Mia. Did she think Alan was having an affair with her? I looked at Sara.

Sara was looking at Marcy. "I heard the ping. Did that work?"

"We're in," Marcy said with a smile. She continued to type, and I wondered if she would change the password. "Do you mind if I poke around a bit? I realize Alan probably has business records on it, so I'll understand if—"

"Don't be silly. Go ahead. Let me know if you find anything interesting. If he's got business stuff on it, I'll probably have to hire someone to help me with it, anyway." Sara pulled sandwiches out of the bag. "I have an iMac at home that I use."

As Marcy typed, she said, "Sara, you know I'll

help you any way I can."

Then a thought occurred to me. "You mentioned Alan's phone. Is it missing? Don't you have a smart phone, too? Family plan maybe?" I added. "He might have a backup in the cloud."

"Family plan: yes. Smart phone: no. My little flip phone is all I need. But Alan loved his. He was always checking out the latest app. Played some game about throwing birds around. Seemed barbaric to me."

"I used to play Angry Birds. Very addictive," I said.

A knock at the door sent Angela into paroxysms of giggles.

An attractive but roguish young man with a lopsided grin was rapping at the glass just below the Closed sign.

Angela bounced and danced as she headed toward the door, wrapping her scarf around her neck and grabbing her purse as she passed the counter. "Sorry, Sara. I've got to go. Andy's taking me out. Do you mind?" She looked very unrepentant.

"Of course not." Sara waved her off. "Have a great time."

Released, Angela skipped out the door. "Bye!"

Andy slipped his arm around her waist, and they moved off down the sidewalk and out of sight.

"Sorry, Sara," Marcy said.

I joined Sara, picked up half a sandwich, and sighed with contentment as I bit into it. I hadn't realized I was so hungry. Then I looked up and noticed Alan's wall safe, now visible after I'd moved things around on the bookshelves.

"Hey, Sara, what about the safe?" I pointed.

Looking where I was pointing, Sara looked puzzled. "That's new. I wonder when he put it in?"

Marcy shut the laptop. "Now that would be fun to look into. I wonder if he bought the safe locally? In any case, I'll bet you can get it drilled open. Want me to call around to see?"

"No, not yet. Maybe the combination is here somewhere," Sara mused.

I had a thought. I have a terrible memory. At home I write things on Post-Its and stick them all over the place. My list of passwords is on a yellow sticky pasted to the bottom of the lift-out pencil tray in my top left desk drawer.

I opened all the drawers on the left side of Alan's desk and checked for Post-Its. No luck. Then my fingertips felt the familiar little yellow square under the pencil tray in his top right drawer. A shiver went down my spine. How easy it must be for thieves. I've got to come up with a better hiding place or break down and buy password management software.

"Hang on. I think I've got it." I held up the yellow Post-It.

Marcy grabbed it out of my hand. "Let me try it."

Marcy spun the knob, and the safe opened. Scooping up the contents, she dumped them on the desk. There were cancelled checks, a deed, some photos of a child, ticket stubs, a graduation program, a few ribbons, a gift box, and other tidbits that would usually have been kept in a scrapbook.

Part of me was repulsed by Marcy's aggressiveness, but, watching her, I recalled my occasional fantasies of Phil dead and me going through his possessions. I glanced back at the safe. "Looks like you forgot something." I pulled a sealed manila envelope out of the bottom of the safe.

"Look at these." Marcy spread the photos out on the desk. "Did Alan have a child? Or niece? Goddaughter?"

Sara shook her head. "Why?"

"He had photos of a girl in the safe taken over a period of years. He's not in the photos, so he either took them or someone took the photos and sent them to him. I'm guessing you'd know who she is if he'd been related to her."

Sara leaned over for a closer look, pushing the photos around to reveal them all. "Nope, although she does look vaguely familiar."

But there was another photo on the desk, one that hadn't caught Marcy's attention but riveted mine. It was a car. *The* car. Doris' car.

My heart pounded as I set the envelope in the rack at the edge of Alan's desk and turned back to the photo. I tried to appear casual as I picked up the photo of the car that was sitting in the shack at my house. Why would Alan have a photo of Doris' car?

Chapter 10

"Look at these checks," Marcy said. "They're all made out to Mia Jamison and span most of the last year."

"The amount is the same for every check and too much for just shelving books." Sara flipped them over and looked at the signature on the endorsement.

The sound of ripping paper made me turn around. Marcy had ripped the envelope I'd found in the safe wide open and dumped the contents on the desk. Angry at her transgression, I bit my tongue. It wasn't my place to say anything. If Sara didn't mind, I reasoned, neither should I. They'd known each other much longer than I'd known either one of them.

My anger evaporated when she dumped the contents onto the desk and I saw what the envelope contained. Now it was my turn to unceremoniously grab Sara's belongings. I quickly scanned paper after paper, photo after photo, forgetting about the others in the room. I was looking at some serious research on my house, my car, my ghost. I felt a hand on my shoulder.

"Cass? Are you all right?" Sara shook me gently.

"You have a weird look on your face," Marcy said. "What's going on?"

Rallying, I said, "These are photos of the house I bought." I showed them the ones I'd been looking at. There were a few recent ones, but most were historical.

While they looked at them, I scanned the papers. Among the research were typed pages of a manuscript. It looked as though Alan had been writing a book about my house and Doris. I could be wrong. Maybe it was someone else's manuscript. But there might be information here that would answer Doris' questions.

"Have you seen this stuff before?" I asked Sara.

She nodded slowly. "Alan was a bit obsessed with the stories about your house. The ghost. I've wondered if that was why he was on your beach that night. The night he was killed." A tear ran down Sara's cheek.

I remembered Sara telling me she knew about the ghost when I'd first met her at Marcy's.

Marcy interrupted her. "Sara, look at this." Marcy held out a gray velvet gift box.

Distracted, Sara took it from her and opened it. "Oh, my gosh! This is beautiful." She lifted a delicate gold chain out of the gray velvet box. A large blue sapphire encircled by tiny diamonds swung free of the case.

"That must have been a present for you," I said. "It matches your eyes."

"Oh, Alan." She sighed and closed the box gently, slipping it into her pocket.

Sara's mood shifted like quicksilver. To me, she seemed ambivalent, even cold at times, and then she'd cry or become sentimental.

After a moment, Sara pushed around some of the other small items and picked up a red plastic bird on a key chain. "Here, you used to play the game. I have no use for this." She tossed it to me.

I caught it. "Thanks. I think." I stuffed it into my pocket.

Sara didn't comment further on the contents of the safe. "I don't think we're going to finish the storage room today. I don't know about you all, but I'm tired."

I really wanted a closer look at Alan's research. "Sara, would you mind if I borrowed Alan's notes about my house? I'm trying to find out more of its history."

She cocked her head at me bird-like. "Have you seen the ghost?"

"I-unh…" I had no idea how to answer that.

I felt Marcy's sharp gaze.

My mind raced. "I think maybe it's just because it's an old house seriously in need of repair. It creaks at night, and before my brother got here, I was spooked and stayed at a B&B."

Sara seemed satisfied, but Marcy continued to watch me, a tiny frown between her eyebrows.

Taking silence as assent, I gathered up the notes and photos, slipping them into the torn remnants of the manila envelope.

I handed the copy of the combination to her. "Here's the combination."

"Thanks."

I jumped at the sound of knocking at the store door.

Sara and I turned at the same time. Mia stood outside with her face close to the glass and her hand cupped above her eyes, peering in, her cape billowing behind her.

"What does she want?" Sara hissed through clenched teeth.

We walked over. Sara opened it a crack and said, "We're closed."

"I know." Mia's eyes flitted to me, but she didn't

allude to the fact that we knew each other. "I did some shelving for Al…Mr. Howland. I thought he might have left me something."

"A check?" Sara turned to look at Marcy meaningfully. "Did you see anything in the desk?"

Mia's eyes strayed to the desk, now messy with items from the safe.

"I didn't see a current paycheck for anyone," Marcy said.

But I thought Mia was looking for another like the ones we'd found in the safe. She'd be hard-pressed to get by without her subsidy from Alan.

Sara turned back to Mia and said, "We're doing inventory now, and we'll be open again soon. Come back in a few days. If I haven't found a check or records of your work, you can give me the information and I'll write you a check."

I could hear the strain as she struggled to keep her voice as normal as possible.

Mia hesitated. "I really need the money." Then she paused again, perhaps sensing Sara's hostility. "Okay, I'll come back." She started to go but then turned back. "He might also have some books and other things he was holding for me—"

"If I find anything with your name on it, I'll hang on to it for you." Sara's voice was dismissive.

Mia left, vanishing around the corner quickly.

Sara's face was set as she watched her go. "Actually, I've got some errands I need to run. Do you mind? You guys are probably tired anyway." She smiled, but there was no warmth in it.

"Sara—" Marcy started.

Sara began turning off the overhead lights.

"Are you sure?" I checked my pocket for my keys.

"You've been a great help. If there's ever anything I can do for either of you…" Sara opened the front door and then locked it behind us as soon as we'd stepped out onto the sidewalk.

"Were we just kicked out?"

"That was weird," Marcy said, pulling her collar up around her ears.

As we walked away, I glanced back over my shoulder in time to see a police car pull up to the curb.

When I got home, Jack and Gillian were waiting for me, sitting side by side on the couch, looking over Mina's books and Doris' diary. They both had their left ankles resting on their right knees, Jack's foot touching Gillian's knee.

I sat down opposite them in the matching chair, pointing at their leg formation. "Do you two realize that your legs make a pattern?"

Gillian laughed and punched Jack gently in the ribs. "Quit copying me!"

Jack broke the pattern and leaned forward to spread the diary open in front of me. "Doris mentions some of her father's friends who visited."

I pulled the manuscript envelope out of my bag. "Alan was writing a book about this house. I have pictures and some of the manuscript that Sara let me bring home to read."

Jack pulled the papers out. "Gold mine."

"I'm going to fix some tea. Want some?" I got up, took off my sweater, and went into the kitchen to put the kettle on.

When I walked back into the living room, Gillian and Jack were both staring at me.

"What?"

"Cass, have you looked at this?" Jack said.

"Not yet. It was quite a day. While we were doing inventory, we found a safe that contained a bunch of cancelled checks made out to Mia, confirming what Mia told us, but Sara and Marcy think she had an affair with Alan." I sat down.

"Did you set them straight?" Jack asked.

I shook my head. "It was awkward and not really my place. There were a bunch of other things in the safe, photos of a child growing up—maybe Mia, tickets that I didn't look closely at, and a gorgeous sapphire necklace that I think was meant for Sara. So I told Sara that I thought it might have been a present, but it might have been meant for Mia. Alan's laptop was there, but it was password protected. Sara said her name was his password, but it didn't work. 'Mia' worked instead. Again, that seems to back up what Mia told us."

"It also backs Sara and Marcy up."

"You don't believe that."

"No," Jack said.

"The shop also contained a lot of vampire books and gear."

"Gear?"

"Stakes, garlic…"

"Seriously?" Gillian said.

"That's quite a mid-life crisis—vampires," Jack said, looking at Gillian with a twinkle in his eye.

"Go right ahead and joke, but don't expect me to pull the ice pick out of your neck. I'll be cashing in your life insurance!"

Jack put an arm around Gillian. "You know you're the only vamp for me."

"Pretty corny, Jack," I said, glad he'd been distracted.

"She loves it." He grinned at Gillian.

I thought for a moment. "You said ice pick. Now that's very interesting. I hadn't considered that."

"While you were gone, we were talking about possible weapons that would leave the kind of mark that mimicked a vampire's bite. An ice pick made a lot of sense."

My cell rang, and I dug it out of my pocket and looked at the ID before I answered. "Hey, Sara. How're you doing?" I listened as she gave me the details of the autopsy in between sobs.

My shock must have registered on my face because both Jack and Gillian were watching me intently.

"Thanks for letting me know, Sara. I'd be happy to drop by for tea. Four? I'll be there." I hung up and dropped the phone in my pocket. "Interesting that you two were discussing possible murder weapons. The autopsy results came back. Alan was murdered."

"Sounds like she invited you over. I thought you just met her," Gillian said. "You make friends fast."

I shook my head. "It isn't me. It's this town. People have been very welcoming. I have my own agenda, though. I'm intensely curious about the autopsy."

"You're not the only one who's curious," Jack said.

"I'm thinking of Mia, too. This will be a shock for her. I'm going to give her a call and then go over to Sara's at four." I pulled my phone out. "After I talk to her, can you guys run by Clem's Clam Shack and introduce yourselves? I'd really like to be able to order pizza."

****

Sara busied herself putting together a tray with cream and sugar. Her kitchen was all white, cream, gold, and rose with red granite countertops.

"Nice tea set," I said. In keeping with the theme of the kitchen, the tea set was rose patterned with gold edging.

"I haven't had much chance to use it. It was my grandmother's. I know it looks a bit odd mixing a fancy tea service with everyday mugs, but I'd much rather have a nice, large mug of tea or coffee than have to refill a tiny tea cup."

"Works for me."

Sara carried the drinks tray into the living room.

Once we had prepared our drinks, I asked, "Do you have a copy of the autopsy report I could look at?"

Sara picked up a report from the side table. "They sent me a password to a web site. I printed out a copy."

I took the papers from her and glanced down.

Sara said, "It sounds so clinical. The weight of the heart, lungs, and spleen." She started to cry again. "It doesn't even sound as though he's a human being. It's so…so cold."

She was right. Alan, a human being who had been alive and walking around not long ago, was now reduced to measurements. I looked up. "The detail is… so specific. I've never seen an autopsy report before. I've only seen TV autopsies. If you had children, this information would be good to have for family medical history."

Sara let out a sob.

"I'm sorry, Sara. I didn't mean to upset you." I knew I wasn't saying the right thing, but I was completely out of my league here. My own life had taken a sudden left turn so recently. Actually, it felt more like I was steering around hairpin turns on a mountain road.

She dabbed her eyes with her napkin. "It's okay. I want you to read it. I'm not sure what it means."

"I don't know how much help I'll be. 'Clinicopathologic correlation.' I don't even know what that means," I said. "It seems to be a summary of the cause of death that includes results of lab tests."

I kept reading. Overinflated lungs. Pulmonary edema. Drowning. Awaiting further test results. Penetration of the jugular and carotid. The bruising on the shins was interesting. Almost as though someone had kicked him. Or he'd run into something at shin height.

Jack and Gillian would be interested in this. "Do you mind if I take a couple of shots of the report?" I picked up my cell and used a scanner app to capture each page.

Sara was looking down, resugaring her tea, and didn't seem to be paying attention. Then I saw the tears falling. I moved nearer to her and hugged her awkwardly. We sat that way for a bit with Sara sobbing as if she couldn't stop.

"It doesn't seem real. It's a nightmare. I don't know what to do."

"I know." I felt so powerless. I wondered if I should tell her about Phil. Although I had been mourning a lifestyle, it was mourning nonetheless.

But the moment passed, and a few minutes later she pulled away and wiped her eyes. "Sorry."

"Don't be."

"I just don't know what to do next."

"I would have said plan the funeral, but," I said. "Sara, does this mean they can't release the body to you?"

She nodded. "Now there will be an official homicide investigation."

"That's right." I looked away. "Now they're looking for a murderer."

****

I arrived home two hours later and stopped for a moment on the front steps of my cottage, turned my head, and closed my eyes to let the breeze play over my face and through my hair. The air wafted its now familiar salty tang.

Opening the door, I called out, "Anybody here?"

"We were starting to wonder if you were coming back," Jack said. "We saved a slice for you."

I took off my jacket at the door and headed for the kitchen. True to his word, there was a nearly empty pizza box on the counter. I grabbed the two remaining slices and tossed them onto a paper plate with a dash of Parmesan. Licking my fingers, I joined them in the living room. "I really have to spend more time getting my stuff out of storage and moved in here while I still have slave labor."

Jack snorted.

"Yum. That was good, and Clem's will now deliver here." Gillian finished the last of her pizza. "There's a stack of linens on the coffee table in the living room that Doris and I sorted out. She'd like you to keep her mother's embroidered set with the cutwork. The rest I'd put in the Goodwill pile unless you think otherwise."

"You and Doris? You're getting mighty chummy."

"Careful," Jack said. "We're all getting cabin fever. Next time we'll leave you here and go off on adventures together."

"You mean you'll leave me and Doris here." I corrected him.

They exchanged one of those annoying knowing glances, and Doris laughed without appearing.

I expected to see a Cheshire smile. "Okay, what aren't you telling me?"

"Doris has learned a new trick. As Jack said, we're feeling a bit housebound. Doris has been trapped within certain parameters for years with her only outlet the occasional mouse or squirrel. Thor is the first domesticated cat in the house since she died. Turns out she has an affinity with cats. Show her, Doris."

Jack held his hands up as if to say that he'd had nothing to do with this. To me, he seemed pretty relaxed given his earlier reaction to Doris. Maybe I had left them alone together too long.

Thor sauntered into the middle of the room and did a flip.

"What the…?" I took a step backward.

"Did you like it?" Thor's mouth moved but not quite in sync with the sound rather like a bad Japanese science fiction movie.

Although lots of strange things had been happening, I realized that I wasn't immune to shock as my heart pounded and my fingers went numb. "Doris? Is this a trick or are you possessing Thor?"

"Don't worry," Jack said. "We don't need to call an exorcist. Thor seems to enjoy it."

"I'm calling her Thoris when she's combined. Like

the Martian princess." Gillian opened the front door, and Thoris sauntered out and down the path to the road where she turned and raised a paw as if to wave.

She looked like the statue of the lucky cat at Phil's favorite Asian fusion restaurant. Banish thought. Banish thought. Banish thought.

"We don't know if there's a barrier or not. We haven't tested it any further than this. Pretty cool, huh? Thor doesn't seem to mind it at all." Gillian echoed Jack. "In fact, he and Doris are getting along swimmingly."

"Word to the wise," Jack said. "If you see Thor weaving back and forth and purring, he's rubbing Doris' invisible legs. A disturbing sight the first time you see it." Jack mock-shivered, sloshing the coffee in his cup.

"Point is," Gillian said. "This could be very handy. Doris has more mobility."

"But she might take my cat and leave," I said, wondering when I'd gotten so attached to Thor.

Thoris sighed audibly. "I can still hear you even in cat form. This is my home. Not leaving unless, you know, I…" Her voice trailed off, but I knew what she meant.

My cell rang. "Excuse me." I answered it.

Ricardo said, "Hi, Cass. How are you?"

"As good as I can be given everything that's been going on." I'd have to fill him in on Doris if he was going to be coming over to my place very often.

"Did I mention that I work part-time at Crystalline, the crystal shop in town?"

"Isn't that one of the two potential clients you mentioned at lunch?"

"Yes. My boss and the owner is Samantha Ross, and she's been filming around town and would like to do some filming on your beach."

"It's a free country." I wondered where he was going with this.

He sighed. "She's a bit unusual."

I barked a laugh. "I'm fast coming to the conclusion that's the norm around here."

He chuckled. "Good. I didn't think it would bother you, but I wanted to give you a heads up. She'll be dropping by. Treat her nice. We want to do her web site…and I want to continue to get paid."

"Ah, it's all about business." I smiled.

"Something like that. Speaking of which, we have an appointment with Brendan down at Dreams and Dust. I'll email you the deets." He hung up.

I pocketed my phone. "Doris, do you know Samantha Ross? She runs the crystal shop in town."

"No, she wasn't invited to the parties, and up until now my ability to meet townies has been limited. Watch yes, meet no."

"Ricardo called to tell me that she might be dropping by to do some filming on the beach. He said she's unusual."

"Unusual?" Jack sipped his coffee.

"She's looking for strange things to photograph on the beach."

Doris said, "There's nothing on the beach."

"This coming from a ghost." Jack rolled his eyes.

"Ricardo told me that the gamers didn't meet on the beach on the night of Alan's murder. Now that I think about it, I believe him."

"Perhaps she just likes nature." Gillian scratched

Thoris behind the ears. "Sunsets. Water."

Thoris purred and stuck her claws in Jack's leg. "Let's go down to the beach."

Jack pulled her claws out of his jeans. "Cat's don't like sand and water."

"I do. Besides, I can get messy and then leave Thor to clean it up."

I couldn't help myself. I laughed. "C'mon, Jack. You're getting pale being shut in all the time. It's chilly but beautiful. We all need some vitamin D. You might want to grab a jacket."

We walked to the hard-packed sand near the water's edge and headed up the shore. The chilly breeze bit at my cheeks, but the lowering sun sparkled off the tops of the waves.

I love the moment when the wave extends as far out as it can reach and that tiny row of pearls appears on the crest right before gravity pulls it crashing back to earth in a white froth.

I remembered how I used to throw sticks into the surf for Rufus. Even as he was growing old, he loved chasing sticks in the surf, snapping at and biting the waves as they attacked his legs. Thoris might like to go with me on walks, but she wouldn't be catching any sticks. I sighed and let the breeze push my hair away from my face.

****

Back inside, Jack looked through the scans on my camera. "Let's download these to your computer." He started reading avidly.

"He drowned," I said, "But you were right about the puncture wounds on the neck. They pierced his jugular."

Jack looked up sharply.

"And his carotid. There was bruising on his shins. Can't figure that one out. The report is so, oh, I don't know, matter of fact. Cold. Clinical. Heartless. It was so poignant, watching Sara grapple with the fact of it." I shivered.

Jack said, "It would take planning to get him onto the beach and bring something along that would make two punctures in his neck. Planning. Premeditation."

Gillian shook her head. "How could he drown if he was bleeding out?"

"Have we completely eliminated vampires?" Jack asked.

"Be serious," Gillian said.

"At the risk of sounding sexist, I don't think a woman—or at least not your average woman—killed him."

"Why not?" Gillian tossed the pizza box away.

He shrugged. "I don't think most women have the upper body strength to penetrate the muscles on a man's neck with... What? An ice pick? And how did he get in the water? It would take a man to drag or carry him."

"Oh, please. That is sexist. Want me to demo my ability to penetrate your neck with an ice pick?" Gillian waved a fork in the air.

"Now you're scary. I'll give you the neck-stabbing point, but dragging a body into the ocean?"

"Hmm. Okay, I'll concede that point."

"It seems as though more than one person might have been involved. It's as though the stabbing was spur of the moment and then a person or persons unknown had to think fast about getting rid of the body."

"Drowning, guys. He died of drowning," I added.

The doorbell rang, and as I got up to answer, they continued bantering behind me.

Chapter 11

Samantha was a vision on my front stoop as we shook hands and traded intros, and I knew from the gleam of the porch light off her chandelier earrings that I would be visiting Crystalline soon to check out the jewelry she carried. The rest of her attire I would not be imitating. She looked like a genie who'd been in a serious fashion accident. Her harem pants were purple and gold. The shoes were elf-style with toes that curled back over the top and had little bells at the end. A plain white shirt set off her purple and gold vest that barely covered her expansive character.

"C'mon in." I stepped to the side to allow her to pass.

As she walked into the living room, she glanced around. "You have some nice antiques here."

"Most came with the place."

"You did well."

I could almost see the wheels turning. "This is my brother Jack and my sister-in-law Gillian."

Jack shook her hand. "That's an interesting camera."

"It's my own design. I assume you're familiar with Kirlian photography?"

"Is that the one that shows life energies? Outlines of leaves that have been torn?"

"That's the one, but the cut leaves turned out to be

detritus on the lens, more's the pity. I designed my own camera with the idea of being able to photograph that which doesn't give off energy."

"Not much that doesn't give off energy. I should think that would be very hard. Even rocks give off heat they gather from the sun."

I cut in. "Ricardo called and said you might be coming by."

"Did he tell you why?"

"He said you were looking for strange things?" I cocked my head to the side.

Samantha smiled. "I'm looking for ghosts."

Jack coughed. "Do you use ghost-hunting equipment?"

"You've been watching too much TV. My camera's more effective. I'm photographing ghosts. The incorporeal remains. Let's call them the non-ectoplasmic residuals of previously extant beings. So far, we have been unable to demonstrate exactly which parts of the total entity survive corporeal death and which parts immediately transcend to other planes. There are some theories that multiple discorporate entities incorporate to share an experience on the earthly plane."

"Aside from shows like *A-Haunting We Will Go* on TV, I thought people gave up on ghosts and trying to film them in the Seventies." Cold rushed around my ankles and I assumed that Doris had tried to kick me.

"I have my own reasons for perfecting the technique. Thank you so much for allowing me to do this. And who knows? We might see what happened to Alan." She looked down at the camera in her hand. "I'm thinking of setting up a Kickstarter campaign to raise money to produce my camera."

There was an awkward silence.

She looked up. "Anyway, I just wanted to let you know why I'll be lurking outside your house. Didn't want to make you nervous." She smiled and looked at me. "Do you believe in ghosts?"

Doris shimmered behind Samantha while I struggled to keep a straight face. What could I say that wouldn't offend Doris yet wouldn't give the game away? "When I'm home alone at night, I believe in ghosts. In broad daylight on the beach, I'm amazingly brave."

The shimmer stopped.

Samantha tucked the camera under her arm. "I'll go find out what lurks on your beach at night."

"Feel free." I opened my door and gestured her out.

She walked down from my cottage, following the gleam of the moonlight off the sand and water.

As I watched, Samantha set up a tripod and pointed the camera down the beach. My eyes played tricks on me again, turning the scene into a moonlit horror show. I imagined that I saw the indentation from Alan's body, but I knew with the rational part of my mind that any trace of him had long since been washed away. I blinked a few times. When I looked again, the beach was a bluish sandy expanse decorated with dark seaweed and gray rocks.

After a few minutes, Samantha picked up the tripod and moved it down by the edge of the sea, pointing up toward the woods. Then she looked up suddenly as if startled. Like spirits of the forest, the vampire gamers emerged single file from the twilit woods onto the rocky grass plateau that ended abruptly in an erosion line at the beach. They didn't see Samantha at first as they threaded their silent dance.

They formed a circle, but then a tall, dark figure seemed to notice her and pointed. They fled back into the woods as one, their capes, scarves, and long skirts trailing like wisps of smoke from a dying fire. Samantha bent over her camera. A few minutes later, as I watched, she packed it all up and headed back for my house.

I held the door open for her and looked for the cat. "Done so soon?" I was pleased that she'd finally be on her way.

"Just for this session. It's too dark now."

I closed the door. "I think you got some pretty dramatic footage when the gamers came down the hill."

"I was more interested in filming the undead companions that were with them."

I raised an eyebrow. "In that case, could we have a look now? Does your camera have digital geo tagging, cloud tech, and a time stamp?"

"That's what Kickstarter is for. When it does, I'll patent the tech, make a fortune, and retire. This is California, after all."

I laughed. I was warming to this strange woman even though I wanted normal like Marcy.

****

The next morning Ricardo met me in the parking lot behind Dreams and Dust and started filling me in with the intensity of a Super Bowl coach as I got out of the car. "Mia will meet us here. This is the south end of the business section of Las Lunas. Dreams and Dust, Brendan's store, is independent. With the takeover by Amazon, Barnes & Noble, eBay, and AbeBooks, he's

156

fighting back to keep his customers, which works for us."

The store glowed with incandescent light.

"It looks warm and cozy."

Ricardo nodded. "Brendan doesn't like the coldness of fluorescent lights or the heat of halogens, and if you ask him, he'll tell you about the radiation the fluorescents give off. A bit paranoid that although he is wobbling a bit over LEDs now that the price is down. I warned him that incandescents are being phased out, and he showed me his stockpile in the storage room."

The old brass bell on the curled spring above the door jangled as we entered.

"I feel as though I've just entered a neighborhood shop from a century ago."

"Good! Exactly what I want you to feel."

Brendan, who could have been called portly, was wearing a corduroy jacket and vest. He reminded me of English professors and Stilton cheese. His dark, shaggy hair curled below his ears. Touches of premature gray highlighted his temples, the center of his beard, and the outside edges of his mustache.

"I'm Brendan Mays, proprietor." He held out his hand, which was soft and warm.

"I'm Cass Peake. Pleased to meet you."

"I hope you like to read."

"Always."

He beamed.

"Everyone comes to Brendan to learn the history and fascinating little bits of detail about a book or author. He told me once that he'd even started writing a mystery novel."

"Now you're telling tales." But Brendan looked

pleased. "Don't mind the clutter in the shop. I'm hoping to add to it soon…if Sara is willing to sell Althea Romeo's collection."

"Didn't Alan buy that recently?" Ricardo asked.

"Yes, but I doubt that it has the same meaning for Sara that it did for Alan."

"And you?"

"Perhaps. Besides, I'll give her a fair price, and she may need money right about now."

We followed Brendan back to some comfy chairs in a reading area. I nearly laughed, remembering Ricardo's words when Brendan turned on some incandescent torchieres.

Brendan looked up over the rim of his glasses. So professorial. I wished that the wrinkles at the corners of my eyes made me look as good. "Now let's hear your proposal."

As Ricardo laid out the rudiments of his proposal, I looked around the cozy store. The wooden bookshelves divided the large room into nooks. Posters of authors, many signed, crowded what little wall space remained.

Ricardo continued, "Lots of collectors do their searching online these days. You need to have a web site up and running so that you can get in on those sales."

"You have to keep up these days or get left behind," I warned.

He smiled and looked around as though he were assessing his stock. "It's not as though I've ever been worried about keeping up with the electronic Joneses. I don't know if anyone outside of Las Lunas would be interested in this stuff." Then he paused. "But I guess we all have to start somewhere."

"I think you should go for it, Mr. B." A young platinum blonde stepped out from behind a bookcase. Mia wore a slinky white dress with a satiny finish, and her pale hair looked wet and slicked back. "Hey, Ricardo. Cass." She smiled and lowered her long eyelashes.

Great look. "Join us."

Brendan turned to look at her over the tortoise shell rim of his glasses. "I didn't realize you were part of this enterprise, Morgana?"

I had to ask. "Morgana?"

"My gaming name."

"Ah."

"She's the brains behind our company. Sit here, Mia." Ricardo pulled a leather chair up for her.

She sat next to him. Her slim, flexible body seemed almost boneless in its pliability. Her large green eyes stood out against her pale white skin.

"Well, you already know my stock, so I'm sure you'll have some good ideas for listing it."

"I'm already working on your database." Mia crossed her legs.

"Unfortunately, a lot of kids' reading has moved to the Internet. There's a lot of fan fiction. You write some of it, don't you, Morgana?" Brendan said.

"And so do I," Ricardo said.

"I stock books for people much the same way tobacconists used to stock favorite pipe tobacco for their customers," Brendan added.

"The personal touch." I pulled out my tablet and took notes. "We could work that into your online service. Customer lists. Most sites have wish lists or something similar."

"I see the new trends by the books being offered. First, there were vampire balls, and now, steampunk balls. The young always have an appetite for the new. Whereas, I prefer the old." He shrugged. "But I like this trend. Anything that gets kids researching the Victorians appeals to me."

Mia opened her laptop and took him through the demo of the interactive web site and ordering system in detail and also suggested that he arrange to sell books by area authors and do more signings in the store: a touch of the new and touch of the old. Brendan looked through the wire frames of the site designs, liking some, discarding others.

"Now we have our sample. We can work up some ideas specific to Dreams and Dust and then get together to compare notes," Ricardo stood. "We want to add a bio on you and an FAQ. Things like where did you get the name for your store. Other things you want your customers to know."

"I can have a penultimate demo in a week. If you like the basics, we can embellish and continually update." Mia stood. "I have to get back."

I shook Brendan's hand. "Great to meet you."

Ricardo and I left by the back door.

"If you can't get me on my cell, come by the Comic Shack. I also work there, and Bobbo knows my schedule. I often have my phone on vibrate when I'm working or gaming. If I'm in character, I won't answer."

"Anachronistic?"

"Got it in one."

****

Even though all three of us wanted to spend the

160

rest of the day reading through Alan's manuscript and Doris' diary, we rented a U-Haul again and headed back to Pleasanton to get the rest of my things and close out my storage unit. For me, it would be like saying goodbye to my old life.

Once Phil and I had announced to our friends and families that we were getting divorced, I discovered just how many—or should I say few—friends I really had. Many women I considered friends had apologetically told me that they were really friends with me because I was married to Phil and he was a friend of their husband's. Some were women I'd laughed and cried with, commiserated with over their own problems, and to whom I had revealed my own issues and problems with Phil. Now I wondered how much of what I'd told them had gotten back to Phil through their husbands. Any issue California law would let him fight, he fought. I suspected that he'd hidden money away long before we filed papers. Nothing I could do about it now.

"It'll feel good to have all my stuff in one place again."

Gillian said, "It'll be good to get this taken care of. Then you can really start over without feeling pulled."

"Do you plan to come back over here for any organizations? Meetings? Friends?" Jack asked.

"Nope. I don't have any of those any more. I'm starting completely fresh. Now's the time for me to change myself because no one really knows me in Las Lunas."

"Don't change too much, Sis."

"Pay attention to the road, Jack. Don't worry. I'll probably be more like the real me now that I'm not constrained by a husband and my concern for his good name."

"Wild times on the coast." Jack pulled into the U-Haul parking lot.

As he got out, Gillian said, "I know it hurts, but you will be happier ultimately. You know that."

I nodded. "I know. I'm just not there yet." It was hard realizing that so much of my life here had been built on air, but I was going to miss that illusion of a happy life.

****

By late afternoon, we were back on the Coast with take out from my favorite Valley restaurant to sooth my tortured soul or at least to provide a little comfort.

Jack backed the U-Haul up to my porch, and we carried the food in to eat and restore our strength before unloading the truck.

While Jack and Gillian got plates and silverware out, I went into the back bedroom to make sure that we could carry all the boxes in there now that I'd relocated my bedroom to the loft and stack them up without blocking anything I would need in the near future. When I'd finished making a few adjustments and carrying out some clothes I thought I might need, I sat down at the trestle table and helped myself to Changsha chicken.

I'd been fairly quiet all day and now felt a bit guilty. "I very much appreciate all your help. It would have been really hard to do this without you."

"Oh, trust me," Jack said. "I wouldn't have missed this trip for anything."

Gillian added some brown rice to her plate. "We've had more fun than Disneyland."

"I'm serious, guys."

"So are we," Jack said. "Who knew? A murderous vampire, an escapee from Aladdin, a neighborhood ghost lady, and a surfer dude."

"Don't forget Doris," Gillian added.

"Wow, when you put it like that… Did I just make a terrible mistake?" A cold, hard knot formed in my stomach.

"No, no, no. I think you just did what a lot of us would love to do," Gillian said. "You're free. You can do whatever you want. No ties. No real obligations. You can recreate yourself if you want. Or better yet, be true to yourself. Personally, I think it's a great opportunity. My advice would be to be fearless. I think you're meeting the people you're meeting and having the experiences you're having because you're open to it. Maybe for the first time."

Jack patted my hand. "Relax. Enjoy."

"We'll come back and visit you."

"For sure," he said. "And you're welcome at our place any time…with a little notice."

I wiped the remains of the delicious chicken from my mouth, feeling stronger. "Okay then. Let's unload and finish up the old chapter of my life."

****

After returning the U-Haul truck, we were too tired to do anything physical. At least, that's what we told ourselves, and it gave us the perfect excuse to do what we really wanted to do.

We spread the manuscript and photographs out on the coffee table.

Doris materialized in trousers, looking a bit like a young Katherine Hepburn with a dark bob. "You can read my diary."

"Thanks, Doris. Join us. We could use some help with this." I started to move over but caught myself, realizing my folly. She could fit in anywhere at any size.

Gillian picked up a picture of Doris' car and placed it on a page of Alan's manuscript that contained a description of the car. "I don't think Howland knew where the car was, so I'm guessing this description is off the Internet. He must have had access to some of Doris' family's old photographs, though, because that picture was taken here." She turned the page and photo around so that I could see it more clearly. "Look at how lovely your bungalow was."

She was right. Although the picture was brownish black-and-white, it looked as though the house paint was crisp and clean. The bushes were trimmed, and flowers bloomed in the beds. "Beautiful."

Gillian continued. "These pages are largely notes, some more developed than others. It looks as though he was finding photos that matched important points in his proposed book. I wonder what got him started on the idea of writing a book about Doris' murder?"

"I'm not sure that it was specifically about Doris; it was about a local unsolved mystery. We don't have enough here that I can see yet that tells us what direction he was pursuing," Jack said.

I leaned back. "I think we need to find out the thesis of his book. Personal interest? History? Local mystery?"

"Maybe an ancestor of his committed the crime," Jack said.

"Maybe," Gillian said, very slowly as she sorted through the pages. "There's stuff on rum runners here.

Some sort of missing treasure or jewelry." She shuffled through more pages.

I fanned out some of the pictures. "This looks like a party. I wish this one were in color. These gowns must have been gorgeous."

"That's me," Doris pointed.

"I know that dress," I said.

"The sea foam green gown," Gillian said.

"The very one."

"I loved that dress." The trousers vanished and were replaced by the gown.

"That is a neat trick," Gillian said.

"That would really save on my clothing budget." I laughed.

Doris flickered.

"I'm not making fun of you." I was beginning to read her moods through her reactions. It made me realize how vulnerable she was. Funny how I'd started caring about her feelings as though she were a friend. "There have to be people in town who know more about your story or at least events or people from the same time, and those stories could shed light on yours."

Jack yawned. "If I don't go to bed soon, I'm going to fall asleep right here."

"Go ahead. I'm going to do a bit more sorting and try to figure out next steps, but I want to enjoy the rest of your time here."

Gillian stood. "We're not leaving just yet. Jack's still got some work to do for you." She patted his shoulder.

He groaned.

Chapter 12

The next morning, I woke up with the strong feeling that much of the mystery surrounding Doris' murder revolved around the people in Alan's pictures. He or someone else had jotted down some nicknames and first names on the backs of the photos, but names like One Eye and Big Al weren't helpful unless I could find anecdotes that revealed who they really were or how they fit into the story. I dressed, thinking of the errands I needed to run.

As I climbed down the stairs, I called out, "Doris? Are you around?"

"Always." She materialized in a loose white blouse and wide-legged trousers.

"Are the pictures we were looking at last night the bootleggers your father dealt with? I'm thinking there must be a local historical society that might have some information."

"Yes, but there were others."

I made coffee and put an English muffin in the toaster. "I'm guessing you can't go through the papers and pictures yourself."

"Not without blowing them all over."

"Please don't do that."

Jack and Gillian came out, and Doris faded away.

"You don't have to leave, Doris."

But she didn't return.

I buttered my muffin, wrapped it in a napkin, and poured my coffee into a travel mug. "I'm going to run some errands. Do you two have enough to do to keep you occupied?"

Jack opened his mouth, but Gillian cut him off. "We're fine. Jack will have plenty to do when you get back with the supplies."

Jack grumbled, but it sounded half-hearted.

On my way to pick up shelving supplies for Jack, I thought I'd stop by Crystalline to see if I could find earrings like the pair Samantha had been wearing when she stopped by.

Looking for parking, I drove around a couple of blocks and found a spot in front of the Comic Shack. I wondered if Ricardo was there today.

When I walked in, I saw a thin aging California hippie with a long, gray ponytail and a receding hairline who'd clearly grown old without managing to grow up, shelving comics.

"Hi, I'm looking for Ricardo."

He straightened, grimaced, put his hands on his hips, and stretched backward. "Oh, man, I need a break anyway. Getting old. Ricardo's helping Samantha out at Crystalline over on Main Street." He held out a hand, "I'm Bobbo, the owner of the Comic Shack."

"I'm Cass. I just moved here." I shook his hand and looked around at all the toys among the comics and graphic novels. He obviously still read his own comics and played with the toys.

"I know. Ricardo told me."

When Ricardo told me he worked at the Comic Shack, he related the story of Bobbo going to Comic-Con as a paunchy Deadman. The story went that he'd bought the wrong kind of latex for his mask before the Con and at the last moment in an effort to salvage his costume, he'd raced into a drugstore and asked for white pantyhose. When the clerk asked what size, he'd famously said, "Doesn't matter. Just something that will fit over my head." He apparently had no clue how the clerk would take his remark. I smiled. Meeting Bobbo, I could picture it all too clearly and understood why Ricardo had told me the story.

"Thanks. I know where Crystalline is. Ricardo has a lot of jobs."

"College kid. He needs the money, and the odd hours suit him. Don't know when he sleeps. Solid worker, though."

"Thanks." I headed for the door, paused, and turned. "Have you lived here long?"

He shrugged. "Since I graduated Santa Cruz. I really didn't want to go back to Iowa. Really bad weather. Sure you don't want a comic?" Bobbo held up an *Avengers*.

"Some other time." I waved as I pulled the door shut behind me.

A good walk can really warm a person up, and by the time I arrived at Crystalline, I was toasty. I pulled my green leather gloves off as I entered the shop and stuffed them in my pocket. The shop smelled of scented candles and incense. The walls were hung with Celtic tapestries and eyelet material from which hundreds of pierced earrings were suspended. Crystals dangled from racks, sparkled off the countertops, and shone from the lighted display cases throughout the store. The net effect was a kaleidoscope of shifting colors and shadows as I moved among the rows.

Ricardo had his back to me as he crouched down, stocking shelves, his thick dark hair pulled back in a ponytail. He wore a black T-shirt, jeans, and black Doc Martens. A plain gold cross hung from one ear.

"Hi, Ricardo." I rested my elbows on the counter next to the 'Do Not Lean on the Counter' sign.

Ricardo took the last crystal from the teakwood box, placed it in the glass display case, and stood. "Samantha mentioned she came by last night."

"She had gorgeous earrings on. I had to come by to see her inventory."

"Glad you came by. Samantha's shop is more classically mystical. We need to think about the essence of each business we do a site for."

"You're the artist," I said.

He smiled, clearly pleased. "Thanks. I'll send you some links so you can get an idea of the range. For example, there are two relatively new gamers who've been hanging around. You might see them on your beach although not with us. They're a bit more cybergoth. They highlight their clothes and accessories with neon. Looks cool under black light."

"Okay. Really feeling old now."

Ricardo laughed. "Relax. It's all about subcultures, not age. They're always morphing. You'll never catch up, but you need to be aware of the range. If you're rich and like craft beer, there's always hipster."

I frowned. "Hipster? Cab Calloway? Bebop?"

Ricardo's look was purely pity. "That's hepster to you. I mean modern urban hipster subculture morphed from alternate and boho. How old *are* you?"

"Thanks, kid. My grandparents had a great record collection. Record cabinet with beautiful inlaid doors.

78s."

"Now I'm jealous. I don't suppose you still have the cabinet and the records?"

"Sorry. Long gone but fondly remembered."

"Pity. Vinyl's the way to go. How do you like Samantha's shop?"

I looked around, nodding and happy to no longer be displaying my ignorance. "Nice. Very New Age."

"She's a subculture all her own and always having visions. She says if she dreams about her father, then we're gonna have the Big One."

"The big one?"

"You know, the Mother of all Earthquakes that splits California off from the coast. Nevada beach front."

"You do know that won't happen, don't you?"

He grinned. "Yeah, I know. Geological time frames and plate tectonics. I did study in school."

My turn to smile. "Glad to hear it. Do you still game regularly?"

"Yeah. I was online last night. There was no game on the beach last night that I know of, but Samantha mentioned seeing vampire gamers or at least she thought they were. By the way, do you know why the beach is such a popular place for the game? There's an optical illusion out by the point. Ever wonder why it's called La Bahia de Las Lunas, the Bay of the Moons, not the Bay of the Moon?"

At that moment, Samantha, Ricardo's boss and the owner of Crystalline, made an entrance. Her sun and moon robes draped off her large body, and her movement shimmered with the metallic thread of the embroidery that made the heavenly bodies appear to be orbiting. Coppery red hair cascaded in fuzzy waves halfway down her back, and she carried a gnarled wooden cane with a large crystal set into the top.

"Cass! How are you? Get to work, Ricardo. No dust. Not a speck on any of my crystals. It blocks their power."

Ricardo sighed. "You do know that crystals are inanimate, don't you?"

Samantha glared at him.

Ricardo turned back to me, a real smile playing across his lips now. "Later?"

"Absolutely." I watched his retreating back for a moment, realizing that their relationship was more mother and son than boss and employee. He had true affection for her, and it was clearly returned. I smiled.

"What can I do for you?"

Samantha straightened some small pewter fantasy figurines on the countertop. A tiny wizard held a staff with a crystal in the end. Surely the smallest crystal in the shop.

"I wanted to see your shop."

She waved an expansive arm to take in her stock. "Feel free to browse. You may want to pick up a few protective crystals and charms for your new place." She leaned close. "Oh, my dear, I dreamt about Alan's murder! I know who did it, but the police won't listen to me."

Samantha's sincerity was overwhelming as she leaned toward me as if to convince me with her sheer presence.

"Oh?" My pulse quickened.

Samantha walked behind the counter, pulled a stool over, and arranged herself on it. "Vampires," she said conspiratorially.

"Vampires?"

"He was drained of blood. There were two holes in his neck."

"How do you know?"

"I have a friend in low places." Satisfaction colored her smile.

"You know somebody who works for the police?"

She nodded.

"What else do you know?" Now I was curious.

"I know that the vampires were on that beach earlier in the evening. Ricardo couldn't work for me that night. They needed a sacrifice so that Mia could go through her rite of passage and become one of them."

"Wait a minute. One of whom? She's a gamer. I didn't know gamers had rites of passage."

She snorted derisively. "Not gamers. Vampires. Blood suckers. The undead."

Okay. "Admittedly, I don't know a lot about vampires, but I thought you became a vampire by being bitten by a vampire. At least that's the way it's done in old movies. You die and rise from your coffin during the funeral and scare the heck out of everybody."

"Hollywood."

"Then how do you become a vampire?"

Again, she leaned forward as if we were sharing secret spy stuff. "You can be born a vampire child—the product of two vampires. Often the mother dies in childbirth, so this is not a popular option."

"I can understand that." Sure wouldn't be my choice.

She went on as if I hadn't said a thing. "Then you can be bitten on the neck. This is uncertain because some never rise again. If you are completely drained of blood, there can be no seed to transmogrify your blood."

Yeah, well, we wouldn't want that to happen. "So you can only become a vampire if you're partially drained?" Drained or not, depending on who you believed, I was pretty sure that Alan wasn't going to be rising from the dead any time soon.

Samantha nodded. "The third way is to go through an initiation."

You'd better hope the vampire had a lot of self-control and wasn't an overeater. "That's what Mia was going through?"

"Yes. A mature vampire, preferably a born vampire, has to drain most of her blood and then let her drink from his veins. A victim must be tethered close by so that, when she arises with preternatural hunger, she can be sated with the victim's blood. The victim: that's Alan." She leaned back, looking pleased with her dramatic presentation and certain that her explanation was the correct solution to explain the murder.

"So that would make Mia Jamison a vampire?"

She nodded.

"What about Ricardo?"

"Hasn't been initiated yet."

"Doesn't it make you nervous having him working in your store? Having the others buy their stuff here?" I had to ask since she seemed so into this.

"They need us. Humans often do vampires' bidding. They think I'm under their control," she said conspiratorially.

"So how can Mia go around in the daylight?"

"It'll get harder and harder for her until she finally

has to become a creature of the night."

"Uh huh. Okay. So you told the police that Mia is a vampire and the murderer?"

"I told them that the entire group must be held accountable." She partially closed her eyes and looked away from me.

"But you just told me that the vampires leave you alone because they need you, yet it sounds to me as though you just betrayed them."

She held a finger up to her lips. "Don't tell anyone I told you. If we don't stop them, they'll turn the entire town into vampires. They've done it before. Have you been in some of the towns further south along the coast?"

"I won't say a word."

"I do happen to have some garlic here if you need…protection."

I shook my head. "Nope. I've got plenty of garlic at home. But thanks. What I really need is a pair of the earrings you were wearing the other night."

She reached behind a counter and whipped out a pair, laying them on a black velvet square.

"Exquisite." I inhaled deeply. "I'll take them." I had a twinge, knowing I shouldn't be recklessly spending my money.

She ran my card, put them in a cute little box and then in a bag. "Here you go."

"Take care."

I left the shop. If it were true that Samantha had told all of her friends and customers what she'd just told me, then she would be the next body on the beach.

Chapter 13

Back at the cottage, I showed off my earrings to Gillian and Doris while Jack unloaded the supplies from the car. Doris immediately materialized a pair for herself.

"That's very handy," Gillian said.

"It's no substitute for being alive." Doris' form wavered.

"Before I finish your shelving, I'd like a break. Maybe see a little more of your new town. How about we go to the upper point and see the college?" Jack asked.

"Works for me." I put my earrings in a drawer. "That's an area I'm dying to explore."

We piled into the car and headed to the campus of Clouston College.

We were talking and laughing as we walked up the sidewalk to the quad and the fountain when Jack stopped suddenly. "Isn't that what's-his-name?"

Gillian said, "Really helpful, Jack."

"George Ho. Again."

Jack snapped his fingers. "That's his name."

I gave him what I hoped was a disgusted look.

Jack coughed. "Wonder what he's doing here?"

"Who's the woman with him?" Gillian added.

"She looks familiar," I said.

"Beach. Cop," Jack said.

Gillian nodded. "When Alan died, Cass. She was the officer on the beach taking pictures."

I nodded. "I remember. How the heck did those two get together?" I felt a sharp pang of jealousy. I hadn't talked to George in years. He hadn't changed. Still the gorgeous Hawaiian I remember.

They hadn't seen us yet as they came out of one of the buildings laughing and talking together.

Then George turned, saw us, and stopped dead. "Cass!"

This time he was the one who looked surprised. "George! What are you doing here?" The woman's arm linked with his.

"What are *you* doing here? Are you and Phil through moving in?" He looked around as if Phil would spring out of a bush at any moment.

"I'm divorced."

"Sorry to hear that. We're in an amateur production of *Chicago* here at Clouston and you?"

That didn't explain the look on her face as she gazed up at George.

"I moved here after the divorce. Bought a place down on the other point of the moon bay. I was showing my brother and his wife around. They're helping me move in. You remember Jack, don't you?"

The two men nodded at each other and shook hands.

George said, "So you bought the haunted beach house."

I was only too well aware of George's superstitions from his childhood in Hawaii. Then I had a flashback of him carrying some wrapped green onions in his pocket at his uncle's funeral to keep his dead uncle's ghost from following him home. Doris would have a field day playing with him. Damn. Now I'd never be able to persuade him to come by my place. "Do you still believe in ghosts, George?"

He smiled at the woman with him. "No. Of course not. I've heard the stories all my life, of course. I was born on the haunted isles full of sentient animals and spirits. Monkey King. Menehunes."

"For some reason, I thought you might have gone back."

"I got a job offer here and have been working my way up the ladder. This is a great place to live."

"I've seen a production of *Chicago*. What parts are you playing in the performance?" Jack asked.

"George plays tympani in the orchestra," the woman said. Then she executed a few sensuous modern dance moves. "I'm one of the prisoners." She sidled up to him. "We got to know each other better during rehearsals."

I ground my teeth. I had to remind myself that I was the one who'd left George to marry Phil. Boy, did he look good. Then I had a thought. It was a bit mean, but I was feeling jealous. After all, all is fair in love. "How would the two of you like to come back to my place for dinner? I'll show you around. I'm here to stay." I smiled.

"We have dinner plans, but thanks," George said. "I hope you do stay and fix the place up. It's a cute bungalow, but it always ends up abandoned."

"Not this time," I said, hands on hips, smile still firmly in place.

The woman looked me up and down. "Have you come in to the station to give us a statement yet?"

I nearly got whiplash from the change of subject. "No, I haven't. No need. I didn't see anything."

"Well, we've got to get going," George said. "Great to see you again, Cass. And you, too, Jack."

"Cass? What the heck was that all about?" Jack asked.

"No idea."

But I found out when we got home.

A phone message awaited me when we got back to my place, asking me to come by the police station in town at ten o'clock the next morning to assist the police in their investigation concerning events that had transpired on the beach near my house.

I deleted the message and turned to Jack and Gillian. "Really?"

"C'mon, Cass. I'm sure it's just a coincidence."

"You saw the look she gave me. She has the power to get rid of the competition."

"She's a cop. She wouldn't do that. George is the detective. He might be the one calling you in. Besides, if questioning you were out of line, her superiors would question it."

"And are you the competition?" Gillian asked.

I let it drop. There was no point in pursuing the argument, but I would be on my guard tomorrow. I checked my watch. My appliances should be arriving any time now. I was sorry that we could only sightsee for half a day, but I was so totally thrilled to have a dishwasher that I almost forgot about George. Almost.

****

When I arrived at the station promptly at ten the next morning, an officer I didn't know took my name and checked a list.

"Follow me."

I followed him back to a claustrophobic little room with a small table and several chairs.

"Please have a seat. Someone will be with you shortly." He smiled and left me alone.

I sat.

A middle-aged officer came in and introduced himself as Detective Daniels and then introduced another officer as Detective Ho. I restrained myself from saying "Hi, George." George sat down across from me.

Detective Daniels sat in another chair off to the side and smiled at me. Not in a nice way.

The table was so small I thought our knees might touch. The room felt hot, and the air was still. This was the perfect room for wringing confessions out of the guilty. I tried to contain my emotions and breathe deeply. I didn't want to give off signals that either detective might misinterpret.

George looked down at a messy file folder full of papers of varying sizes, shuffled them a moment, and then started to ask questions without looking up at me. He started with name, address, what I'd seen on the day in question, and what I usually saw on the beach. "Are you familiar with vampire gaming?"

"I've heard of it. I wouldn't say I'm familiar with it." What was that all about? He was obviously reading the question from a list. "Why? Do you suspect the gamers?"

"Do you engage in this gaming?"

"No."

"Are you familiar with the people who do?" He shoved a list toward me.

I scanned it as though it were a timed test. "Some of the names are familiar."

"Which ones?" he asked in a monotone.

"Ricardo Santiago. Mia Jamison." I didn't know most of the names.

Then he looked up at me with a completely straight face. "Are you aware that there is a statistical link between gaming and violence?"

That was an odd question. I had heard about the link on the news recently regarding a mentally ill young man and a gun attack, but there was no gun used in Alan's death unless there was something I didn't know. What answer did he want from me? "My understanding is that some studies show a link between those who play ultra-violent games and those who commit violent crimes, but that so far no one has established whether violent people like to play violent games or whether violent games teach people to be violent."

This time when he looked up he studied me for a few moments, giving nothing away. Detective Daniels leaned forward, reducing the tabletop space by half.

I leaned back away from both of them, raising my hands. "In any case, I don't endorse violent games."

He shuffled a few more papers, pulled one out, and set it on top of the others. "Do you know Sara Howland?"

He already knows, I thought. "I met her recently. I just moved here. I don't know any locals well."

"Do you like her?"

"So far."

"Are you aware that the victim…" He shuffled more papers. "Alan Howland sustained two wounds in his neck in close proximity, imitating the bite of a vampire?"

For a moment I thought I was going to be sick. "Yes." It didn't come out well, so I cleared my throat. "Yes." That explained his vampire gaming questions.

He stared at me for what seemed like several minutes. "Do you run a web site for a local vampire gaming group?"

I'm sure he saw my body jerk. Ricardo had a list of potential clients, and there were several gaming groups on the list, including his own. "My partners and I are in early negotiations to develop a web site for them. It's my business. I'm doing the same for several shop owners in Las Lunas."

"Do you know the law around liability in the case of cigarette manufacturers versus lung cancer patients?"

"Why does that matter?"

"Just answer the question."

"No."

George closed the folder and stood up. Detective Daniels straightened up. They both looked down at me, still sitting at that tiny table and feeling very small. Then they silently walked out of the room.

Well, that was rude. But I didn't move.

A few minutes later the officer who had shown me to the room came back and led me out.

I walked to my car, got inside, and just sat for a few minutes. The questions hadn't been tough, but I had difficulty trying to figure out what they'd been getting at. I felt bullied, and that pissed me off a bit. I took out my cell and called Jack.

"George had a list of questions. I got the impression that he was asking everyone the same set. He seemed to want to tie Alan's murder to the gamers."

I frowned. "He did ask some questions that implied some sort of liability. I'm not quite sure what he was getting at."

"We'll get lunch started. There's still some ham, right?"

"I think so, but anything's okay. I'll be home in a few minutes."

****

I went into the bathroom when I got home and splashed cold water on my face.

When I joined them in the kitchen, Jack asked, "You didn't let Thor out this morning, did you?"

That surprised me. "No. In fact, I haven't even seen him this morning." Which was true, but I hadn't paid attention. "He may be hiding. He could be sleeping behind a box or maybe he went walkabout with Doris."

"Thor," Jack called out.

Nothing.

"He can't be inside. He'd come to me. Thor!" He snapped his fingers.

Maybe I didn't know Thor as well as Jack did, but I'd learned a thing or two over the last week. Feeling as though I could finally do something right, I took a can of tuna out of the cupboard and popped the top. Ten seconds later, Thor was at my feet, looking up expectantly.

I poured the juice into a bowl and set it in front of him, putting the meat in a container for later. He purred as he lapped.

Jack stared at the cat. "Traitor!"

"Thor seems to be governed largely by his stomach," I said.

Jack looked disgusted, but that little ploy had

returned life to normal.

"Sit down, you two. I can tell you about it now." I sat, took a deep breath, and picked up half of my ham sandwich. "It didn't last long, but it seemed like forever."

"What did they ask you?" Gillian asked gently.

I shook my head. "Nothing important. I think George was stirring the pot at that woman's instigation, but I have no idea why other than her warning me off George. He kept talking about gaming and violent gaming and the link to violence. He seemed to be trying to tie me in with the vampire gamers."

Jack stopped chewing and took a swig of beer. "They probably suspect anyone in the vicinity of a crime. Clearly, this house has a rep as we found out when Marcy told us we had to convince Clem's Clam Shack that we were alive not ghosts and would pay them if they delivered. I'd almost forgotten how superstitious George is."

Gillian shook her head. "I think you're misreading it, Cass. It sounds more like the cops were trying to establish a connection. He was probably fishing. You live near where the gamers meet and the scene of the crime. He might have been trying to see if you remembered something you'd seen if he made the connection for you."

"I think he's out to get me."

"Cops are people, too. You had a pretty intense look on your face when we ran into them."

"I did not. I was warm and welcoming."

Jack snorted.

Gillian shushed him. "I think George felt very uncomfortable. It must have been a shock to find out you're living here."

"I'm sorry if I made you uncomfortable. It was a shock seeing *him*. We used to be so close, planning a life together. When George and I met, he was pre-law, so I assumed he'd go to law school but he dreamed of becoming a cop." I shivered, remembering my fears back then. "You know the story, Jack. He wouldn't give up on his dream. I broke it off. Told him I couldn't live with the fear."

"I remember," Jack said. "We were so sure you two would marry."

"He told me that if I loved him, I'd share in his dream instead of trying to kill it. We both did love each other, but neither of us realized how valuable that was at the time." I paused.

"And so you married Phil," Jack said.

Gillian looked sympathetic. "It sounds as though you're feeling some regret."

"Maybe."

Jack got up without a word and headed for the kitchen. I watched him go.

"I guess I shouldn't be talking about this in front of Jack. He and Phil were close. I think he also felt betrayed by Phil's philandering." I cast a worried look at the kitchen. "I don't think George ever married, but what if…"

Jack reentered the room with a steaming cup of tea. He set it down in front of me. I could smell the peppermint.

"Relax. It's all coincidence. George has his own life now." Jack sat back down and reached for the plate with his half-finished ham sandwich.

We'd all forgotten about Thor until he landed in

the middle of the table, sending the magazines flying and making us all jump.

I grabbed him before his jaws could close on the ham. "Nice try, furball." I set him on the floor.

"Thor!" Jack yelled.

"Doris?" Gillian called.

"Not me." Doris materialized over by the circular stairs.

Thor jumped to a chair but didn't make another move to get on the table.

"Good choice. If you behave yourself, I'll give you the scraps." Thor leaped down and followed me into the kitchen, so I put the bits in a saucer for him, glancing at the wound on his head. It was healing nicely.

Thor ran his pink tongue over his nose and around his mouth.

"Trust me. It's delicious."

He only looked at me for a moment before digging in.

Jack watched the entire proceedings in stunned silence. "I guess I don't have to worry about leaving Thor with you." There was a touch of hurt in his voice.

My cell rang. "Hello? Oh, hi, Ricardo." I caught Jack's eye. "Mm hmm. Yes. Really? Okay. What's the URL?" I jotted it down. "Thanks." I disconnected and turned to Jack. "Mia created a web site for Samantha. Not for her store, but for her photography project. It's linked to a bunch of other sites he thought I'd be interested in and," I paused for dramatic effect, "Samantha wants her vids accessible online when she starts her Kickstarter campaign. For now, this is all private." I grabbed my MacBook Air and sat in the glider.

Sure enough. The site reflected Samantha's personality—larger than life. Lots of links went to like-minded sites, but I wanted the one to her videos. I wasn't convinced that it was a good sales point to make her videos available. And there they were. In a moment, I was looking at a video listing of films taken with her special camera. Jack pulled up a chair and leaned over my right shoulder. Doris hovered at my left.

The first two were labeled Alan's Book Shoppe and dated the day before Alan's murder and the day after. Why was Samantha taping Alan's store the day before he was murdered? One was labeled vampire gamers, and another was shot on my beach the night before Alan was found there.

The opening image showed the front of Alan's store at twilight. It looked as though it had been shot from the alley across from the entrance to the bookstore. The brightly lit storefront made the surrounding sidewalk and street seem murky and threatening, ominous. I was able to make out Alan moving around inside, waiting on a middle-aged man that I didn't recognize. Then out of the surrounding darkness, a slight figure approached the store.

As soon as she stepped through the door and into the light, I saw that it was Mia. She walked straight back to Alan, who looked up and jerked, apparently startled. He finished his business with his customer quickly and then escorted him out the front door, locking it, and flipped the sign to 'Closed'. Then he grabbed Mia by the upper arm and practically dragged her into the back of the store. I watched until the end but only saw the blurred forms of pedestrians as they crossed in front of the camera, hurrying about their business.

The scene disturbed me because of its implication of violence. Alan was not gentle when he grabbed Mia; it was not a loving father's embrace. Was there something between them that might be a motive for murder? I shook my head. Mia had set this up, but she wouldn't have posted this if it implicated her in her father's murder. It wasn't just that I trusted my new partner, but I respected her intellect. Regardless of what it looked like, it must be harmless.

"I'm not sure there's any value to using these videos to demonstrate her camera's capabilities. She should rethink that plan," I said.

"Agreed," Jack said.

The second video, labeled two nights later, was taken from almost the same position. The storefront, dark by comparison, was clearer for not being backlit. I was able to read the name of the store and see the pedestrians a bit better. Traffic in front of the store had picked up from two nights previous, and I wondered how many had heard by then and were rubbernecking.

There she was again: a pale white ghost against the blackness. She seemed terribly thin. Then I realized that her black velvet cape swirled around her as she moved, truncating her form. Mia stopped at the door and leaned her head against the framework. Her shoulders shook as if she were crying. The scene lasted only a few minutes before she looked up as if startled, turned, and ran off camera. It said something about Mia's character that she would put these out there for anyone to see her grief.

Within seconds, a portly figure entered the frame from the other direction. I recognized Brendan. He stared in the direction that Mia had run. I assumed he was watching her flee although I couldn't be sure.

Then he removed a key ring from his pocket, opened the door to the shop, and went in, carefully locking the door behind him. The store remained dark. A couple of minutes later, through the front window I saw a rim of light that appeared around the door to the rear storage room that I had looked at the day I'd helped Sara do inventory.

Why did Brendan have a key to Alan's store? "Oh, I definitely think we don't want to make some of these videos public."

The two of them were rivals, friendly rivals, but rivals and competitors nonetheless. I assumed they jealously guarded the secrets of their businesses and that each would have died before giving the other access to his business. Poor choice of words.

Did he get the key from Sara? Was there some business that she needed him to take care of as a professional? Or had I misunderstood the nature of their relationship? I doubted that Sara had sent him, based on the way Sara had acted when we were doing inventory at the store. She hadn't hovered over the papers and the desk as though something important were going on. Quite the opposite. She had seemed to be uninterested in anything that the laptop contained.

Then I looked at the video Samantha had made on my beach. It contained some lovely footage of the ocean, the hill, and the graceful line of gamers, but no undead companions to the vampire gamers. I thought about downloading this one. "Now this one is lovely although I still don't see any ghosts."

"I'm tellin' ya. No ghosts on the beach, and I

should know," Doris said.

Gillian came through the door with a bag of groceries that she carried into the kitchen. She started removing groceries and setting them on the counter. "What am I missing?"

Without looking at her, I said, "Mia set up Samantha's camera web site with links to her videos." There was a good shot of the woods on the tape. The gamers looked even more ethereal on tape than they had in person. "I like this one. These are the local gamers, and this was shot on my beach. Some or all of them game online as well. They're probably the people that George suspects...after Sara, of course." I turned back to the screen and counted. "Nine."

Jack laughed. "The nine walkers."

"Boo," I said.

"Lighten up."

I leaned, closer, looking for Ricardo. "That's funny. Samantha said that Ricardo begged off tending the store for her, that he was with the gamers the night before Alan was killed. I don't see Mia, either. So much for the whole vampire initiation thing."

"Better question," Gillian said, "is who was minding the store if it wasn't Ricardo or Samantha, who was clearly filming?"

"Interesting thought," I said. "But I'm guessing she has other part-time help. Probably another student."

"And that's the second time you've mentioned a vampire initiation," Jack said.

"That was one of Samantha's speculations about why Alan was killed. And before you ask, no, the gamers don't hold blood sacrifices on my beach. There seems to be some cross-pollination among the various gaming and cosplay groups."

Jack relaxed.

"That I know of."

He stiffened again.

"Kidding. I recognize a few of the others in the group, but some are strangers."

Their figures in the reddish glow of the fading sun, moved rhythmically among the trees, seemingly performing a ritual or dance.

As I squinted at the screen, I saw something that caught my attention. "Do you see that?" I pointed at the screen.

There was someone else up among the trees, perhaps a latecomer who didn't descend all the way because the group was retreating. The figure was slightly built and short. It could have been either a small man or a woman. Whoever it was turned toward the camera for just a few frames but was too far away to make out clearly, and the resolution was rotten. Then the figure stepped back into the trees as the gamers retreated back up the hill.

After the gamers had gone, the figure followed their trail up the hill and over the other side into Las Lunas State Park. All I could tell was that he or she was dressed in dark clothing and had short hair or was wearing a cap. He or she had made no attempt to get their attention or join them. Just the opposite. As they had retraced their steps through the woods, the figure had stepped deeper behind the trees to avoid being seen.

"Probably nothing," Jack said. "Makes you wonder what she's videoed over the years."

"I wouldn't know. But if other people know she's filming them…" I let my voice trail off.

"Wouldn't make her too popular."

After dinner as I put the dishes in the dishwasher, I looked out over the bay and saw the lights twinkling on the boats in the harbor.

"Just right," Jack said, looking out the window over my shoulder. "Let's go for a walk."

The sky was clear but for a few wisps of softly curling fog that played around the edges of the treetops.

"It's a beautiful night," Gillian said. "Chilly but beautiful."

We walked down the beach. Ahead of us the moonbeams glittered off the water at the point, and we finally saw the illusion of the moons. Watching the moonlight on the breaking waves, I felt like an eavesdropper, listening to the shushing of the ocean on the beach like two old friends sharing a secret. The smell of wood smoke reminded me of summer campfires when Jack and I were children. "This place is magical. I'll be sad when you two leave."

"Cass, we're across the Bay. What? An hour away?"

"Wish that were true. I cannot believe how bad the traffic's gotten."

"You were in a bubble over in Pleasanton. Hey, Gill, you're awfully quiet."

She turned a thoughtful gaze to us. "There's been so much going on. I was taking a quiet moment to reflect. We've accomplished a lot. Got Cass moved in. Cass even has a job."

"Now I just have to make some money."

"True, but one step at a time. I...my world has been changed by your change, Cass. I've always enjoyed a good fantasy, but never in my wildest

191

dreams…I mean, ghosts."

Jack put his arm around her shoulders. "But haven't you always believed they were real? I mean, you always want me to turn on the lights. You sleep with a night light—"

"Oh, there you go, revealing my deepest, darkest secrets." She pulled away and punched his arm softly.

"Seriously, don't most people believe in ghosts somewhere deep down? Otherwise, why are we afraid of the dark?"

"Maybe that's the real reason I don't want you to leave."

Jack snorted. "Somehow I think you're actually safer with Doris around."

Gillian stopped walking. "OMG. I never thought I would hear something like that from you."

Jack turned to face her. "What? I always believe the evidence of my own eyes. In fact, I'm believing it now." He pointed. "Although I'm not sure what it means."

Gillian and I turned to see what he was pointing at. The hillside glittered with tiny lights like a million fairy lanterns.

"Fireflies?"

I shook my head. "No fireflies in California."

"Not strictly true," Gillian said very slowly as she continued to watch the lights. "Some aren't bioluminescent. Some are dim. But there are fewer fireflies here because it's so dry and even drier than usual during this drought."

"Then what…?"

I really had no idea, so I went with my initial impression. "Fairy lanterns? I don't know if I'm scared or enchanted."

A voice out of the dark made me jump and scream. "I hope you're enchanted."

All the little lights went out at once.

"Too bad." Dave looked up the hill. "Fear drives away the light and allows the dark to move in."

"Dave, you scared the wits out of me." I clutched my chest, wishing he'd be less cryptic.

Maybe it was a trick of the shadows, but he looked sad in the moonlight. His eyes were hooded, and the corners of his mouth turned down. Even his voice sounded melancholy almost toneless.

"I had hoped you'd be enchanted by our little community on the coast. Its old name is *Finisterre* or earth's end. Many of us were outcast elsewhere but have found community here. I'm so sorry that you're frightened."

"Dave, I didn't mean—"

He cut me off. "It's okay. After all, you're only human." He turned and walked back to his deck.

Jack watched him go. "What did he mean by that?"

Gillian tucked her arm in his. "I think he was sitting there all the time, watching us."

"That's a bit creepy."

"He seems so sad. I feel as though I hurt him somehow." The magic had gone out of the night. "Let's head back. I'm cold."

Chapter 14

Early the next morning Samantha stood on my stoop, unbidden, looking stunning in emerald green gypsy gear with brass bangles hanging from her ear lobes that set off her red hair perfectly.

I tucked an unruly strand of my own hair behind one ear. "Hi, Samantha, come on in." I yawned and waved her in.

Jack poked his head out of the kitchen. "Oh, hello."

Gillian's smile was early-morning, pre-coffee brittle. "So what are you filming today?"

Before she could answer, the phone rang.

I pushed past Jack and Gillian and answered, "Hello?"

"Hi, Cass. This is Brendan. How are you?"

"I'm fine, Brendan. Thanks."

"I called to see if you wanted to go to dinner tonight?"

"Oh, you know, I'd love to under ordinary circumstances, but Samantha and Jack and Gillian are here and we have plans for tonight."

"Sounds crowded. Maybe another time." The disappointment in his voice preened my ego. "I was hoping for a little company after visiting my father at Brindale Nursing Home today. It's always a rough visit. They treat their patients pretty well there though he complains about not being home." He paused. "I think he's more annoyed that I moved into *his* house. We were always at sixes and sevens with each other."

"Maybe he's glad that someone is looking after his house."

"I tell him about every improvement I make. You should come over to see it. It's an old Queen Anne house that I'm restoring. I've really been getting into it. I ordered reproduction Victorian frieze papers and medallions for the ceiling."

"It sounds lovely, and I would like to see it sometime."

"Then we'll have to find time for you to come over. Feel free to bring your brother and sister-in-law. Say hi to everybody. I'll call you later." Brendan hung up.

As I hung up, I thought that Brendan might be a good source of historical information about the town and perhaps also about Doris and the photos in Alan's file. Clearly, his family had been here for at least a couple of generations. "That was Brendan. He'd like to show us his house before you guys leave the area."

Jack rolled his eyes and turned to Samantha. "I keep telling her that it's not as though we live across the country. Just Berkeley."

Samantha smiled. "In a way, Berkeley is another country."

"Not you, too!" Jack said. "And don't start with Berserk-ly, either."

"Well—"

Jack held up a finger and frowned.

Samantha let loose with a serious belly laugh that was contagious because Jack joined in after an initial reluctance.

"Okay, I guess Berkeley is unique."

Samantha snorted.

"I'm just worried you won't come visit," I said.

"Oh, don't worry, Cass. We'll lure them back."

"Can we help you with something, Samantha?" I asked.

"Oh, no. I thought I'd let you know that I'll be prowling around outside. With everything that's been going on, I didn't want to spook you."

I saw Jack bite his tongue rather than pun, but he was having a hard time of it.

"Thanks, Samantha. I appreciate it."

"Well, I'll just go film then." She turned and headed down the steps to the beach.

Then Jack said, "Nice of Brendan to think of us."

"Yes, it was. Ricardo mentioned the gossip that Brendan threw his dad into a nursing home so that he could take the house away from him. I think that alienated him from people who liked his dad. Folks assumed that he hated his dad. But Ricardo said that it was Brendan's pride that had kept him away from home, seeking his fortune, and when he returned, he found his dad in a sorry state and near death. He put him into the nursing home for the nursing part."

"Don't let him know that you know all that stuff. Let him tell you."

"Why?"

"It's a guy thing. Seriously. He'll think you were snooping."

"Okay." I hoped I wouldn't slip up.

Jack poured himself another cup.

"Can I have some of that?" I held out my mug.

Jack filled it. "I haven't figured her out."

"If you mean Samantha, I think something else is going on. Ricardo really cares about her, and he has good instincts. She's a bit sad, but I don't know why. Is she really looking for ghosts? Perhaps a specific ghost? I don't know her history, so I have no idea. Except for her eccentric vampire theories, she doesn't really seem to be connected to the murder at all. The thing is, nobody seems to be connected to the murder. I don't really see any suspects."

Jack said, "I don't really see any motivation for the gamers once you eliminate any vampire hocus pocus."

"But they might actually believe that hocus pocus."

Gillian sat down at the kitchen table. "Maybe nothing is going on. Maybe it really was an accident."

"Nice try, Gillian, but someone rather viciously jabbed Alan in the throat. Want to play a game? Let's find out what we know." Jack sat down with a pad of paper and several pencils. "Anyone want a sheet?"

"We really should be finishing things up so that you guys can go home." But I sat down on the other side of the table and accepted a couple of sheets of paper and a pencil.

Gillian took a sheet from Jack and a pencil. "We're nearly through. Jack and I will be out of your hair tomorrow."

"I really do have to get back to work, but I think we have time to have a bit of fun with this."

"Will there be a test later?" I asked.

Doris materialized, and I jumped.

"What? You're working on the shiny new murder? You haven't got time to figure out who bumped me off?"

"Let's do both, Doris. If we make some notes about

both murders, that might get the juices flowing." Jack sat at the trestle table.

Doris sat on the kitchen counter.

Gillian got up, refilled her mug and mine, and sat back down next to Jack. "What do we know now?"

I wrote on my paper as I talked. "Alan was murdered near my house. The location could be accidental or deliberate." I doodled a cliff. "Maybe there was intent to have the body found in the same location as yours, Doris, to keep the reputation of Murder Beach alive. He could have fallen off a boat." I drew a boat.

"Or the cliff." Gillian wrote column titles: location, weapon, motive, opportunity.

I added their thoughts to my list next to the picture of an ice pick. "He could have been killed on the beach and been dragged or fallen into the water. Possible he'd been there long enough for the tide to come in."

Jack leaned back. "You'd think someone else would have noticed him."

"My house probably blocks the view of the beach from a lot of places."

Jack wrote Suspects.

"Sara's the most obvious," I said. "If you suspect family first. He does have other family. A cousin inherited a boat, a cousin Sara didn't know about. It's possible there are a whole slew of people we're unaware of."

"Maybe. Maybe not. For the sake of argument, let's stick with those we know about." Jack wrote names under Suspects: Sara, Ricardo, Mia, Marcy, Samantha, Brendan, Vampire gamers. "We'll get their names later."

"Hey! What are you doing?" I said. "We don't know if any of them were involved."

Jack shrugged. "We have to start somewhere. We can always eliminate them or add others. Better not to overlook anyone."

"I almost forgot. When we were taking inventory at the shop, Sara gave me this." I pulled the Angry Birds keychain out of my pocket. "I don't think she knew what it was."

"How could you forget something like that?" Jack asked, taking it from me and examining it.

"Shouldn't you turn that over to the police?" Gillian said.

"I don't see why. Surely, they looked through the shop."

"Interesting USB drive." Jack pulled it apart. "Girly."

"Geek," I said.

"Pull out the laptop, Gillian. Let's have a look," Jack said.

Gillian got his laptop from the bedroom.

Jack booted it up and shoved the little bird into the USB drive. Jack leaned forward and started opening directories.

"Ricardo wouldn't kill anyone. I don't think Mia would, either. I just went into business with both of them."

"How would you know that?" Gillian asked.

I doodled a guillotine. "I don't, I guess. It would just suck."

Jack smiled. "A little vampire humor?"

"I'm going to set up a spreadsheet."

Jack copy/pasted the information we'd

accumulated so far.

"There's some interesting stuff on this USB. Looks like he kept his research on here. Backup, anyway. I want to capture some of it along with what we have so far from other sources." He opened a few more directories. "This is fascinating background on this place." He looked up. "And you, Doris."

Doris' bored façade faded away, and she rematerialized next to him, one ghostly hand on his shoulder. "Show me."

Jack opened Picasa and sucked the pictures into an album and ran a slideshow for her. If ghosts could cry, she'd have been in tears.

"My father. My car!" She wrapped her arms around herself.

Jack quickly labeled the photos and then gently disengaged. "Most of the material on this flash drive isn't relevant to Howland's murder, I'm afraid." He watched Doris as she drifted away into nothingness.

"What about Samantha?" Gillian asked. "She seemed awfully interested, and she did return to the scene of the crime. Maybe she's trying to throw everyone off with the vampire stuff."

"Maybe Jack's right. Let's add everyone we can think of. We can always take them off later, and we may find there's evidence against someone who looks innocent on the surface." I added her name to my list. "Let's add Brendan, too. He lost a business deal to Alan. Angela is Marcy's assistant." I was getting into it.

"He's on the list. I'll add her," Jack said. "Now we have to consider motive."

"Sara suspected that her husband was having an affair with Mia Jamison. Even if he wasn't," I said, putting "jealousy" in the motive column for Sara.

"There doesn't seem to be much on this USB drive so far that would provide motivation for Alan's murder."

"I keep everything important in my life on my phone. Sara said he had a smart phone, but they didn't find it."

Jack looked up. "The police may have taken Alan's with them."

"Or it's in the ocean," I said. "He probably backed it up in the cloud, so the data may be found."

"In any case, there'll be a copy of everything that's on the phone on his computer if he synched up with it."

Gillian said, "Sara also has the motive of gain. She inherits Alan's possessions. Unless you know otherwise?"

"Sara had a copy of the will at the store. There were a number of people that got stuff, but she inherited the bulk of the estate."

"Continuing then. Motive for Brendan would be revenge over that lost business deal and getting rid of a rival."

I added to my notes. "Oh, and he has a key to Alan's shop. He was on one of Samantha's videos letting himself in."

Jack whistled. "I remember, and that's gonna get him into trouble."

Discomfort over her safety niggled at me again.

"Let's move on or we'll never get through these. Motive for Mia?" Gillian prompted.

"If she can prove she's his natural daughter, she stands to inherit," I said.

"Has she made a claim?" Jack asked.

"Not to my knowledge. Are we out of ideas for Alan's murder? Shall we scope out Doris'?"

Doris clapped her hands and swung her feet. It was so odd watching that silent clapping. I grabbed a blank sheet of paper and set up the same grid. Jack glanced at her and started another Excel workbook.

"Doris, was the land up the hill on the other side of me a state park when you lived around here?"

"Oh, yes. The land was part of a bequest."

"So no neighbors there."

Jack added, "There were probably far fewer people in the region then, but bootleggers obviously used the area and probably the beach. Doris, you may have seen or heard something you weren't meant to."

The cliff by my house was the point end of the shorter of the two arms and was the near side of the Las Lunas State Park that stretched south down the coast. The heavily wooded top of the cliff contained a picnic area and campsite. It also had one of the best views around when you reached the cliff itself. I wondered what Doris could have seen.

She shook her head. "No idea."

I set my pencil down. "I think we're going to have to do some research. Maybe it's time we looked through the old papers we've gathered up in those boxes." I inclined my head toward the plastic boxes stacked in a corner of the living room. "Maybe you guys will stay a little longer."

"Tantalizing," Jack said.

"Clear the table. I've got several boxes of papers and one of pictures and oddments, Doris' diary, and my own notes. Oh, and Wilhelmina's two books."

Gillian wiped the table down. Jack set the first box

on the table. I set Doris' diary on the table, and although I could no longer see her, the pages turned.

Gillian took the lid off the box. "That was creepy."

"Thanks, Doris," I said to the air. "That reminded me of an old movie, a ghost story from the Thirties in black and white. *The Uninvited* with Ray Milland and Gale Sondergaard. In the movie, that's how they discover the murder. The ghost opens the doctor's medical notebook to the page that describes the murder. I don't suppose you've done that for us, Doris." I looked down at the page she'd chosen for us and read aloud. "Uncle Stanislaus came over today. I don't like the way he looks at me. He's a palooka. My father sez I must call him 'uncle' whenever there are strangers here." I wondered why Doris wasn't visible. "Are you all right, Doris?"

"I wonder if Stanislaus is in Alan's manuscript." Jack rifled through the manuscript.

"Jack, this could really be due to a breeze. Don't get too excited."

Gillian pulled some pictures out of the box and read the backs. She sorted them into piles. "It would help if you could identify some of these people, Doris. Are they people you know? Doris? Are you here?"

"I'm afraid we've upset her."

Jack set out the picture of Doris' car from the manuscript envelope.

Gillian pulled the identical picture out of the box. "On the back of this one, someone's written 'Breezer.' Some of the pictures in the box are from Doris' generation, but this collection is a mashup of all the pictures we found in the cottage. Hindsight is twenty-twenty. We should have put them in separate piles."

"Don't worry about it, Gillian. We'll do what we can now. Jack, there's a box of archival sleeves on the table by the front door. Can you grab it? You're nearest."

Jack pushed the chair back, startling Thor, who'd curled up next to the chair. He brought the box back to the table and opened it. "When did you get this stuff?"

"I've had archiving supplies for a while now. I was going to put Dad's letters from when he was in the Navy and Mom and Dad's love letters in these sleeves. I have binders and labels, too."

"Do you throw anything out?"

"You've been helping me move in. What do you think?"

He snorted. "Are you planning on archiving everything? Should we be putting the papers in sleeves, too?"

"It could get expensive if we have to buy more sleeves, so let's start with the most fragile stuff. I bought them with the idea that we shouldn't keep handling our parents' letters. There are a couple of ring binders. These letters are a lot more fragile."

"Look at this." Gillian had laid out a patchwork quilt of photos of the cottage. A variety of folks peopled the photos, and a very young Doris was in most of them, often the center of attention. "This place had an actual yard! Look how far away the ocean is."

Jack leaned over for a look. "Lots of erosion. You might be out a house soon."

"Not with the park there. The government will move to save it."

"You wish."

"Gillian, there are sleeves for a couple of sizes of

photos. Use whatever makes sense."

She stuffed a few sleeves. "Good idea, Cass." She flipped through a few more piles. "I think I've found Uncle Stanislaus." She handed me a picture of a hefty man, clean-shaven, face shaded by a big brimmed hat. "Says Uncle Stan on the back."

"Doris! It's going to take us a long time if you continue to absent yourself. We really need your help here. Is this the guy from your diary?"

Jack sat back down. "She's as stubborn as you are. I'll look for a reference in the manuscript. If we had a last name, we might be able to Google him."

"Doris? Last name?" She was pissing me off. I had a mind to stop wasting time on this…except that I was also curious about what happened to her and how it tied into my house.

"Hey, look at this." Gillian pulled a diamond solitaire engagement ring out of the bottom of the box.

Then Doris joined us, at least audibly, wailing as if her heart would break. The sound was everywhere at once. It echoed off the walls and seemed to roll from room to room as if a gauzy wind blew it through the house. It broke my heart and terrified me all at once. I picked Thor up and looked him in the eyes. "Doris, are you in there?"

A watery chuckle emanated from everywhere and nowhere. Then a hiccough and Doris appeared wavery and indistinct. "I'm sorry. The r-ring. It was from Lemuel. For a moment, it was as if we were there on the beach. It's my last memory before I…I…"

I put Thor down. Had Lemuel, whoever he was, killed her? Finally, a real clue! "Doris, do you think Lemuel…uh…was responsible for your death?"

"He adored me. He proposed to me that night. On his knees and everything. Roses. Moonlight." Then her eyes widened. "Lemuel! What happened to him? How did my ring get into your box?"

"It must have been in between papers in one of the drawers. I'm really surprised that no one took it," I said.

"The haunting rumors must have helped to save it from thieves," Gillian said.

Jack opened a browser. "What was his last name?"

"Lemuel Clemens."

"Seriously?"

Doris drew herself up and hardened her edges that had softened at the mention of his name. "And what's wrong with his name?"

"Lem Clem?" Jack's typing faltered. "Never mind."

I think he muttered something about parents.

He focused intently on the screen, adding search terms. "Nothing. We need more information. I'm guessing he wasn't important enough to warrant being digitized."

"He was important to me!"

"I know," I said. "We'll find him. We just need to do some more basic research. Google crawls more places all the time. There could be something in a newspaper morgue that isn't online yet. We can check genealogical sites. Do you know anything about his family?"

"I've got more pictures in sleeves. Do you recognize any of these people?" Gillian spread out half a dozen sleeves on the table.

"My father and Lemuel." His name came out on a sob. "He was a sailor, but he often did bodyguard work for Daddykins and me."

I looked at the photo. Lemuel was tall with broad shoulders and a shy smile. Nice looking in an old-fashioned way. Hair parted in the center. Wore his pants too high for my taste. Pleated. Thin belt. I wondered if, perhaps, "Daddykins" hadn't thought Lemuel good enough for his little girl. "What did your father think of Lemuel?"

"He trusted him with his life."

That wasn't what I asked, but I let it pass.

Doris took a closer look at the pictures. "More."

Gillian dutifully spread out some more picture sleeves.

Doris nodded and bit her ghostly lip as she looked at them. "These are my father's business partners."

She identified several men who appeared in many photos.

I'd already been able to sort out those who worked for him from those who worked with him by their clothes. These days fashion equalized people's status considerably. I suppose there's a difference between those who can afford haute couture and those who can afford Wal-Mart, but so many people of high and low status dress the same these days that class distinctions are less obvious than they were when Doris was young.

"This is Mary Ann Deluria. She was Dad's fancy woman."

Jack frowned, but Gillian nudged him and whispered in his ear and he got it.

"These two men always seem to be with Lemuel." I pointed to two equally tall and muscled young men.

"Daddy's bodyguards." She began to tear up again.

"Can you remember more names?" I turned on my

recording app, wondering if ghosts could be recorded. Maybe I'd better write the names down as well.

"Timothy O'Reilly. Elijah Jones."

"Good Irish and Welsh surnames." Jack typed them one at a time into Google along with an early century date based on a letter that looked like the right time frame. "And we have a hit with Mary Ann. Leave it to the fallen woman to show up on Google."

"Crass, Jack."

"Maybe, but scandal is a researcher's friend."

"True but still crass."

"You, too." Gillian leaned over to read the screen. "What does it say?"

Jack leaned back. "She took over everything!" He scrolled down. "Uh oh."

Chapter 15

He glanced over his shoulder at Doris and then up at Gillian.

She read where he was pointing."That's odd. All at once."

Our obtuseness and lowered voices caught Doris' attention. But as she moved to read the screen, Jack closed the laptop. Her anger was potent as she dove through the laptop but didn't come out the other side.

"Oh, crap." Jack lifted the lid, but the screen no longer held the image of the newspaper article. It looked as if all the pixels had gone crazy. He moaned. "I really liked this laptop."

"Glad we weren't using my Mac," I said.

"The ghost in the machine." Gillian rubbed his neck. "You were only trying to keep her from pain. Is she trapped in there?"

He shook his head. "I doubt it."

"Lemuel is dead. But that was the case, anyway." She had to have known that.

"At least they died together." Gillian sighed. "I'm a little surprised she has no memories at all of that moment. I would have guessed that her senses would have been heightened. The fear alone…"

"She may have blocked it. Traumatic amnesia."

"You mean dissociative amnesia."

Jack waved a dismissive hand. "You know what I

mean. But her father, too! That's shocking." Jack lifted the lid again and peeked, shook his head, and closed it.

"And Mary Ann inherited the whole kit and caboodle. Rather casts her in a suspicious light," Gillian said.

"And her granddaughter is still around. I wonder if she knows the story of this little cottage?" I shivered.

Jack nodded. "I'm sure of it. I think that's why she's made a friend of you, Cass. Something else is going on."

"Why didn't the granddaughter get the house?" Gillian asked.

"I don't know if Doris' father actually owned this place. Doris only said they lived in the area. They may have visited here," I said. "I should be able to find that out pretty easily. They had to make sure the title was clear before I bought the place. If Doris would show herself, we could just ask her."

A hollow knocking emanated from inside the laptop. We all looked at each other. Jack fumbled as he tried to open it up. A tiny Doris emerged, dusting off her virtual skirt and sleeves. As she stepped forward into the room, she grew larger. Jack continued to lift the lid, relief apparent on his face when he realized that the computer was now back to normal. Just to be sure, he flipped through a few files and apps. Then he patted the lid affectionately.

"Now you have to solve all our murders." Doris lifted her chin. "But I suspect you know who did it."

"Mary Ann Deluria?" I ventured.

She gave a sharp nod.

"It's a place to start. But I have a couple of questions for you, Doris. Is this your cottage?"

"No."

"Ah." I'd been hopeful that we'd solved at least one mystery. "But if it belonged to Mary Ann, why didn't Marcy claim it as her granddaughter?"

"It was never Mary Ann's. It belonged to my mother," Doris said.

"Your mother?" Gillian asked. "Who's your mother?"

"Her name was Shelagh. You have a picture of her."

Gillian sorted through the photographs, laying them out on the table one at a time.

"There." Doris pointed to one of the pictures we'd been looking at of Doris and her father in front of the cottage. On closer inspection, the woman with them did bear a strong resemblance to Doris.

"Why didn't your father marry your mother?" The three of them looked like a happy family in front of the cottage.

"He asked her, but she refused. She was a bohemian. She was an advocate of free love and believed that the government had no business in the personal lives of its citizens. She was a feminist and didn't like what the law allowed a man to do to his wife."

"She didn't trust men," I said.

"No, she didn't although she loved my father."

"You said you don't trust men."

"Yes."

"Did your mother raise you?" Gillian asked.

"No. My father did, but we visited her often."

"So she owned the cottage in her name?"

"Yes."

Jack cut in. "So I'm guessing you're haunting the place because, in a sense, it was your home, but you died before you could inherit it."

"My sister Francine inherited it. She was born after I died."

"Shelagh and Francine or Francie, the writers who used to live here. Remember the séance where they wanted to call up Shelagh's ghost as a muse, but they got Doris instead?" I asked. "Now it makes sense why you appeared, Doris. You're the one with unresolved issues."

"Wait a minute," Gillian said. "How do you know about Francie? You died before she was born."

"She was part of that first séance and the writers who called me here."

"How does that work exactly?" Jack asked.

"Not now, Jack," I said. "Doris, your mother must have kept some of your things after your death. That's why your ring and your car are still here."

"It didn't occur to me until now," Gillian said. "But you asked us to keep your mother's cut-work embroidery. I'm sorry that I didn't understand when you said it."

"Please let us know which of your mother's possessions you value, and I'll keep them, of course," I said.

"Thank you," Doris said. "The writing desk was hers. I remember her sitting there, writing."

"She was very beautiful," I said.

"Yes, she was." Doris faded away.

I turned to Jack and Gillian. "I think we should give her some time to herself."

"Makes me a bit suspicious of Marcy's motives,"

Jack said.

"It does cast her interest in you in a different light," Gillian said. "Are you going to confront her?"

I shook my head. "No reason to do that. I want to spin it out to see what kind of game she's playing."

"I think you should give Dave and Mina another go. They've lived here a while, and they live in proximity to the crime scene...scenes." Gillian put her hands on her hips. "Should I pack some of this stuff up neatly? We could do some sorting and organizing, but it's going to be hard to top that revelation."

"Yes. Thanks. I'm thinking I need some more plastic file boxes and folders to sort into. Who knows what other gems are in here."

I took Gillian's suggestion to heart, gathered some of the photos into a plastic sleeve, and went in search of my two nearest neighbors, leaving Jack to finish the pantry shelving and Gillian to sort through and organize the paper remains of Doris' family's lives.

As I walked between our houses, I glanced up at Wilhelmina's, but it was dark and the curtains were drawn. I'd never seen it so uninviting.

Dave's lights were on, so I knocked. A moment later he opened the door. "Hey, there. My favorite neighbor. Come on in."

It was as though the other night had never happened. I thought about asking him what he'd meant but decided it might be more prudent to forget about it...for now.

He shut the door behind me and then quickly moved into his living room ahead of me to offer me a chair. "What would you like to drink?"

"Iced tea?"

"The Long Island variety?"

"No. I don't think I could handle alcohol right now."

He frowned, and I knew he was dying to ask but wouldn't allow himself until he'd satisfied his hosting duties. In many ways, Dave was transparent and his emotions played across his face, which made me like and trust him. However, there were other layers to him that were not so easy to ascertain. Sometimes he seemed to be speaking in code. He didn't express hostility, but he seemed to expect me to understand.

While he puttered in the kitchen, I looked around his funky beach house. He owned lots of unusual things, such as oil paintings of a Moro pirate and his mate, five-foot turned antique candle stands, and a lava lamp. He seemed to like lots of open space because there was no clutter, paper or otherwise, and all the furniture had low, clean lines.

When he set an iced tea with sprigs of mint in front of me on a cork coaster, he asked, "What's going on in your life that's fraying your edges?"

"I was worried about being lonely here, but my place seems to have turned into Grand Central."

"You've been partying without me? I'm hurt!" Dave put his hand over his heart.

I laughed. "Hardly. You know I'd invite you if I were actually throwing parties." Then I had another thought. "Dave, what do you think of the gamers?"

"I don't have an opinion of the online stuff. I don't do it. I'm a live action kinda guy." He winked at me.

"That's a no-brainer." I laughed. "No, I meant the bunch that occasionally inhabits our beach."

"There are several groups of gamers and cosplayers

at the college, and many of them like our beach. The vampire crowd." He thought for a moment. "The steampunk group, but they also hang out at a Victorian club in town. The superhero bunch doesn't hang around down here."

"Okay, so riddle me this, Batman, what about the gamers believing they're vampires?"

"Not the steampunk crowd. Totally wrong vibe. The others…" He shrugged.

"That was pretty definite."

He paused again. "Perhaps that was a bit cut and dried." He laughed, a gentle, easy sound. "Look, there are certainly people up in the City who think they're vampires and people who want desperately to be vampires and there are blood drinkers, but I don't believe your average gamer, even the vampire gamers, thinks for a half-second that he or she is really a vampire. They're just suspending their disbelief for a while to play the same as you do when you read a book."

"There is a lure to wanting to live forever," I said.

"You could also argue that authors write books and painters paint pictures in order to live forever. To live in memory. Forever young. And isn't that the essence of the vampire legend?"

"So you think part of the reason for pretending to be vampires is a desire for immortality? Wouldn't that buy-in make them more likely to have murdered Alan? To play out some ritual? To get in touch with other planes of reality? I've heard about things like it in the news."

Dave got up and paced over to the patio window. I could tell he was really uncomfortable, and I wondered why. Some childhood memory, perhaps?

Finally, he turned. "I think you're really barking up the wrong tree. I don't care what you see on TV or read in the papers, a fantasy life is not a sufficient motive for murder. Look for a motive of passion. Love, hate, gain, or jealousy."

I remembered the list of suspects we'd been working on before I came over. We'd listed jealousy and gain for a couple of people.

"So you agree with Brendan," I said. "The gamers are disillusioned romantics, creating a world that's more interesting to them than the one they're living in."

"You could say that. We all try to recreate our everyday lives with a little..." He shrugged and smiled his lopsided grin. "Pizzazz."

Now was the time. "Dave, what's your take on Marcy."

The laid-back Dave visibly jumped. "She's...ah...we need a vet in the area."

That was about as noncommittal as you could get. "How long have you known her?"

He shrugged and regained his composure. "Her family is from the area but moved north when they came into money. I know she moved back relatively recently. I don't really know her." He put a slight emphasis on the word know. "I don't have animals, so I have no need to visit a vet. I enjoy the free animals who live around me, and they have no desire to see a vet."

"But she attended the séances."

"Yes."

Clearly, he wasn't going to tell me anything more.

"I have a few photos of some people who might have lived or worked near here a number of years ago."

I sensed reluctance. "They're probably a bit before your time." I spread them out quickly on the coffee table.

Dave thumbed through them, shaking his head. "Not really my time period."

I gathered them back up. "Thanks, Dave. You've given me a lot to mull over."

He walked me to the door. "You're welcome anytime." But he seemed much more serious and contemplative than when I'd arrived.

I hadn't found out much about the history of the place, but I walked out to the lane and turned uphill to Mina's place and was glad to see it open and radiating welcome. Mina met me at the door and gestured me in.

I followed her into what I would describe as a parlor as opposed to the living room. It was a lovely, formal room of chairs, plants, small tables, and framed pictures. On the table between two Queen Anne chairs, a tea service awaited us, the teapot adorned by a purple quilted cozy.

Mina removed the cozy and poured two steaming cups of tea. Then she offered me a plate of lemon bars. My stomach growled. It was lunchtime.

I only sipped the tea, having just had an iced tea, but I selected a lemon bar and took a bite. Yummy. "Did you make these?"

"I did. My mother's recipe handed down. I'm glad you like them." She sipped her tea. "Are you ready to hear a little of the history of our town?"

"Absolutely. How did you know?"

She tilted her head. "You've been here long enough to have gotten through the essentials of moving in. I thought you might be ready for a little depth."

"Exactly so." The tea was delicious and nice and

hot. I wondered if she had tea by herself if she received no visitors. Either that or she was seriously psychic.

Mina settled back in her chair with her cup. "My family has been here for many generations, and I've seen many changes. It's an unusual little town in many ways, and just like every other small town the world over in many others. There are layers of folks here. The old ones form the spine of the community. As new groups arrive, they become the sinews, the flesh, and our communications, our sharing is the blood."

I took a sip to give myself a moment to think about her metaphor. "I like that. It's very inclusive that people are incorporated into the body and life of the town. I recently acquired some photographs of people who either lived in my cottage or spent time in the vicinity. Some have partial names or nicknames on the backs. I'm wondering…"

"If I know who they are." She shrugged delicately. "I might. Do you have them with you?"

I opened the plastic sleeve and pulled out the photos.

Mina took them from me, looking over each thoughtfully and then reading the names on the back. "This is Al Hanrahan. Big Al. He knew my father, but he left the area after some business deal went bad. I don't really know much about it. My father never mentioned him again after he left." She flipped through a few more, pausing at the car. She flipped the picture over and laughed. "Breezer. That's an old term. Nice car. I don't care for today's chubby cars in their boring neutral shades." She finished the stack. "I'm afraid I wasn't much help, but maybe something will come to me later or perhaps you have other pictures?"

"I do have some others back at the house." I slipped the photos back in their sleeve. "I was wondering if you could tell me a bit about my cottage, its history, and the people who lived there. Maybe you know something about the first woman who died on the beach?"

Mina refreshed our tea. "Oh, Doris wasn't the first person to die on your beach. Hundreds of people have died there since the dawn of time."

"Good point, but I'm interested in Doris and how her story is intertwined with the cottage."

Mina nodded knowingly. "I see you've gotten to know your ghost."

I stared at her, thinking back to her first nervous visit to me in the cottage. She knew Doris was there. Why had she been nervous about her?

Chapter 16

In her uncanny fashion, she said, "The last time I saw her, she was a hurricane of anger, rampaging through your house. When I visited you, I expected a repeat performance. I'm delighted to be wrong."

"The last time you saw her?"

"I was there at the séance that conjured her, and I was there when she chased us all out with death threats if any of us ever returned."

When she smiled, I could see hints of what she must have been like when young. "Can you tell me anything more about her?"

She shook her head. "I'm afraid I don't have the answers you seek. At least not those particular answers. However, I may know some others who can help you. Let me see what I can do. This is a complicated little town with some well-hidden secrets."

I finished my tea. "Thanks. I really appreciate it." I stood. "If you want to see some of the other things we found in the house, please come down whenever you can."

Mina stood. "I will."

The wind was picking up as I walked down to my place.

I let myself in and found Jack and Gillian sitting at the table, still going through papers. "Are you guys still at it?"

"We couldn't stop ourselves from diving a little more deeply than we'd intended into the papers. Doris joined us while you were out. Even Thor fell asleep in one of the boxes." She stretched and yawned. "I think we satisfied our curiosity. There are some tantalizing bits and pieces. Doris' family was one of about half a dozen who've been here for generations. Their histories are entwined to the point that some legends grew up around some of them. Hers reminded me of Romeo and Juliet except that they were murdered instead of killing themselves."

"That's kind of a major difference." I picked up the coffee pot and topped off her mug.

She shrugged. "True, but the significance is that their families were against their relationship. That always leads to trouble."

Jack added, "Trouble. Death. Dismemberment."

"You are so cheerful, Jack. Give me your cup."

He held it out to me, and I topped it off.

"According to Mina, Big Al is Al Hanrahan, and he was a businessman down here but ran into some trouble. Mina's father knew him." Gillian made a note. "We can try to find him."

"Did you get the shelving up in the pantry and over the washer and dryer? If so, I'll let you guys leave and go back to your lives. Thank you so much. I can't believe how much work we've gotten done. I feel at home now."

"No problem, and I am ready to sleep in my own bed."

"Tell you what. I'll treat you to a late lunch if you haven't eaten. There's a fruitarian restaurant called Melon-choly I'm really curious about. There's a vegan place called Callie's Flower. And Soupçon for sandwiches…and soup!"

"I like the sound of Soupçon. Let's go there," Gillian said. "Have you eaten there?"

"Yes, actually. I like their food," I said, picking up my keys.

****

When we got back from lunch, I parked my Subaru at the curb in front of my cottage and turned off the engine. "Looks like we have company."

"Is that Ricardo's boss?" Gillian asked.

Jack opened his door and Samantha turned around. This afternoon she was wearing a golden cowgirl outfit. On the top of her head sat a gold felt Stetson with a conch band in copper. Her pale yellow blouse flowed like silk. The suede skirt was dark gold, long, and fringed as was the vest. She even wore cowboy boots. Jack raised an eyebrow.

She smiled and walked toward the car. "Hello. I was about to go up on the hill. Want to come?"

Jack and Gillian shook their heads. "We're headed for home in a little bit."

Something inside me dropped when they said that, even though it had been my suggestion. But I was a big girl, and it was time I worked on building my new life by myself. I was grateful to them for staying so long. I'm not sure how I would have handled everything without them. Probably not well.

I didn't think Samantha had really expected an affirmative answer, but her eyes saddened. I felt a kinship because I could identify with that lonely, bleak feeling that had invaded my life post-divorce and crept all the way down to my bones, paralyzing me at times.

"So okay. See you later." Her voice as flat as a Kansas plain.

A few minutes later we saw her trudging up the hillside toward the picnic area at the top and the state park beyond.

"While we were working on Brendan's plan, Ricardo told me a few things about her. Her family is dead. She's an only child. A few years ago she met a wonderful man, and she finally thought she had what she wanted—another family. He was a widower with a young daughter. Samantha can't have any children of her own. Anyway, last year he died slowly and painfully from cancer. He divided his money between Samantha and his daughter: a trust fund for college for his daughter and enough money to start a small business for Samantha. She opened Crystalline."

Thor sauntered into the kitchen, stopped, and looked at me.

"Speak of the devil." I looked down at the not-so-wee beastie.

Thor opened his mouth and uttered a cracked meow.

Jack scooped him up on one forearm, flipped him over, and stroked Thor's belly until he got a good purr going.

I could tell he'd miss the beast, and I was glad Thor seemed to have forgiven him.

"Where's the medication for Thor's eyes?"

"It's in the fridge. The directions said to keep it refrigerated, but you might want to warm it up a bit." I chuckled. "He really jumped when I tried to put it in cold."

We spent the rest of the afternoon stocking the

shelves, stacking boxes, and cleaning up. Our efforts substantially reduced the clutter in the cottage.

I stepped back, hands on hips. "Job well done, guys. This is enormously helpful."

"I need a beer. Want one?" Jack asked.

"I'll take one." Gillian washed her hands in the sink. "We can even make it home by suppertime."

"Speaking of suppertime, I wonder why Samantha hasn't returned?" I asked. "She usually doesn't spend this much time photographing."

"She probably just drove home without saying anything," Jack said.

That hadn't occurred to me. I went over to the door and looked out. "Nope. Her car is still sitting over by the road."

Then we heard sirens and saw flashing red lights up on the ridge.

Ricardo ran toward us. Disheveled and out of breath, pale, and panting, he pulled to a stop at my steps. "It's Samantha…"

"Is she all right?" I asked, alarmed. "I just saw that her car is still here."

"No, she's not. She's… There's blood everywhere. Is Mia here?"

"No, I haven't seen her today. I thought we were getting together tomorrow to finish up Brendan's web site. Why?"

"Hearing about Samantha made me worry about Mia. She's not answering her cell."

"Samantha. Is she…?" I asked.

He shook his head. "I think she's dead." He crossed himself and then bent over, head down, resting his hands on his knees, and caught his breath.

"The cops are questioning everyone in our group. They came to my mother's house, yanked me away from dinner. My mother is really upset. I left with them before things got out of hand. A hiker said the 'crystal lady' was dead in the State park. Since I work for her, they took me along to…" He broke down. "Who would kill her?"

But I could think of a couple of people who might kill the woman who was filming all over town.

"Want a lift back home?"

Ricardo shook his head, not speaking, not looking up, and walked slowly to the gravel and the road beyond. I watched him go, my heart aching for him, then I closed the door and turned to Jack and Gillian.

"I feel so sorry for him. Ricardo is devastated." The wooden chair scraped as I pulled it out and sat down, suddenly weak in the knees.

Jack and Gillian exchanged looks. Then Jack said, "You know, it's getting late, and I'm really tired after putting up your shelves. If you don't mind, I'd like to spend one more night."

I smiled. "Jack, you are such a sweetie. I'd be very grateful."

"Let's order pizza now that Clem's is delivering."

Gillian started clearing the table. "Works for me. No anchovies."

"Spoil sport. Let's get two. I love leftovers. Meat lovers and veggie?"

"Go for it, Jack," I said.

He called and then joined us at the trestle table. "We never did finish our little whodunit game."

"True, but do you guys really feel up to it? I know you're both tired."

Gillian sighed. "Yes, but we'll have pizza to replenish our flagging whatevers soon."

"All righty," I said. "Where were we?"

"We were going to consider that Brendan may have killed Alan for profit or jealousy. Now I think we have to consider that he might have murdered Samantha because he found out she'd been filming him," Jack said.

"No, I don't have to consider that. Not when he's a paying customer." But my head was spinning. "Besides, I'm still planning to go have dinner at his house and pump him for local information for Doris."

"You certainly picked an interesting town to move to." Gillian laughed.

It was a thought that had been running through my own head. Pleasanton was never like this.

"We need to find out exactly what happened to her…" Gillian sat staring at nothing.

"Gill?" he said gently.

"Who her?" I asked. "Samantha or Doris?"

"I was thinking that you seem to be a focal point, Cass." Gillian started ticking things off on her fingers. "If Samantha was murdered, then two murders have taken place within yards of your house. Three if you count Doris."

"You should always count Doris," Doris said, joining us.

"Hey, Doris," I said.

Gillian continued. "Now you know everyone involved and most of the suspects."

"That's a bit of a stretch. I didn't know them before I moved here. I don't think this has anything to do with me. If it did, this place wouldn't be called Murder

Beach."

"But," Jack added, "if the videos go online for all to see, it's fairly obvious that many were taken on your beach or nearby."

"Oh, great!" My mouth went dry.

"Cass, relax. Gillian's not accusing you of anything, but are all those things true of your next door neighbor?"

"She may not be accusing me, but she's scaring me, nonetheless."

Gillian put her hand on mine. "I'm sorry. I didn't mean to, but Jack has a point. Is there anyone, such as your next door neighbor, for whom all these events would be as related as they are for you?"

"Dave? Sort of. I think. Maybe. Oh, I don't know." I couldn't think.

Jack persisted. "Did he know Alan?"

"Yes."

"Samantha?"

"No, I don't think so. Maybe. Lots of people who weren't into that stuff went in there for scented candles, crystals, and aromatherapy oils. But I don't think Dave has anything to hide that Samantha could reveal."

"You don't know him well enough to determine that." Gillian added gently, "You said that Dave said he didn't do Internet gaming."

"If the murders are linked, this would seem to let Sara off the hook. No motive for Samantha's murder," Jack said, "unless she really hated Samantha's crystals."

"Let's see if we can get up on the hill. I want to see for myself."

"Where Samantha was killed?" Gillian asked.

"Why?"

Jack shook his head. "That whole area will be sealed off. It's a crime scene."

"I know, but I'd like to see how close I can get. Maybe something will make sense up there. I've wondered if Alan was thrown off the cliff."

"Cass, we don't know if the two murders are linked. For all we know, Samantha may have been mugged."

"Too coincidental." I started to get up.

"Nope." Jack put his hand on my arm. "Pizza."

"Oh, yeah." I sat back down.

"Don't worry. We'll go with you tomorrow to keep you out of trouble, but let's at least wait for the excitement to die down," Gillian said. "Personally, I'd rather you didn't become a victim."

"Not after all the work we've done around here," Jack said.

"Gee, thanks, Jack," I said.

"Back on track, kids," Gillian said. "Tonight we can haul out our lists to see if there's any similarity between our suspects for the two murders."

"After pizza," Jack reiterated.

****

The parking lot at the top of the hill by the picnic area was deserted the next morning. We pulled into the parking area as close as we could get to the picnic tables and the built-in grills that hadn't been adequately cleaned. Bits of tin foil and unrecognizable burnt flesh beaded the rods like an infernal necklace suspended over the fire pits.

Jack was wrong. There was no sign of crime scene tape or barricades. At least we wouldn't be breaking the law. The wind whipped up the hill, thrashing my hair and whipping the ends of my scarf as I climbed out of the car slowly.

"Cass, I'm still not sure this is a good idea."

"There's no tape up." I gestured at the picnic area.

"Yeah, I noticed that. I guess they're through with the area."

I couldn't ask them to do something that ran counter to their consciences. "Look, guys. I really have to do this for my own peace of mind because when you go I'll still be here, but you two can stay with the car. If the cops come along… I don't know. Tell them I became hysterical or something and dragged you up here against your will."

Jack laughed.

Gillian glanced down and picked a piece of lint from her crisp gray wool trousers.

Jack closed his eyes briefly and pinched the bridge of his nose.

"It's okay," I said. "Really."

Jack came to a decision. "No. We'll help you." He looked at Gillian.

She nodded reluctantly. "It feels creepy to me."

Once committed, they got into it, helping me look around. Gillian and Jack moved on ahead deeper into the trees. I followed slowly, looking around for any signs or belongings that the police missed around the tables and grills. I expected a certain amount of detritus but didn't see any.

As I moved into the woods on the other side of the picnic area, I noticed stains on the trees. I reached up to touch one, but stopped myself. What if it were blood? Is this what Ricardo meant when he said there was blood everywhere? I followed the trail of stains, and it led me to the edge of the cliff. I looked down at the waves swirling over the rocks below and started to lose my balance. Strong hands grabbed me from behind.

"You almost went over! What are you doing?"

When the vertigo subsided, I said, "Jack, look at the trees, the bark. I think that might be a trail of blood from the picnic area to there." I pointed at the cliff.

"Samantha wasn't attacked here."

That stopped me. "How do you know?"

"Because we found the crime scene tape. It's down below on the other side. She was close to the public beach when she was attacked. Gillian took one look and headed back for the car. I came to find you."

"What if this is where Alan was attacked?"

Jack bent down to check the stains, which had gotten progressively closer to the ground as the trail approached the cliff. Then he straightened. "Cass, how tall was Alan?"

"If I'm remembering correctly, according to the autopsy report, a couple of inches taller than me. Shorter than you."

"That wound was in his neck."

I nodded.

"The stains closest to the picnic area are about the right height for a neck wound on someone his height, but we don't know if these are blood stains. Kids could have been out here marking the trees with paint. We know the gamers use these woods."

"They do, and they are vampire gamers. Maybe they were trying to simulate blood," I said.

"Or using animal blood. You can buy dried blood at gardening supply stores to keep pests out of your garden."

"Maybe we ought to tell the police. Let them test the stains."

"Cass, I'm sure they've seen all this and taken samples. Seriously. They do this for a living." He put an arm around me. "Let's go back to the car. Are you satisfied? Have you seen what you needed to see?"

I nodded. I really didn't know what I was expecting. Jack was right. Of course the police would have checked all this. They were trained, had equipment, and knew the sorts of things they should look for. I may have felt as though I should be doing something, but now I knew there was no point. It was going to take a cooler head than mine to sort all this out.

Chapter 17

The message light on the landline blinked at me when we got back. I pressed the play button as Jack and Gillian followed me into the kitchen.

George's noncommittal voice said, "Got your message. Nice to hear from you. What made you think Samantha Ross was murdered? She's at County General recovering from a beating. Listen. I'm heading out to rehearsal. I'll call you later. Next time, leave your cell number, and I'll text you. Check with the hospital. She may be seeing visitors."

I'd left the landline number precisely because the cell somehow felt more immediate and intimate. I had such mixed feelings about George, but I immediately texted my cell number to George, knowing he wouldn't be able to answer right away.

"Thank goodness!" Gillian said.

The second message was from Brendan. "I hate leaving messages. Talk to Ricardo."

Jack laughed.

So much for putting my landline on our flyer. "I'm going to call the hospital." I looked up the hospital on my phone.

"Let's get some flowers and go visit if they'll let us in." Gillian set out the mugs and put the kettle on.

"Great idea." I called the hospital. When reception answered, I asked, "Do you have a patient by the name of Samantha Ross? She would have been admitted late yesterday, the victim of a beating."

The woman asked if I was a relative.

"No, just a friend. She parked her car at my house. She was doing some filming in the woods above my place. I was wondering if she's there and if I could see her."

"I'll see what I can find out." Then she put me on hold.

The woman came back on the line. "I talked to your friend. She regained consciousness an hour ago. They'll have her in a room where you can visit her shortly. I'm listing you on her chart. Visiting hours are over for the morning and she's already been given a sedative, so you couldn't see her right away even if they get her settled. Why don't you come down after lunch?"

****

We entered the hospital lobby at 1:30 in the afternoon. When it comes to hospitals, I always prefer coming in the front door on my own two feet.

Hospitals smell funny. There's no way around it. Anyone who's spent any time in one associates that smell with illness and death. After all, you only come here if you're sick, dying, or visiting someone who is. If you're the one who's sick or dying, you don't much care what the place smells like.

Samantha had formally added all of us, including Ricardo, to her accepted list of visitors although the receptionist told us that they only checked if they had been alerted to a problem, such as a rowdy ex-husband or ex-girlfriend. I fought hard to keep the smile on my face when I saw Samantha. The bandage on her nose tented outward like a bird's beak. Her eyes were bloodshot and set in a raccoon's dark mask.

"Hey, Samantha, how're you doing? I brought Jack and Gillian, but if we tire you out, let me know."

Samantha adjusted her position slightly and winced. "Everything hurts. I feel as though I've been run over by a truck."

"Tell the nurse. They'll give you something stronger."

"Blocks the vibes."

"Samantha," I said in exasperation. "Take the meds."

Her grin was lopsided and swollen.

"You can joke about this?"

"What else can I do? Someone just tried to kill me. If I don't laugh, I'll cry." Her voice was nasal through the bandages.

"Have you talked to the police?" I looked around for a chair.

"Apparently they've had someone here since they brought me in. They talked to me as soon as I woke up."

I scooted the chair up close to her bedside and sat. "What do you remember about yesterday?"

"I'd rather not remember it."

"We know," Gillian said. "It must have been horrible. All alone with no one to help you. You must have been terrified."

Jack added, "We thought if you could remember, perhaps we could go back and look at the site. Maybe find something the police had missed."

That surprised me after his comments to me, but I appreciated his attempts to support Samantha.

Samantha nodded and then winced with pain. "I'd just run into a significant cold spot and was filming when I heard a shuffling sound behind me. I turned with the camera still in front of my face. I saw him, bundled in a heavy jacket, scarf, and hat. He reached out and slammed the flat of his hand against the lens of my camera and that knocked me down. I don't remember anything else. The doctor told me that you don't feel the blow that knocks you out. My concussion was caused by a blow to the back of my head, not the camera in the face, bad as that looks."

I thought back to her camera design. No display screen. I guessed that refinement would come with investments.

Jack frowned. "That means there might have been two of them."

"Or she hit the back of her head when she fell. But at least you got them on film," I said.

Samantha looked away. "Bill Daniels said they didn't find my camera." She started crying.

"I'm so sorry. I know it was your prototype. We were up on the top of the hill this morning and didn't see your stuff. Your car is still parked on the road. At least, it was when we left."

Samantha sobbed. "I just don't understand why."

"They didn't...I mean, you weren't...uh..." I cleared my throat. "You weren't raped, were you?"

She looked shocked. "No!"

I was embarrassed. "Sorry, but I had to ask. The person who hit you must have taken your camera intentionally. Maybe the motive was robbery." But that didn't make sense because they wouldn't have known if it had any value. It clearly wasn't a smart phone.

Whoever it was hadn't wanted to be filmed and suspected he had been.

A nurse came in through the open door. "You have another visitor. One of you will have to leave."

Jack said, "Gillian and I will go down to the gift shop. Take care, Samantha. We'll see you later."

Samantha said, "Thank you."

I stood up. "I'll go, too. But I had to make sure you were okay. If you remember anything else, let me know. I'll be back tomorrow to check on you."

"Look for my stuff? Okay?"

"You bet." I turned to leave as Ricardo came in. "Hey, Ricardo. If you come by my place after you leave here, we could use some help checking the park for Samantha's camera."

"Absolutely. I figured I'd come by to see if the boss wanted me to close up shop while she's laid up." He winked at me as Samantha squawked in the background.

"Careful. You'll raise her blood pressure."

"I'm so happy she's okay, that I'd keep it open twenty-four-seven if she wanted," he whispered. "Oh, dinner at Brendan's tonight." The door closed behind him.

I took the elevator down to the first floor and found Jack and Gillian in the gift shop. "Ricardo's with her now, and I guess we're having dinner at Brendan's."

"Bummer. I was looking forward to pizza again," Jack said.

****

Someone knocked on the door.

"That must be them!" Jack swung the door wide. "C'mon in. Cass is getting her stuff together. Let me

236

take your jackets. This could take a few minutes. Want anything to drink?"

Ricardo followed Jack into the kitchen. I looked up from my computer. Mia was stunning in a green silk, off the shoulder maxi with a handkerchief hem.

"Hi Mia. I think I'm underdressed."

She laughed. "No, I'm just desperate to wear this vintage dress I found in the City."

"I never fit into vintage. Too hippy." I hit Command-S. "I'm almost finished here. Did you bring the sketches?"

She held up an envelope as she walked over to the table. "Right here." She set the envelope down and picked up one of Mina's books. "I think I've seen this in the bookstore."

She flipped through the book as I saved the file to a flash drive.

"Hmmm. 'Is Las Lunas haunted?' Yeah, I'd say so. Ever since I moved here, there've been weird goings on."

I leaned back. "What do you mean?"

"I was so frightened, so insecure when I tracked my father here. Then unexplained things kept happening. At first, I thought my dad was protecting me. Then I thought I had a guardian angel, keeping me from harm. But when I started dating Ricardo, he kept telling me that I was imagining things, and because I was falling in love with him, I let it go." She glanced toward the kitchen. "But I never believed that this town was normal, so I kept investigating on my own." She leaned closer and lowered her voice. "I even started to wonder if Ricardo was in on it."

Jack and Ricardo came into the living room,

carrying beers.

"Don't spoil your dinner. I suspect Brendan will have put in a lot of effort." I scolded.

Mia read through the table of contents. "For example, 'The Woman in Black.' I swear one night around midnight when I was on my way home after one of our meetings, I saw a woman suddenly appear ahead of me. There one minute, gone the next. Then I heard a cat meow. The story is that she turns into a cat and runs away."

I thought about the cat I'd seen in the fog. "I think I may have seen her, too. What else?"

The air behind Mia shimmered, and I was so tempted to introduce her to Doris, but now was not the time.

Mia raised an eyebrow. "The murders on your beach and all the ghosts."

"You're going to scare her, Mia."

If only Ricardo knew, I thought. "Oh, don't worry about me. I'm more curious than scared."

But Ricardo continued to look worried. "Mia hasn't lived here very long. I've lived here my whole life. You can destroy the reputation of a whole community—"

Mia cut him off, waving the book in his face. "Hello! Published! I'm not spreading any stories that a tourist can't read him or herself."

"And that gives me an idea." I opened my laptop again and started making notes. "What if we incorporate some of the local legends into our designs?"

Gillian nodded. "Not a bad idea. It could be a theme tying the web sites together into a community. Do they still do webrings? I haven't seen one in a while."

Mia quirked a smile. "The concept's a bit dated now. Very Nineties. But that's not to say that we can't develop our own structure for the community around a theme. Personally, I like the idea of using legends." She cast a glance at Ricardo. "But we'll have to think it through. It might not work for all businesses. For example, no ghosts for real estate agencies."

I laughed to cover up the ghostly chuckle from just over my left shoulder. "Got your point." I glanced over my shoulder to let Doris know that I was aware of her presence.

Jack took another swig of beer. "Ricardo, you're the only one in the room who grew up here. Is this book accurate? What are the local legends?"

Ricardo looked at all of us solemnly in turn. "They aren't to be mocked."

That got my attention but Mia rolled her eyes.

He ignored her and continued. "Most people have talked to a ghost without realizing it."

And then there are those of us who do.

"They usually aren't wispy, nor do they moan and drag chains around. But ghosts aren't the only creatures that live here in Las Lunas."

I realized I was leaning forward. "What else is here?"

"I'm guessing sea monsters and mermaids." Jack dropped his bottle into recycling, breaking the spell.

Ricardo stopped, and I sensed the tension in him.

"What? You're at the seashore. Ergo..." Jack shrugged.

I was annoyed at Jack for his flip attitude that I usually found so endearing. I had really wanted to hear what Ricardo was about to say. I hadn't forgotten the strange noises and bumps in the night and the fireflies that weren't fireflies.

Ricardo slipped his jacket on and picked up Mia's coat, holding it open for her to slip her arms into the sleeves.

I stood and picked up my laptop and Mia's envelope. "Ready to go. Who wants to drive?"

In the creeping twilight, the warmly lit Queen Anne beckoned and Brendan met us at the door. "I'm so glad you could come." He held the door open for us as we walked into the entry hall.

"Brendan," I said, "I have to ask you about the color scheme. Is it a guy thing to paint a house so dark? I mean, black, maroon, and bronze hardly seem like cheerful house colors."

Brendan's laugh was deep and rumbly. "While this house is a lovely painted lady, as Victorians are referred to in the Bay Area, and are usually brightly painted around here, I did some research on paint colors in Victorian times. Why own a bookstore if you can't use it for research? I discovered that these are typical colors for a house during this part of Queen Victoria's reign during which it was built. I thought long and hard about it, but in the end, I went for historical accuracy. I must admit that I've really gotten into restoring her authentically. It's become a bit of an obsession."

I looked around. "You've done an amazing job."

"Thanks." He showed us into the living room. "For example, the long drapes that outline the tall windows are pulled back with reproduction brass pulls. Looped over the pulls are silk tassels I found in a repro catalog. When I could find original hardware, I grabbed it."

I handed him a bottle of wine in a green velvet sack.

He untied the cord, slid the bottle out, and examined the label. "My favorite vineyard."

"You flatterer. I'm waiting for someone to write a book called *Wine for the Palate-Challenged*."

"What a beautiful Oriental carpet," Jack said.

"And I love the lace doilies," Gillian added.

"That doily is an antimacassar. Macassar was oil that men used on their hair."

"Yuck," I said. "I'm not a fan of a lot of hair product."

"Most women don't like oil staining the upholstery, so they tatted antimacassars to prevent the oil from being transferred to the upholstery."

"Is this macramé?" Mia asked.

We turned our attention to a shadow box that contained earrings and a brooch that looked like fine macramé.

"That's hair jewelry," Brendan said. "Victorian women would collect hair from a loved one—often deceased—into a hair keeper and weave or braid it into jewelry as a memento."

"Gross!" Jack leaned closer.

"This is like a museum." I wondered why Brendan hadn't become a teacher.

"Would you like the grand tour?" Brendan asked.

We all looked at each other and nodded.

"Good. Let's start at the top and work our way down." Brendan led us up two flights of stairs to the top of the house. The Persian runners on both flights were held in place by brass rods along the backs of the steps. Underneath the runners the hard wood was beautifully polished. I thought about the work all this must have taken.

On the third floor, the rooms were untouched and full of old furniture, boxes, and trunks. Brendan pointed out the rooms and their histories without taking us into them. The second floor showed evidence of recent construction.

Brendan said, "I'm working on a suite of rooms for a new English professor who starts at the college in the fall. I'm putting in a few amenities, such as a whirlpool bath, for her. I'll fix up the wooden fire escape at the back of the—"

Though we were on the second floor, the hammering at the front door made us all jump.

Brendan frowned and hurried down the stairs. "They'll damage the door pounding like that. I'm coming! I'm coming!" he shouted.

We all followed him down. By the time we reached the front hall, George was handing Brendan a folded sheet of paper. His eyes widened when he saw me, but he was all business.

"I have a search warrant."

Brendan shook his head. "But why?"

"We have reason to believe that you had unusual access to Alan's Book Shoppe." He pushed past Brendan, followed by two police officers. He pointed to one. "You start upstairs. You," he pointed to the other, "in the back."

By the time the officers moved off to start the search, we had stopped behind Brendan. Brendan opened the warrant and read it.

I was uncomfortable and tapped him lightly on the arm. "Perhaps we should just leave."

Brendan looked up. "Wait a minute." He turned to George, who had moved off into the living room. He turned back and held up a finger. "Wait just a minute." He went into the living room.

I said to Ricardo and Mia, "I don't know if we should stay and offer moral support or get out of his way."

Jack said, "If we stay, we may find out something."

"I'm sure he spent time and money on dinner," Mia said. "It would be impolite to leave."

"Okay then," I said, swallowing my feelings. "Let's tag along."

But there was no need because George pushed passed us and went out the front door.

Brendan followed him but stopped next to me. "He got a call. Seems they found the young man, the missing gamer, they were looking for. I guess searching my house dropped to a lower priority for them. That's a good thing. Anyway, the two officers will search—"

The officer who'd started searching at the back of the house interrupted him. "We're through with the kitchen and dining room." He went into the living room.

"That was fast, thank heavens. Let's have dinner." Brendan herded everyone out of the hall and into the dining room.

Despite Brendan's patter, we were a quiet group as we ate the salmon pâté and sipped a nice light Chardonnay. One of the officers stuck his head through the door and told us they were leaving. Brendan got up to escort them out and lock the front door. He looked distinctly relieved as he served the main course with a flourish.

I turned to Brendan. "Okay, so what were they looking for and how do you tie into the murder?"

"Ah, subtlety."

"Brendan."

"Oh, all right. You did say you wanted a little local history, Cass."

I'd been thinking Doris' history, but I'd take what I could get.

"Alan and I were rivals. Say, I wonder if Sara would consider selling me Althea Romeo's collection now that Alan's gone to his reward?"

I made a speed-it-up motion with my hand.

"Just a thought. To make a long story short, I have…had a key to Alan's. Undoubtedly, the police found out as it was listed on the warrant. They apparently have evidence that I used it, which I did, but not to commit a crime."

That answered one question. "So you didn't know that Samantha videotaped you using a key to enter Alan's store?"

Brendan nearly dropped his wine glass.

"Why do you have a key to Alan's store?" There was an edge to Mia's voice.

"To spy on him, of course. While it's not really a secret, I had no idea there was a video of me using it."

He looked so shocked that I believed him.

"Why did you need to spy on him?" She furrowed her brow and cocked her head sideways.

"What does it matter? My reputation is probably ruined now."

"I doubt that anyone will notice. Too much else going on," Ricardo said.

Brendan brightened. "Do you really think so?"

"Unless you're arrested for murder, of course," I added.

Brendan's face fell.

"Oh, you're a big help, Cass." Jack shook his head.

I shrugged. "There's always the possibility that a little scandal might help. They say all publicity is good publicity."

"That's optimistic." Brendan removed our plates to the sideboard and set a small stack of fine porcelain dessert plates and a cherry cheesecake down then proceeded to cut pieces for all of us.

It was hard to resist diving immediately into the cheesecake, but I had to know. "Oh, you're not getting off the hook so lightly, Brendan. How did you get a key to Alan's shop?"

Had Brendan been a cat, the cream would have been dripping off his chops. "You know I've been writing a mystery?"

"Yeah."

"In one scene I have my protagonist acquire a house key by bribing a parking attendant to let him have the key ring while the target attends a gala."

"So?"

"So I did some research to see if it would actually work, and it did."

"A valet gave you Alan's key ring?" That was the last time I was leaving my keys with valet. "He could have been fired! What if Alan had wanted his car while you were copying keys?"

"I gave him more than he would have made for the entire night, and he kept the car keys with him. The keys were tagged and put on a pegboard, so he could have pled ignorance if challenged. Besides, it only took me a minute to take impressions of all the keys. That wasn't the hard part."

"Okay, I'll bite," I said. "What was the hard part?"

"Finding somebody sleazy enough to make the keys and then sneaking around at night to try them out on the door. It's amazing how honest people are on the coast."

Jack laughed. "Next time take pictures of them and print them out on a 3D printer."

Gillian poked him in the ribs. "Don't give him ideas!"

"What a great idea!" Brendan looked like an overgrown boy recounting a favorite adventure. "I can use that."

I said, "Samantha caught you on camera."

He was incredulous. "People who live in glass houses shouldn't throw stones. Filming people without their knowledge has to be illegal. I should turn her in."

That settled the question of whether Brendan had known he'd been videoed and whether he'd attacked Samantha for it, at least in my mind. I believed him. "Brendan, she didn't turn you in. She's in the hospital. She was attacked in the same area where Alan was killed."

"What?"

He looked so stunned that I couldn't believe he'd had anything to do with it. He was either the best actor I'd ever seen or he had absolutely no control over his face.

Ricardo said, "We don't know much about it yet, but she was attacked close to the beach on the other side of the hill from Cass' house."

"Having that key makes you a suspect," Mia said.

"In case you hadn't noticed."

Brendan sat down heavily. "I'm doomed. No wonder they're searching my house. I need a lawyer."

Jack said, "That can wait until morning. Right now I want another piece of cheesecake."

"Delighted," Brendan said, brightening again, and cut him a second piece.

Mia took a last bite of cheesecake. "That was delicious." She hesitated. "Do you still want to view your new web site tonight?"

"I'm sorry," Brendan said. "Much as I've enjoyed having you here, I'm afraid that being searched and knowing that there are videos of me breaking and entering has put a damper on my high spirits. Can I have a rain check? You all need to come back for a real tour of the house. We can view the web site then."

Mia caught my gaze, and I knew she was thinking that we couldn't go live without his okay. We would have to wait for the big launch. We needed his web site to sell our work to others. No. It would be too easy to put this off and leave Brendan to stew in his fears.

"No, Brendan. I know I've only known you, Mia, and Ricardo a very short time, but you're my friends. We are not about to abandon you when you need us, but we also need you. You're our marquee customer. We want to launch based on your web site as the cornerstone for our Las Lunas business sites." I put my napkin on the table. "Let's finish that tour and then take a few moments with the web site. Nothing heavy, but if we can get your feedback, we can move ahead. I know you want to help us be successful."

He set his napkin next to mine and sighed. "I do."

Mia stepped in. "We don't want to pressure you,

and we do want you to be happy. But we do need to launch soon."

"We can also do your author web site when you're ready," Ricardo added.

Brendan laughed, a genuine belly laugh. "You drive a hard bargain. Okay, let me show you the rest of my home." He stood.

Jack and Gillian exchanged a relieved look and rose, followed by the rest of us as we chatted over each other and trooped out of the dining room behind Brendan.

****

I got up early the next day to get started on Brendan's suggestions. I even planned to put in some time on a proposed mystery book author site for Brendan.

The house was dead still. No people. No ghost. No cat. I took a quick shower and pulled on jeans and a black Henley.

I was running a comb through my hair when there was a knock at the door. Cautiously, I looked out the window before opening the door.

George stood on the stoop.

Chapter 18

I had a moment of panic before I opened the door. "George, you'll have to stop dropping by so often."

"Sarcasm. Some things never change." He stepped into the living room and looked around. "I never figured you for antiques."

"And I never figured you as hypercritical." I put my hands on my hips.

"Some things do change." He turned to face me. "Look, I'm sorry we interrupted your dinner last night, and…" He broke eye contact. "I wanted to see if you were okay."

"And why wouldn't I be?" I walked into the kitchen. "Follow me. I need caffeine to wake up." I started making coffee. "Jack, Gillian, and Thor either aren't up or aren't here. I'm assuming that he got out, and they're looking for him, but everyone could be asleep for all I know."

George stopped in the kitchen doorway. "I can tell you where they are."

"Where? Do you want eggs? I'm famished. I've got some dill and cream cheese left for scrambled." I opened the fridge and took out the ingredients.

"They called me to come and watch over you while you slept. I'm a bit surprised to find you up. They took the cat to the vet."

I got out the mixing bowl but hesitated. "Now why

would they do that?"

"I don't want to alarm you. Why don't you call them before you start cooking?"

I wiped my hands on a red towel and frowned. "I will, given that you're being so helpful." I tried to keep the annoyance out of my voice and went into the bedroom to get my phone off the charger and called as I walked slowly back to the kitchen.

I hung up and tucked the phone into my pocket as I walked into the kitchen. "Went straight to voicemail."

"Don't worry. I'm sure they'll be back soon. I have some information. Want me to wait for them to return before I share it?"

"No." I poured two cups of coffee and handed him one. "I don't remember; do you take milk and sugar?"

"That hurts."

Was there a trace of humor there?

"Keep cooking. I'm hungry."

Definitely humor.

He sat on a chair at the trestle table. "This is one convoluted case. We picked up two out-of-town gamers for questioning, and one gave Brendan up for trying to sell a rare book he'd stolen from Alan's shop. Samantha's video from her computer places Brendan there, and his fingerprints are all over Alan's store. We got a warrant, and sure enough, there it was. He hadn't even hidden it. That brings him up a notch on the suspect list. You may want to steer clear until the situation is resolved."

"He didn't do it. I'm guessing he's being set up and probably by those two. Are you seriously taking their word over his?" I set a plate of scrambled eggs and toast in front of George. "Can you be telling me this?"

He made a face. "Mostly. I'm just saying that on purely evidentiary grounds, he looks guilty. I'm telling you a bit more because of what happened here while you slept."

I put my plate on the table and sat down. "While I slept? What are you talking about?"

"Cass, there was an incident here. You slept right through it."

A thrill of ice ran through me. "What? What happened?" I heard noise at the front door.

Jack and Gillian came in, carrying Thor in his carrier.

"Would you guys like to tell me what's going on? George seems strangely reluctant."

Jack said, "Sorry. We needed to get Thor to Marcy. He tried to take out the vandal."

"Vandal?"

Gillian nodded and turned to George. "You haven't shown her yet?"

"Shown me what?"

George made a quiet down motion. "I haven't had a chance."

I turned on Jack. "Why didn't you wake me?"

"We figured whoever did it was long gone, and we weren't planning to be gone long," Jack said.

"Whoever did what?"

Gillian put a hand on my arm. "We'll show you. I'm sorry we didn't wake you. That was clearly a mistake."

Jack added, "We had a visitor last night. Thor got hurt defending house and home."

"Oh, poor baby!" I took the carrier from Jack and set it on the couch. I opened the door of the carrier.

The way Thor stalked out and surveyed his domain told me that he wasn't alone in that furry body. I looked up at George and back at Thor. I swear Thoris raised an eyebrow at me.

I whispered, "I'll get George out of here as fast as I can, Doris."

Thoris seemed satisfied and rubbed against me before running off.

"He'll be fine. More scared than anything," Jack said. "Come round to the back. We want to show you something."

I stood up and slipped my boots and jacket on. The four of us went out the back door. Someone had painted graffiti on the back side of my cottage nearest the woods, and my screens had been slashed. I read the graffiti.

U wanna keep ur nose on ur face, bak off

Chills went down the backs of my thighs. "Were they in my house?" While I slept upstairs?

"No, but you can thank Thor for that. He got kicked for his trouble."

"How do you know that?" I asked.

"Marcy, your vet, felt that was the most likely scenario based on his injuries," Gillian said. "Thor hissed at her, so she knocked him out and X-rayed him to be sure."

"I'm surprised he's as alert as he is," Jack said.

"How did I sleep through this?" I asked.

Gillian said, "You were exhausted, and your bedroom is at the top of the house. Whoever it was slit the screen in our room. We'd opened the window for some fresh air. Thor went flying across the room and out the window."

"He must've gone for the guy's face," Jack added. "We heard Thor howl, some swearing, a hollow sound, and Thor wailed."

"We turned on our light," Gillian said.

"I went out with a flashlight," Jack continued. "Thor was lying on the ground wheezing, and there was no one in sight. I swung the flashlight around and saw this lettering."

"I went to the window," Gillian said. "Jack told me to get dressed. He called George to come over to watch you and the place. We tried Dave first because he was closest, but he wasn't home, so we left a note on his door, warning him that someone might be prowling around but also letting him know that he should come over to check on you if he got the note before George arrived. Then Jack carried Thor in and made a call to your vet's cell phone. We met her at her office."

"Sorry, but we didn't want to wake you. You were sleeping so peacefully, and George said he could be here in half an hour."

Interesting that George would come. "Don't worry about it. You did the right thing. Is Thor all right?"

"Bruised ribs. He'll be fine."

Someone rapped out shave-and-a-haircut on the back door.

"I'll get it," Gillian said and went to the door, opening it wide.

"Gillian." There was consternation in Jack's voice.

But she stepped away from the door, revealing the visitor. "It's Dave."

"C'mon in, Dave," I called.

"Hey, guys. I got your note. Is everything okay? I didn't see anybody prowling around."

"Whoever it was took off after slashing our screens and leaving a nasty message scrawled on the side of the house."

"Sorry I wasn't around to help. I just got in." Dave grinned. "Do I smell coffee?"

"Have a seat. I'll pour you a cup," I said. I handed him a mug of coffee and looked at the remnants of breakfast. "I can make more eggs."

"Yeah!" Dave said.

"I will. You sit," Jack said. "We've been up a while."

"I'll help," Gillian said, coming over to the counter and pulling out a clean mixing bowl.

Dave leaned back in his chair, balancing on the two rear legs. "Part of why I dropped by was to see if there was any more news. Like, did they catch the murderer?"

"Dave, you're going to break my chair legs."

He brought all four legs to the floor. "Did you know that the Shakers invented a swivel for the bottoms of the two back legs that lets you lean back without torquing them?"

"No, I didn't. If you come over a lot, I'll check it out. By the way, this is an old friend of mine and a Las Lunas police detective, George Ho. George, this is my neighbor Dave."

"I gathered as much. Pleased to meet you, Dave."

"Likewise."

"Murderers," Jack said, steering the conversation back. "Two of the vampire gamers are under suspicion and…" At a hand signal from George, Jack changed direction. "Except they're outsiders, not our coastal gamers. Not originally from this area."

"Whoa! No shit! I guess I missed all the excitement again."

"You've really got to quit partying and stay home once in a while," Jack said, tightening his mouth to suppress a smile.

Dave looked stricken.

"He's joking, Dave," Gillian said over her shoulder as she stirred the eggs.

I looked around. "Dave, have you noticed anything unusual lately? Anyone hanging around who shouldn't be?"

Gillian passed plates of dilled eggs and toast.

George had been quiet until now. "You should know that I called the station and an officer will be out to handle the vandalism. I expect he'll be by pretty soon. Don't worry."

The fear hit me again. Whoever it was had been right outside while I slept, and I'd be alone soon. I had nearly been alone last night, but I didn't have time to dwell on it because there was a knock on the front door.

"Timing is everything," George said, getting up and heading for the door.

I heard a woman's voice, and a moment later she followed George into the kitchen. "You seem to be a target for almost everyone these days, Ms. Peake." But she said it sympathetically.

I recognized the friend of George's who'd taken the pictures of Alan's body on the beach. "I have no idea what the vandals think I know, but this was obviously designed to scare me. And so far, it's succeeding admirably. Would you like to have a look?"

She nodded. "Yes, ma'am."

Jack and George walked out with me as we showed

her the cut screens and the graffiti. She had a small digital camera with her and took pictures of everything, including the ground around the windows and the wall containing the graffiti.

She finally finished. "I'd like to look at your doors and around the perimeter to see if there's any evidence that your house was entered. The threat is another matter. Given the murder of Alan Howland and the attempted murder of Samantha Ross, we're taking this very seriously. I'll be checking back from time to time." She handed me a card. "Please do not hesitate to call if anything happens or you think of anything. And I mean anything." She left to walk around the house.

I was getting tired of starting my days off with crises.

When we re-entered the kitchen, a heavy discussion was underway.

"Ah, the vamp chick," Dave said through a last mouthful of eggs.

"That's the one," Gillian said.

"She wasn't the type, anyway."

Gillian stared at him. "There's a type?"

"Not so much a type to commit murder, but there's definitely a type to *not* commit murder and she's it." Dave finished the last of his toast. "There's a vibe." He waved his hands in the air.

"Elaborate."

His boyish grin lit up his face. "Okay. Let's see. Wild chick. Out on her own. She's probably got a record, right? Juvie?"

"Possibly," George said.

Dave waggled a finger. "But no violent crimes. Property stuff, right?"

George sat down. "I have no knowledge of anything else."

"I rest my case." Dave reached for the toast.

"That was a bit slim," Jack said.

"No, no," Gillian said. "Dave might be onto something. There are people who are willing to hurt other people and those who will take what they want—property crimes—but draw the line at violence. Unarmed burglars, for instance."

"So we're all safe now?" Dave pushed his plate away.

"Yes, Dave," I said.

"Then I can run up to the City for a party tonight."

I frowned. "Haven't you been up to the City every night?"

"Sure have," he said, digging in. "There're so many parties, I don't want to hurt anyone's feelings by not showing up."

"Silly me."

"Well, I'm outta here! Thanks for breakfast," Dave said as though he didn't have a care in the world and got up, pushing his chair back under the table. "I'll check back on you later." He bent over and kissed my cheek. "Now you take care of yourself. No more chasing murderers. Promise? And you call me if you need anything."

"I promise."

The screen door banged behind him.

"Okay, guys, can you help me fix the screens before you leave?" I gathered up the breakfast plates and put them in the sink.

Jack and Gillian shared a look.

"Ever practical," Jack said. "Where's your local

hardware store? Gillian and I can go. I'll just take some measurements."

I gave him a tape measure, directions, and money, and they both went out the back door. Several minutes later, a car motor started up and slowly faded into the distance.

"George, will you come with me while I check the lights? I want the place well lit tonight."

"Sure thing." He took a last sip of coffee and stood up.

We went outside. Several bulbs had been unscrewed enough to turn them off. I tightened them while George flipped the switches, checking and double-checking.

"You're good to go for now, but I think you should consider hanging safety lights that are caged. Makes it harder to unscrew them. Also, a safety light on a pole would be good. You might also consider investing in an alarm. Maybe some cameras."

"I'd have to check with the neighbors about the safety light."

"I'd better go." He reached out and held my upper arms. "Take care of yourself. Someone will be back to check on you. Be prepared for a team to show up to ask questions and collect potential evidence."

It wasn't exactly a hug, but I'd take what I could get. "Jack and Gillian are going home."

"Ask them to stay for a few more days."

"I hate to impose on them, but even if I ask, they may have to say no. Work. Lack of vacation. Exigencies of modern life." I half-smiled.

He returned my smile. "Ask anyway."

I closed the door behind him and looked for Thoris.

Doris appeared. "Thor is tired and very sore. I left him on your bed to sleep."

"Thank you, Doris. Do you know who the intruder is?"

"Not sure. The scent was familiar to Thor, but I don't share his memories, at least not in any useable form." She shivered. "I hope he'll be all right. I had no other way to chase the guy off."

"Only one guy?"

Doris nodded. "Slim and muscular, but remember my recollections are from a cat's perspective. Black pants, black sweatshirt, black balaclava, dark eyes, gloves. Seems Haile Selassie if ya ask me."

"Stop, Doris. Wasn't he an Ethiopian Emperor? What are you talking about? Your slang is driving me crazy." I rolled my eyes.

Doris pursed her lips. "Hello? See you later, alligator. Are you actually an alligator? No. It's a rhyme. Word play. Y'know. Fun. You know what fun is, right? Haile Selassie. Highly suspicious. Police car. Policy car when you pronounce the silent e." She held her hands out and moved her shoulders up and down. "Work with me here!"

I shook my head but smiled. "Okay, but you're going to have to give me a clue occasionally. Anyway, George didn't find anything when he was out there. The message was obviously disguised as illiterate. It creeps me out and pisses me off at the same time. I don't know if I can get any sleep tonight."

"I'll stand guard. I don't need sleep. You've got plenty of moxie." Doris quirked an eyebrow. "Solving a certain murder would give you loads of confidence."

"Being attacked does provide an element of

motivation."

"You're frail, but you ain't no weak sister!" Doris did a shimmy, and ghostly fringe swung every which way.

"Thanks, Doris. I don't get why someone is threatening me."

She shrugged her ghostly shoulders. "Beats me. It's not like you've solved the crime."

"Thanks," I said wryly.

"Y'know what I mean. Maybe someone doesn't want you here. You know. In this house. It's been empty a long time."

"I've been wondering who paid the taxes and did the basic upkeep myself. I would have thought it would have been sold for taxes long ago."

"Check the tax records."

I nearly slapped my forehead. "Doris, you're genius."

"Naw." But I could tell she was pleased.

Chapter 19

I did an Internet search and figured out where I needed to go to find the records I required. By the time I had what I wanted, a couple of officers arrived to gather evidence, fingerprints, and whatever else they needed. I showed them around the back and let them get on with it.

As they were leaving, Jack and Gillian returned and I realized that I was okay. I had a plan, and I wasn't going to put up with being harassed. Surviving Phil's infidelity had changed me, and I wasn't going to sit around and let anyone else set the agenda for my life. I belonged here, and I wasn't leaving.

"Cool. If the cops are through, we can get to work."

I frowned. "Do we need permits or anything?"

Jack laughed. "No structural changes. Just repairs. No problem. All of your screens are different shapes, so it's a good thing that no frames were splintered."

"That's good."

"Want to help," Gillian asked. "Or do you need to rest?"

"I'm fine. Really I am. I have something else I need to do, though. I want to know who has an interest in this place, who's been paying the taxes, who might want to scare me away."

"Come straight back here," Jack said. "Don't go

off half-cocked. Someone clearly doesn't mind a little violence."

"Don't worry. I'll come back and share." I grabbed my keys and headed for my car.

****

Jack was cleaning up and putting tools and paint away when I returned. "We painted over the graffiti. The new paint stands out, though. Good thing it's along the back, but you were planning to paint the whole place, right?"

"Thanks. Just what I need: another expense."

Gillian called out from the living room. "What did you find out?"

"The taxes were paid by Dave."

"Seriously? He couldn't have told us and saved us some angst?" Gillian said.

"I called him after I checked the records. It never occurred to him to say anything. He was quite happy to have a vacant, haunted house next door on the beach. Keeping it vacant gave him privacy. He did some work around the place so that no one would complain and have it condemned. He thwarted several attempts by builders who wanted to buy it as a teardown. He was very concerned at first when he heard that a divorcée from Pleasanton had bought the place. He was prepared to scare me away if I proved to be trouble, but he decided he liked me and was happy to have me next door. He found out from the realtor that I had no intention of replacing the house with a monster home."

"Too bad he won't keep paying the taxes." Jack had washed up and joined us in the living room.

"The reason the garage is in such bad shape is that he never ventured back there, assuming it was empty."

Jack looked thoughtful. "You know, I'd better do a little repair work before we leave. I want to make sure my car is safe."

The air next to him coughed.

Jack swiveled to face Doris, who half-materialized behind him. "Look, I know it's your car, but it's not like you can drive it."

"But you could drive Thoris around in it," Gillian said.

Doris silently clapped her hands.

"Guess you'll just have to come back to visit," I added. "Okay, so there was nothing sinister in the tax question. I'll have to try to figure out other possibilities."

"If Jack is going to spend a little more time fixing up the garage, we should go back to visit Samantha before we leave," Gillian said.

"Speaking of which, I promised George I'd ask you to stay. I told him you probably couldn't..." I let my voice trail off.

They looked at each other.

Jack sighed. "I totally get it. I was thinking you should come back with us or take a vacation or stay at a hotel."

I shook my head. "Can't afford it."

"I'll make some phone calls to work," he said. "I hope they catch this jerk fast." He pulled out his cell and headed out the back door.

"I should check with Ricardo to find out what's going on with Samantha before we just go over to the hospital." I took out my cell and phoned. "Ricardo, it's Cass. I was wondering how Samantha is doing. We were thinking about visiting her."

"She'd love that. She's a bit put out with the cops right now. They should be releasing her soon, so you might want to call first. The police have been to the shop and to her house. They took her computers."

"Can they do that?" I asked.

"That's her argument. She's getting a lawyer lined up. They may suspect her of something. They may be trying to protect her. Who knows? But it's motivating her to get out of the hospital."

"She'll give the police what for, but I want her to get better. This is a lot of stress. She has no advocate, though."

"She has us," Ricardo said. "I agree that someone needs to stand up for her while she's incapacitated, but I'm trying to do that. I shut Crystalline down for now, so the best way to reach me is by phone. I'll be putting some hours in at Bobbo's, but the rest of the time Mia and I will be finishing Brendan's site."

"I'm afraid I've been slacking. There was some vandalism at my cottage. Jack's making repairs."

"Are you all right?" His voice was heavy with concern.

"I'm fine. I wanted to ask you about the situation at Brendan's. When the cops left there, it was because they found a missing gamer. What's happening with that?"

"The buzz among the gamers is they picked him up. Out-of-towner. I never liked him, and I do think he's capable of murder. He tried hitting on Mia. At first, she was open with him, telling him some of the stuff about her family. She told the whole group part of her story, but he really focused in on Alan, declaring him to be evil. He told Mia he could kill Alan and make it look like a vampire got him. There was a similar case in Louisiana that he'd heard about."

"Looks like we have our murderer."

"Not really. Mia begged him to stay away from Alan. After Alan died, she confronted him. He told her he plotted it out but never did anything."

"But the cops don't believe him?"

"No idea. It's not like they tell me what they're doing. This is all hearsay, what Mia told me, and what I found online."

I paused to think.

"Cass?"

"Sorry. They took him in for questioning at the very least, so I'm guessing they do suspect him. But you aren't convinced?"

"He had motive, means, and opportunity, but it's pretty weak."

"Have you heard anything about what made the wounds?"

"Wounds didn't kill him. He drowned. That was on the news. Look, I've got to go. Let me know if you find out anything."

"Will do." I hung up. "I just remembered what I saw at Dave's a few days ago. Gillian, what did we see hanging off the grills in the picnic area?"

She picked up on it right away. "Hot dog forks. But weren't they chained to the grills?"

"Two evenly spaced holes," I said. "Dave had the same type of long, two-pronged fork hanging from his grill, and it wasn't chained."

"But they're so ubiquitous in a picnic area, who'd notice?"

"The killer," I said.

Gillian asked, "Good point. Did Ricardo have anything new?"

"Just some information on the gamer the police wanted for questioning."

"I have a question for you. If Alan is Mia's father, is his wife her mother?"

"Good question. I have a feeling the only person who can answer that without a test is Sara and maybe not even then."

"Has anyone said anything about it?"

I shook my head. "Not that I remember. I would think that, if she were, Alan would have said something to Mia, but she talked about Alan as her father but not Sara as her mother."

"Do you feel that it's something you can discuss with her?"

I thought about it. She'd been pretty open about the autopsy, but it wasn't as though we were bosom buddies. "I can ask. Now that you mention it, it seems odd that Mia wasn't mentioned in his will."

"Unless there's a later will."

"Now that hadn't occurred to me. For that to be true, I'm guessing that either Sara or her lawyer would have had to know about it."

"Unless there's another relative or friend that Alan was closer to. That someone might have had a reason not to come forward. Protecting Alan's memory?"

"Or the person doesn't like Mia. I'm remembering the conversations we had while helping Sara with her inventory. Sara didn't know about Alan's relationship to Mia. When we talked about the reading of the will, Mia wasn't mentioned, and I had the distinct impression that Marcy thought Mia and Alan were having an affair. Now I'm not saying this is fact, but it doesn't seem to me that anyone except us, Ricardo, and Mia has a clue that Mia is Alan's daughter."

"That makes me wonder if the person who killed him had any idea. Didn't Ricardo mention that Alan had taken a DNA test for paternity?"

"I think he did." I sighed. "I'm going to have to pursue this."

"You need to tell George."

"True. And then I need to talk to Mia and Ricardo." I hesitated. "I also have to tell Sara if no one else will."

"You do realize you're not responsible. I think Mia and Ricardo will understand, but Sara may think you're poking your nose where it doesn't belong."

"I know, but it's the right thing to do."

Gillian raised an eyebrow. "Then start with George."

"You're right." It wasn't how I'd pictured our next conversation. "What constitutes obstruction of justice? It's a small town and they're cops. They probably already know, don't you think?"

"Take three deep breaths and make that first call." She got up. "I'm getting a drink."

I phoned George. "Hey, George."

His voice sounded cautious. "Did anything else happen? Do I need to pay you another visit?"

"You're always welcome here."

"Even with a search warrant?" At my silence, he continued, "Just a little cop humor."

Gillian set an iced tea in front of me and took a sip of her own.

I looked up at her, mouthing thank you, and

continued. "How's the case going? Anyone confess yet?"

She gave me a thumbs up.

"It should be that easy."

"Listen, George. I remembered something I probably should have mentioned before."

"Oh?" His voice tensed up.

"Mia told me that she's Alan Howland's daughter."

"Go on."

"You should talk to her. I'm just repeating what I've been told, but I gather that Alan had a paternity test that confirmed it."

"Would you happen to know if Sara Howland is her mother?"

"I don't know, but if she is, she doesn't know as far as I can tell. I know that Mia wasn't mentioned in the will. Sara mentioned some of his relatives that she didn't know about; surely, she would have mentioned a daughter."

"Is there anything else you haven't told me?"

"Not that I can think of." I looked over at Gillian.

"Thanks, Cass. I have to go now. Talk to you later." And he hung up.

I set my phone down and took a big swig of tea. "That was weird. All of a sudden in the middle I forgot why I was telling him that."

"Don't worry about it. It's up to him what he does with the info. As you said, they may already know."

"Good point. He was pretty noncommittal."

There was a knock at the door. I started.

Gillian got up and answered. Ricardo and Mia followed her back into the room.

"We just dropped Samantha off at her house and

wanted to come by to tell you so that you didn't make an unnecessary trip to the hospital."

"Thanks, Ricardo. Have a seat." I gestured toward the couch. "How is she?"

Gillian said, "Want some iced tea? Or anything else to drink?"

"Yes, please," Mia said and followed Gillian into the kitchen.

Ricardo sat down on the couch. "Where's Jack?"

"He's making some repairs to the outbuilding. It's pretty run down. He'll probably be back soon."

"I have some interesting info about Samantha's injuries. She was telling me about it as I drove her home. Remember Alan's neck?"

"No!" I said.

He nodded. "Yes."

"Two holes?"

Ricardo nodded again.

"No way!"

"And there was a note pinned to her body. It said that she'd been spying on the gamers, had turned them in to the cops, so she had to pay. The police questioned her in the hospital about it." He leaned forward and cracked his knuckles.

"That doesn't make much sense. You're a gamer. She knows you. All the gaming groups are playing in public places when she videos them. They have nothing to hide. It's not like she's creeping around and peering in windows."

"That's what I told her. Her feelings were hurt at the thought, but I told her we were being framed. The police seem to think that Alan's murder and the attack on Samantha are related."

"So now the police are focusing in on the gamers."

He nodded.

"I'll bet capturing the two gamers they were looking for has helped them zero in. The thought had occurred to me that Samantha's pointing the finger at the gamers over Alan's murder might have repercussions."

"I don't think we should guilt her out over that," Ricardo said. "Samantha was unconscious when the note was pinned to her, and it was removed by the police before she regained consciousness. In all the pain she was suffering, she was also unaware that someone had stabbed her in the neck. The wound was superficial, unlike Alan's, which may point to two different attackers. I think we have a copycat."

"Gillian and I were discussing a theory about the holes in Alan's neck. We realized that a hotdog fork would make those lovely, evenly spaced holes in his neck. My neighbor, Dave, has a pair hanging on his grill, and there are some on the grills up at the campsite on the crest by the cliff with implements chained to the sides."

Thor, sleeping on the throw rug under the coffee table, yawned, exposing his two long white fangs.

Mia and Gillian joined us, bearing a pitcher of iced tea and glasses. Mia sat as Gillian poured.

"Did you two get any more done on Brendan's site?"

Mia took a glass. "Thanks. We did. We made a bunch of changes, and I think we're ready to go. I'd like to send Brendan a password and walk him through viewing it."

"I think we should offer to walk him through in

person, particularly the first time. I want him to be comfortable checking our updates without having one of us present all the time," Ricardo said.

"That's a good point," I said. "But he is a cornerstone client, and we should work to keep him happy."

When Ricardo looked a bit mulish, I added, "For now. We'll train him to be more computer savvy."

"Okay," he conceded. "I can do it."

Mia put a hand on his and smiled. "I think you'd better let me do it."

"I agree," I said. "Brendan might be stressed over the police focus on him because of Samantha's videos, so having a live human who cares about him help him out is a good thing."

Mia set her glass down. "I'll get on it right away. We need to go live."

My cell rang.

Ricardo got up. "We have to go, anyway."

"I'll get the door," Gillian said.

I answered the phone. "Hello?" It was a local number, but one I didn't recognize.

"Cass? It's Sara. I'm down at the police station again. Can you pick me up? Marcy was supposed to, but she had an emergency."

"Sorry to hear that. Of course I can come get you. Are you all right?"

"No. I-I don't want to talk about it here. I'll tell you when you pick me up."

"Okay. I'll be right down." I hung up. "Gillian, I'm going to pick Sara up. She's at the police station, and I'm wondering if it's because of the call I made to George." I pulled on my jacket and grabbed my gloves and car keys. "See you in a few."

"I'll go see how Jack is doing." Gillian walked me out.

I parked and dodged a light rain as I entered the police station. Despite the double doors, the room was chilly from all the people going in and out.

"May I help you?" the officer on duty inquired politely.

"I'm just picking up a friend. Thanks."

"You can sit down over there." He gestured toward a bench against the far wall.

"Thanks again." I walked over to the bench as he turned back to his computer.

After ten minutes Detective Daniels came out, stopped, and stared at me. "What are you doing here, Ms. Peake? Do you have information for us?"

I stood. "No, I'm picking Sara Howland up. Do you know if she's ready to go yet?"

He frowned and thought for a moment. "Let me take you down the hall. There's a little room where you can wait privately."

"Thanks, I appreciate that. It's a bit chilly out here by the door. Is she all right?"

"She's fine. She'll be out in a minute."

He escorted me back through labyrinthine corridors to a bare and dingy room with the sort of metal furniture that used to make offices so bleak before brilliant young programmers demanded more luxurious working conditions.

"Coffee?"

"Yes, please. Cream and sugar." I sat on the hard metal chair.

Detective Daniels brought me coffee in a paper cup

that immediately transferred its heat to my fingertips. Then he left me to wait. Before long, footsteps drew my attention to the hall.

Sara saw me and came into the room. "Ready to go?"

"Let's get out of here." Once in the car, I said, "What did they want you for?" I turned the key in the ignition, started the car, looked both ways, and pulled out of the parking lot.

She hesitated a moment and then said, "They wanted to question me about Mia's…" She swallowed hard and then exhaled audibly.

I waited.

"The police feel… Apparently, Alan had a child. Mia. They asked a lot of questions about what I knew and was she my child." Sara burst into tears.

I glanced over at Sara. "Do you want me to pull over?"

"No, that's all right." She turned to stare out the window, wiping her eyes. Then she said in a thin, small voice, "I had a daughter once, but she's dead."

"What?" I nearly ran a red light.

She cleared her throat. "My daughter died at birth."

When she finally turned to look at me, there were tears in her eyes.

The car behind me honked, and I looked up to see that the light had turned green. I hit the gas.

"I'm sorry. I didn't mean to open up old wounds."

"It's okay. I haven't thought about Holly for years."

"Holly. That's a nice name." But I didn't believe that she hadn't been thinking about her. The grief was too raw. The loss of a child. Does anyone ever forget?

"Was Alan her father?"

"We weren't married. It was an accidental pregnancy, but I—I didn't want to give my baby up. My parents wanted me to, ah, get rid of the baby and go back to school. But I loved Alan."

"Looks as though he stuck by you." I turned the corner.

"Yeah," she said softly. "My parents were wrong. They said he would leave after Holly died, but he came to me secretly."

"Forgive me for prying, Sara, but how did your daughter die?"

She hesitated. I almost regretted asking her. Almost.

"She died shortly after she was born. I don't know what happened exactly. I heard her cry. At least, I think I heard her cry. I called her Holly because… because…" Her voice got high and tight as she pulled a tissue out of her purse and wiped her eyes. "It was Christmas."

I wanted to comfort her, but I kept my eyes on the road. "How do you know your daughter is dead?"

"My mother told me."

In that moment her voice sounded very young to me, girlish.

"And my father and…Alan."

"Did you see a death certificate or…" I hesitated to say "a body." I glanced at her for a second. "Did you have a funeral?" An idea was forming, but it was so fragile that I didn't want to express it yet.

She shook her head. "I was very ill…afterward. She was cremated. After I was better, we had a memorial service and sprinkled her ashes in the"—she swallowed—"ocean."

"So you never saw any official documentation?"

"It was so cold that day. The ocean was dark. The ashes just…went away. It was as if she'd never been."

"Sara, when exactly was she born?"

"Christmas morning. My parents were so upset. I ruined Christmas." She wiped her eyes again.

Crummy parents. But it wouldn't do Sara any good for me to voice that opinion. "How many years ago?"

"She would be nineteen. It's so hard for kids when their birthday is at Christmas time. No birthday presents."

She was rambling, maybe a sign that the pain was too great for her to handle. "Where was she born?"

"St. Luke's."

"What city?"

"Santa Dolorosa."

Santa Dolorosa was a high-end, mid-peninsula town. They should have good records. I'd learned a bit in my search for the person who paid my cottage's taxes. "Is that where your parents live?"

She nodded. "They want me to come home."

"I'll bet," I said.

"They don't think I can make it on my own without Alan. They've never thought I was strong enough to be alone, and I know they'll take care of me." Again her voice had a child-like quality. "Did I already tell you that?"

"Is that what you want to do?"

"They have a huge house. Belong to the country club." Her voice went all soft and dreamy. "It would be safe there."

"You've been through a lot recently, and I

understand if you don't want to answer any more questions, but I'm curious. Why did you marry Alan? I mean, you didn't have to at that point. You could have taken your time. Made sure he was the right one. Recuperated a little after the baby died. There was no longer any pressure to marry quickly."

She turned to stare at me, wide-eyed. I watched her peripherally, keeping most of my attention on the road.

"He was very sweet and gentle. He brought me flowers and candy. Like a romantic hero." She smiled. "Not like my dad who yelled and bullied us into doing what he wanted us to do."

"Your parents didn't like him." I was struggling to make her description of her father jibe with the rosy picture she had just painted of returning to her parents' home to live.

"No, they *hated* him! But when I got pregnant, they relented. I think they liked the idea of being grandparents."

I pulled up in front of her house and put the car into neutral. "Sara, if there's anything else I can do, please let me know. I mean that. I hadn't realized… about your daughter. That must have been awful."

"Thanks for picking me up and for everything else." She unbuckled and turned toward me. "I told them about you."

"Beg pardon?"

"I told my parents how you were helping me, going through things, doing inventory, and trying to find out who killed Alan. I told them all about you, that you were my friend, that you would figure it all out. That you wouldn't let the police arrest me."

"I seriously doubt that you'll be arrested, and I'm

happy to help in any way I can."

"I know you will." Sara smiled and got out of the car. Halfway up the sidewalk, she turned and waved.

I waved back but waited at the curb until she went into her house. All the way home I tossed around family combinations and motivations. I must have been concentrating a bit too hard because, when I opened the front door and stepped inside, a black furball hit me on the ankle with a spring-loaded paw and ran off to sulk under the table.

"Hey! What was that all about?" I closed the door behind me. "Jack, your cat just hit me on the ankle."

Jack and Gillian turned around from the table where they were both huddled over the laptop.

"You must have been ignoring him, Cass. He always does that when he wants attention. Besides, he's your cat now."

"So he is, but he may have to wait a bit longer for attention. Is the garage all fixed?"

"It's as good as it's going to get without a lot more time and effort," Jack said.

Gillian asked, "How's Sara?"

I sat down in the chair opposite them. "She had a baby right after she married Alan, but she said it died shortly after it was born. Holly. That was the baby's name. Born Christmas morning."

"Was Alan the father?" Jack asked.

"Yes. She didn't see the baby after it died. No funeral. No viewing. She took her parents' and Alan's word for it."

"And you don't think that's good enough?" Jack said.

"I guess I just have a suspicious nature," I said.

"If the baby survived and they put it up for adoption, wouldn't they need Sara's signature?" Gillian asked.

"If they took her baby, then they're sleazy enough to forge her signature," I said.

"They might have been trying to protect her at a time when she was emotionally fragile. It doesn't mean that they spirited the baby away and put it up for adoption. There's no motive to do that. Alan would have been in a stronger position as the father of Sara's parents' only heir. Money wasn't a problem, and Alan and Sara got married so legitimacy wasn't an issue."

"I know. I know." I sighed. "Something is bothering me, but I don't know what it is."

Chapter 20

Someone rapped on the front door.

Gillian opened it. "Hi, Marcy."

"Hi, Gillian. Is Cass here?"

"C'mon in. She's in the living room."

Marcy joined me there.

"Hi, Marcy," I said. "I heard you had an emergency."

Gillian shut the door and followed Marcy.

"Catfight. It was brutal. Looks like you had company."

Gillian picked up the dirty dishes and carried them into the kitchen.

"They've left. Would you like something to eat or drink? Did you come to see your patient?"

"No, actually, I heard what happened to your place and wanted to see how you're doing."

"Oh, I'm fine. No idea why the vandal picked on me. Illiterate vandal. Probably some mentally ill type."

Her face tightened. "They can be very dangerous. You should be careful."

"Thanks, Marcy. I picked up some pepper spray. I'll be ready if he comes back." Given Marcy's propensity for gossip, maybe word would get around town, and whoever it was would leave me alone in future.

"I heard you picked Sara up from the police

station. I was supposed to pick her up. Sorry you got stuck with that."

"Yes, she told me, but she said you had that emergency and I didn't mind."

"In addition to checking on you, I wanted to ask you over for a small dinner tonight." She glanced at Gillian's back as Gillian carried a tray of glasses into the kitchen. "It's impromptu, just you and Sara. I don't want her sitting alone, thinking about Alan's death, but I don't want to overwhelm her with people she doesn't know. I want her to feel that she has friends she can talk to. So many of her friends were Alan's friends. He was very outgoing. Sara's more shy."

That struck a chord with me after my own recent experience with people in Pleasanton who I thought were my friends. "I understand. Sounds good. What time?"

"Six?" She rose. "I'd better get back to the office."

"If you don't mind my asking, you and Sara are good friends. How did you meet? I didn't see any pets when I dropped her off."

"We go way back." She smiled. "We were college roommates and kept in touch." Her smile faded. "As to the pets, Alan was allergic, but don't worry. I'll remedy that. There are a lot of animals that need a good home."

"See you tonight," I said as I let her out the door.

"I hope you two don't mind." I walked into the kitchen to help Gillian.

"She probably thought Jack and I had left by now. She and Sara have been friends for a while."

"Being old college roommates actually explains a lot about the familiarity Marcy showed toward Sara and Sara's unconcerned reactions. I feel more at ease knowing that."

"I can finish this up if you want to change," Gillian said. "Looks like Jack will finally get that pizza he wanted when we went to Brendan's."

****

Marcy's lights were on when I pulled in front of the clinic behind her red Jeep. I got out of the car and closed the door. Marcy must have heard me because, by the time I got to the front door, she'd turned on the porch light and opened the door.

"Come on in. You're the first one here." She shut the door behind me.

I followed her into the waiting room and up the stairs to her living space on the second floor. She led me to the living room.

"Want a beer? Glass of wine?"

"A glass of wine would be great. White if you've got it."

I sat on the couch.

"Sweet or dry?" She was still standing.

"I prefer sweet." I shivered.

"Sweet it is. I'll turn the fire on." Marcy flicked the switches on the gas fireplace and went to the kitchen and got a couple of glasses and a bottle out of the fridge. "Sara prefers sweet whites, also." She handed me a glass and poured a small amount of white wine. "Let me know if this is to your taste."

I took a sip. "This is quite good." I held my glass out for more.

Marcy filled it. "Thanks for coming. I worry about Sara. She is so naïve sometimes. Alan was a bit of a control freak, so she's never toughened up." Marcy sipped her own wine.

"Is that why you wanted us to be friends?" I looked around her living room. Her bookshelves were filled with police procedurals, true crime, and high tech thrillers.

She sat down. "At first I thought it would be good to broaden her circle of friends. Then she was weakening under her parents' pressure for her to move into their home where they would have turned her into a child again, and I thought if she had more anchors here, she'd stay."

The doorbell rang.

Marcy got up. "That should be Sara."

I followed Marcy to the door. Sara stood on the stoop, shifting from foot to foot in the cold evening breeze. Her face was drawn and pale.

"Sara! What's wrong?" I said.

She threw herself into Marcy's arms, ignoring me. They looked like lovers. If they were this close, why did no one seem to know about their relationship? Marcy hugged her tightly, made soothing sounds, and stroked her hair.

"It was terrible! She raged at me that I was a liar," Sara wailed.

"What happened, Sara?" Marcy said gently.

"I called Mother." She sniffled into Marcy's shoulder.

Marcy made an exasperated sound.

"I know. I know. It was a terrible mistake." She started to cry again.

"Shh. Let me take care of your mother."

She settled Sara on the couch and then walked to the fridge and pulled out a chilled glass. She uncorked the bottle of wine and poured a glass. I sat down next to

Sara, and she noticed me for the first time.

"Sorry. My mother and I have a difficult relationship," she said. "When the police questioned me, they asked about a child, Alan's child. I asked my mother if that was Holly." Her voice broke on Holly's name.

Marcy sat down on the other side of her, handed her the glass, and hugged her. They both seemed to have forgotten me again.

"I'm going to call Andrea." Marcy disentangled herself from Sara and got up.

I was torn between leaving them to sort out whatever issues Sara was having and sticking around to find out what was going on. Marcy took her cell off the charger and called Andrea. I wanted to know more about Sara's parents, and Marcy calling them made up my mind to stay.

"Andrea," Marcy said. "Yes, I know it's been a long time." She listened for a few minutes. "No. I understand. Sara's here. She said she spoke to you." She turned away from us and said a few things under her breath.

I couldn't hear her conversation clearly, but I thought I heard something about an arrangement. Sara couldn't take her eyes off Marcy.

"Andrea, what does—" She listened for a moment. "I understand, but—" She frowned. "You did *what*?" She sat down heavily in a chair opposite Sara. "Oh, my—" She closed her eyes and rested her face in her hand, still listening to the phone. "Do you have any idea what you've done?" She was no longer listening to Andrea; she was looking at Sara, and there were tears in her eyes.

Her expression did not make me feel all warm and cozy.

"Marcy?" Sara's voice was very soft.

"Andrea, you and I will finish this conversation later." She clicked the phone off and put it in her pocket.

"What is it? What's wrong?" Sara's body stiffened and she leaned forward.

"Sara, honey, your baby didn't die." Tears leaked from the corners of Marcy's eyes.

"Then the police were telling the truth..." Her voice trailed off.

"Your mother lied to you. She lied to all of us." Her voice was very low.

"But my baby—" Sara looked bewildered.

"Sara, baby. Your daughter's alive. Your parents placed her with a friend of your father's cousin, if I heard that correctly. That way they could keep control of her. They could have put her up for private adoption, but they might have lost the ability to keep track of her. Foster care was out of the question because of the oversight. They couldn't explain who she was, and if they left her anonymously, they wouldn't know what happened to her. She thinks she was in foster care. That's what they were paying the couple to say."

"I have to find her." Sara stood up. "I have to go. I can't stay." She headed for the door.

Marcy met her there. "I'll help you find her. Trust me. Everything will be all right. I promise."

But Sara pushed past her and left.

Marcy turned back toward me. "Looks like dinner's postponed. Sorry about that. I hope you understand that I'm very worried about her mental state."

I was already on my feet. "I think that's a valid concern. Please let me know if there's anything I can do." I moved toward the door.

"Stay for a few minutes. If you want to help, maybe you'll have some suggestions. I want to go after Sara, but I think she needs a little space to process having a child."

I'd set my glass on the coffee table. Marcy picked it up, poured more wine, and handed it to me.

"Andrea lies. She always has. At first, I didn't believe her, but she said some things..." Marcy sighed. "I believe what she said this time. Maybe if she'd let me in on these little family secrets," her voice dripped venom, "things would have turned out differently. I could have advised her."

"What do you mean?"

"Andrea isolated Sara after her baby died or rather after Andrea faked her death. What a thing to do! It's not like they didn't have plenty of money to raise the child. Who does that to their grandchild?"

"Do you have any idea why?" I sipped the wine slowly and set the glass back down.

"The Petermans are used to order and efficiency. That's Bob Peterman's area of expertise. He's a management consultant, and he travels all over the world. Sara was an accident, and they let her know it. They weren't planning to have any children, and she was an inconvenience. They sent her to boarding school and then on to college where I met her. I'm guessing having to raise a grandchild was another problem, so they disposed of it."

"Why do they want Sara to come home now if they

spent so much time pushing her away?"

"That's a good point, and one I can use. Thanks." Marcy turned toward me.

I wasn't sure how much I should tell Marcy. "I know that Alan had a child that was in the foster care system. I assume the child is Sara's missing baby, but I could easily be wrong. For all I know, he may have a number of children."

She snorted. "That would be just like Alan. He deserved what he got for the way he treated Sara. He never understood her. He never made any attempt to understand her. He was after her family's money."

"You didn't like him, did you?" But I thought I already knew, and the chill penetrated to my bones.

She didn't need my questions to urge her on. I recognized rationalization when I saw it. I'd done it often enough myself. I kept quiet as she justified herself.

"Sara was my roommate at college. I spent Christmas our freshman year with Sara's family and got to know them pretty well. Alan and Sara slept together freshman year and Sara got pregnant." She shook her head.

"Could your family have taken Sara in?"

"No." Her grin was more of a rictus. "I also come from an old, old family that made their money right here in this very town but I'm the black sheep of my family. I was always in trouble. That's what happens when you give kids money instead of love. My father disinherited me when I dropped out of college and ran off and joined the Navy after Sara left me and married Alan." She smiled at that memory of her rebellious youth. "I liked the discipline in the Navy. Something I wasn't used to at home. And I learned skills that have been useful."

I understood why these two women at odds with their own families would have formed such a close bond. "You told Andrea on the phone that she should have told you about all this. Don't you think you should give Sara the same opportunity to run her own life?"

"It would be more than she can handle right now."

"Maybe Sara married Alan because she needed someone to love after the loss of her baby."

"She had me! Sara could have been anything. I would have helped her."

This time I could see the tears in her eyes, but they might have been from anger, not grief.

"They wanted to punish Sara. They always were control freaks—just like my father. It pretty much broke Sara. And you, you're living in a house that should be mine."

"Excuse me?"

"The man who bought this house was my grandfather but he gave it to his mistress. My mother and I should have inherited your house. Alan got interested in the house because I talked to Sara about it and she told him."

There was a knock at the door.

Marcy opened it. "Yes?"

"Is Cass here?"

"I'm here, George." I got up and walked to the door.

"I'm sorry to have to interrupt your plans, but she's needed at home." He gestured toward me. "C'mon, Cass, we have to go."

"No problem. Dinner's canceled anyway." I turned

to Marcy. "Thanks for inviting me."I followed him out and paused before getting in my car.

George said, "Follow me to your house."

I did and pulled up next to his car in front of my house. The lights were all on. George waited for me, and we walked up to the door together.

"Maybe I should leave," George said.

"No! You're not getting away from me again that easily. You stay. We have lots to talk about." I opened the door and immediately smelled pizza. "They may have saved some for us."

George grinned and stayed, grabbing a slice of pizza. Ricardo and Mia were there as well as Jack and Gillian. That explained the number of pizzas.

"Partying without me, I see."

"Enjoying my last chance for Clem's pizza until our next visit," Jack said.

"How was the dinner?" Gillian asked. "George came by to see you, so we sent him over to get you in case you felt obliged to stay longer than you wanted. How'd it go?"

I glanced at Mia. "It was interesting. Sara and Marcy were college roommates and very close. Marcy didn't like Alan." I didn't want to say too much in front of Mia. "Marcy mentioned that she should have inherited this house."

Jack handed me a piece of pepperoni and onion pizza. I took a bite. It was delicious.

"So she knows about her grandfather's mistress," Gillian said.

Then a thought occurred to me. "Guys, I don't think we should wait any longer to confirm to Sara that she has a daughter and she's right here. Sara was pretty torn up." I looked at Mia again. "That is if Mia is up for it."

Everyone turned to look at Mia.

Ricardo put an arm around her. "Even if the DNA matches, you don't have to acknowledge her as your mother if you don't want to. Blood isn't everything."

George said, "That was a line of police inquiry. There is no maternal certainty."

"We have to get Sara's permission to run tests on her," I said. "What if we ask her to come over and tell her what we know. Mia's results are already on file. Mia?"

Mia nodded slowly. "Alan said she wasn't my mother, but I'd like to know for sure."

"Good. Tonight was pretty traumatic for Sara, so I'd suggest that we wait a few days to pursue this."

George put his arm around my shoulder, and I looked up at him. "I'm going to steal Cass away for a few minutes." Then he said quietly to me, "Is there somewhere we can talk privately?"

"My aerie."

He smiled. "Your what?"

"It's the loft where they used to hold the séances." He blanched. "We could go outside instead."

"No, that's okay. Let's go." He followed me upstairs.

"I've turned it into my bedroom. It has a great view of the ocean. I love waking up here every morning."

George looked around. "Very nice."

"What did you want to tell me?" I put my hand on his arm. It was so nice to touch him again.

"What's your impression of Marcy?"

Not what I was expecting, but okay. "I think she's

driven by very strong feelings for Sara. At one point, I wondered if they'd been lovers."

George raised an eyebrow at that. "How so?"

I shrugged. "Just the way Marcy held Sara. With tenderness. I'm not sure that Sara reciprocates in the same way. From what I've seen, she loved Alan." I frowned. "I got the impression that Marcy might have killed Alan for love of Sara."

"That's interesting." George's voice lost some of its warmth, and I felt him go all cop on me. "In what way?"

I dropped my hand to my side. "The way she talked about him. She has an angry streak. Thinks he mistreated Sara, cheated on her, wouldn't let her have pets." I thought about my conversation with Marcy. "She was in the Navy, so she has training."

"That came out in her background check."

"Background check? Did you run one on me?"

"Why? Do you have something to hide?" But he was smiling.

"I'm an open book." I paused. "Also, Marcy called Sara's mother, Andrea Peterman, while I was there. I didn't catch everything, but there's something else going on, I'm pretty sure. Can you question Marcy?"

"There is no evidence against Marcy, Cass. This is all speculation on your part." He tucked my hair behind my ear. "You shouldn't encourage Sara to have that blood test just yet."

His fingertips felt nice on my cheek. "Why not?"

"You should wait until we close the case."

"Why? Are we in danger?"

His face didn't give anything away. "It's possible. You've already had a warning scrawled on the side of your house. As Alan's daughter, Mia might be vulnerable, depending on the killer's motives."

"If Marcy's jealous of Sara and killed Alan," I said, "then she might want to get rid of Mia. She might see her as competition."

"I didn't say Marcy was the killer."

"You didn't say she wasn't. You said you didn't have any evidence."

George was silent.

"We need to get evidence."

"Cass, stay out of this and let us do our jobs."

"I can help."

"You could get yourself killed."

"Would you care?"

He held my gaze for a long moment and then pulled me into a hard embrace. His kiss was hot and deep. His lips were as soft as I remembered. I wrapped my arms around his neck and didn't want him to stop. When he let me go, I leaned into him and caught my breath. He put both hands on my arms and gently pushed me away.

"I'm sorry. I shouldn't have done that." His voice was breathy.

"You're not on duty. You can do that anytime you want."

"I have to go now." He walked to the stairs.

"Are you sure?"

He stopped and looked at me, his half-smile letting me know that he'd enjoyed our embrace, too. Then he left.

Chapter 21

When I came downstairs, everyone was looking at me. "What?"

"George just left without a word," Jack said. "Did you two have a fight?"

"Nothing like that." I couldn't stop the smile.

Gillian got it and nodded at me, smiling herself. Jack looked puzzled.

"We need to start up the séance parties again. I think Marcy is guilty, but there is no evidence against her. But we can find out one way or another if Alan confronts her and accuses her of murdering him."

Mia inhaled sharply.

Ricardo put his arm around her. "Alan's dead."

"Which is why we're having a séance." I moved closer to Mia and Ricardo. "There's something you don't know, but if we're going to work together, you'd find out eventually. Better I should tell you now so that you won't be upset by what we're going to do, Mia. I can leave you out of this if that's what you want, but I'd like you to know the truth and be able to make your own choice."

"I'm not sure this is a good idea," Gillian said. "If you're planning what I think you're planning."

Mia looked back and forth between the two of us. "I don't know what the two of you are talking about, but my whole life has been nothing but secrets. I'm tired of not knowing what's going on. Please don't try to protect me. Tell me the truth."

I looked at Gillian. She shrugged.

"Okay, please do not think I'm crazy, and please listen until I finish. Then you can laugh and leave if you want." I took a deep breath. "First, my house really is haunted."

Ricardo laughed.

"Seriously, and with her cooperation, I'll introduce you to Doris tonight. Second, if she's willing and can do what I think she can, we can hold a séance with her help. Third, I'm hoping that Mia and Ricardo can set up some cameras to record the séance."

Jack interrupted. "In California, recording someone without their permission is against the law."

I nodded. "I know. I would have to tell people that we were recording it for fun. If Marcy, Dave, or Sara balks, then we're left with eyewitness statements. I'd be worried that they wouldn't be allowed in court."

"Will a jury believe a video? People are used to seeing special effects," Jack said.

"I don't know for sure what we'll catch on the recording, so it may be a moot point."

"Who are you planning to invite?" Ricardo asked.

"I thought all of you plus Marcy, Dave, and Sara. Too many and we're taking a risk that someone will blow it; too few and Marcy might be suspicious. It's better that you and Mia know the truth ahead of time so that you'll be prepared. I have no idea what you'll be able to see on a monitor or what will record. Samantha hasn't been able to record ghosts on her camera. Only Marcy, Dave, and Sara won't know anything in advance."

"You mean Gillian and Jack think there's a ghost here?" Ricardo asked.

"Oh, they've already met her." I looked around. "Doris?"

Jack stepped toward me, shaking his head and waving his hands. "No, no. Remember what happened when you introduced me to Doris? You can't do that to Mia. It's a real shock to the system."

Gillian said, "Jack dropped his beer."

"You might be right. Doris, if you're willing to go along with this, would you shimmer near me?"

Mia and Ricardo both gasped when she did.

"You saw that?" I asked.

They both nodded and didn't protest. I guess they were as ready as they were going to be.

"Doris, could you fade in gradually?" I expected her to ignore me and pop in, but she didn't. She phased in slowly.

Mia and Ricardo were holding each other tightly.

"You see her, right?" I asked.

They nodded.

"Are you okay?" Gillian asked.

Ricardo said, "No." He took a deep breath. "But I will be. How cool is that?" He laughed nervously.

Mia put out a hand tentatively and withdrew it quickly when she felt the clammy cold. She shivered.

"Yeah, I've felt that, too," Jack said.

"I can't help it," Doris said.

Both Mia and Ricardo jumped.

"Takes a little getting used to," I said. "I needed you to meet Doris right away because she's part of my plan. Will you help us, Doris?"

"You bet your sweet patootie!"

****

When we decided to go ahead with what Jack called my hair-brained scheme, we realized some of our seemingly insurmountable difficulties, such as getting Marcy to come.

As Jack pointed out, "What makes you think Marcy will show up for a séance at your house? Or that she won't show up with an ax?"

"Hubris," I said. "She believes she's right and she's after justice. Twisted justice, to be sure, but in her mind killing Alan was because he didn't take care of Sara. I think the logic of this is because Alan never had to follow through on anything, never actually had to work hard, he always took the easy way out, which meant he left Sara in the dark. Because Sara's parents were used to getting their way, they did what they wanted with their daughter's and granddaughter's lives. Because Sara chose to believe the obvious explanations and out of fear chose not to dig any deeper, the truth has taken this long to uncover."

"So she's fixing things? Setting them right?" Gillian asked.

"I think so. To me, it sounded like justification for eliminating the obstacles to her relationship with Sara. And that's why she'll come to the séance. She won't want to be left out of anything I'm doing with Sara."

"Does Marcy even believe in the supernatural?" Jack asked.

"Now that is a really good question," I said. "She attended séances here in the past. We need a certain level of belief for this to work."

Gillian nodded. "If she's a skeptic, this won't work. She seems pretty hard-nosed to me."

"She knows she's the granddaughter of Mary Ann and she told me that this should have been her house so she must know Doris' story. That might be the chink in her armor. It's possible we might get some information about Doris' murder."

"Let's not forget our goal here, Cass," Jack said.

"You're right," I said. "We need to spend some time trying to restore the loft to its previous séance setup. We'll need Dave for that. Also, maybe if Dave attends, Marcy will feel more comfortable about coming."

"Even if George weren't superstitious," Jack said, "I don't think it would be a good idea to invite a cop. That would pour cold water over any chances we have of getting a confession."

Gillian agreed. "This has to be spooky and otherworldly. It has to be effective. We'll only get one shot at this."

I thought about George. He couldn't be part of this because he was a cop but also because of his fear of ghosts. I had no idea how he would react when I finally told him about Doris. Her prize for leaving him alone until I was ready to tell him would be the fun she could have with Marcy at the séance.

"We need Dave, Marcy, Sara, Jack, Gillian, myself, Doris, and Thor in the room. Everyone except Doris and Thor is known even if slightly to Marcy. She should be completely comfortable and feel in control. Nothing will happen unless she's confident." I took a deep breath.

"Okay, let's get this show on the road." Gillian clapped her hands.

****

It was nearly midnight. The loft was perfect. The multi-colored, gauzy scarves adorned the lamps in the far corners. Pillar candles sat on the turned wooden stands. Drapes covered my personal belongings that were pushed up against the walls. Pillows, beanbags, and rugs were spread in a circle around the Ouija board that was placed on a low table in the center of the room with a few candles and some incense.

Thoris was ready and sat in a corner of the room. Most of the participants didn't know about our secret weapon. She'd be inhabiting Thor until she manifested. We wanted a few people to know so that they could calm anyone who freaked out, but we also wanted some genuine surprise. Marcy was bound to be suspicious. I was shaky and trying to remember to breathe deeply. So much was riding on this. I wanted justice for Alan, Sara, Samantha, and Mia. I also wanted to avoid being stabbed in the dark by Marcy. There was a reason I put ambient light in the corners of the room. I had pepper spray in my pocket.

The doorbell rang, and I nearly peed my pants. Gillian would be letting people in downstairs and directing them up here. Deep breath. Deep breath.

Sara's head came up through the loft entrance. She paused and looked around. "Very nice." Then she came all the way up.

"Thanks for doing this, Sara."

"I want to know the truth."

"No matter what happens, just let it happen. Oh, by the way, I'll be recording the séance so that we can replay it and discuss it afterward. Any problem with that?"

"Not at all."

"Have a seat anywhere in the circle. There's a bottle of water next to each seat if you need it."

Sara smiled but continued to stand next to me.

I heard a knock followed by Dave's deep voice. Then I heard Marcy's strong voice greeting Dave. That was it. They were all here, and we would begin soon.

Marcy's laugh preceded her up the stairs. She hoisted herself up through the opening and turned to Dave. "Need a hand?"

"Nope. I'm fine."

"Take your places anywhere in the circle," I said. "By the way, I'll be recording the séance so that we can all review it and discuss it later."

"Cool." Dave sat down near the window, folding himself gracefully onto the large red satin pillow.

Marcy plopped down on the green corduroy beanbag next to him. She didn't give explicit consent, but she also hadn't objected to being recorded.

Dave said, "I'm glad you're restarting this tradition."

Jack and Gillian came up through the opening. Marcy patted the cushion next to her and looked at Sara. With a quick glance at me that I was sure Marcy saw, Sara walked slowly over to Marcy and sat down next to her. I sat next to Sara on her other side and saw the frown on Marcy's face. Jack sat next to me followed by Gillian on his other side. I used the remote to lower the lights as Gillian lit the remaining candles inside the circle.

"I think we're ready to begin. Turn off your cell phones. Does anyone need to use the bathroom? No? Okay." I'd read up on séances and had a long, oblique talk with Dave about what went on at those earlier séances. My thinking was that I wanted to make Marcy's experience here as familiar as I could until she was relaxed. I kept my voice low and mellow. "We must all have open minds and welcoming hearts. We want our compatriots no longer in the flesh to feel at home and communicate with us. Let your every day worries fade away and focus on breaking down barriers and preconceptions." I paused and waited for the rustling of shifting bodies to settle down. "Please remember that we are unlikely to get clear answers to our questions. You may only get a feeling."

Gillian leaned forward and lit the sandalwood incense.

"You may get an impression. I hope we experience a physical manifestation, but we are here to support one another. We are sitting close together so that we may use the Ouija board. Sometimes yes or no questions are the best way to get clear answers."

Some people shifted so that they would be able to reach the planchette.

"I'm not a medium, but I have some sensitivity to the spirits."

Marcy and Dave shifted.

"I could have hired a professional medium, but I thought inviting a stranger in might be more disruptive. More than anything, we want a warm, supportive atmosphere here. Let's open with an invitation." I bowed my head and closed my eyes. "May we all be safe in this circle of friends and like-minded people. May any who have gone before us into the great adventure of the next plane of existence now join us to provide us with their wisdom and knowledge." I looked up and spread my hands to either side. "Let us now close the circle and connect our energy into a ring of power."

Everyone clasped hands around the circle, and a tremor of anticipation passed through the group.

"Is anyone here?"

Nothing.

"Please join us whether you are known to us or not. We welcome you. Is there anyone here who is attached to this house? This place?"

A breeze passed through the room, the scarves on the lamps moved, and the candle flames flickered, causing the dim light to play across the walls and ceiling. Gasps echoed around the group.

I nodded. "Thank you for joining us. Do you have a message for someone in this gathering?"

We heard an audible sigh. As if on cue, Gillian gasped. Then the planchette moved of its own accord to "Yes."

"With whom do you wish to communicate?"

An exhalation of breath from everywhere and nowhere seemed to form the word "you."

It was so effective that I jerked, and I felt other tugs on my hands. "Do not break the circle," I intoned somberly. "What is your message?"

Another exhalation of breath. And then: "Beware…you…danger…" The words were breathy and indistinct as if it took great effort.

"What danger?" I said.

But there was nothing. It was as if all the energy had left the room.

Marcy said, "I think that's it."

"No, no, wait!" Sara cried. "Alan? Alan? Are you there?"

Marcy visibly stiffened and hissed. "Sara! No!"

"Alan?"

I said, "Alan, if you're there, please move the planchette."

It was as if the room had been reenergized. The planchette moved slowly and jerkily toward "yes."

"Oh, Alan. I knew you'd want to contact me."

Marcy stood up.

"No, Marcy! You broke the circle," Sara cried.

A wind whipped around the room. The scarves shimmied on the lamps, and two candles went out. Marcy turned toward the circular staircase. We all turned toward her and saw the mist hovering over the opening. Several of us gasped, and Marcy froze where she stood.

The mist advanced slowly toward her. She backed up, and others scrambled out of the way. The circle was broken, but everyone was transfixed as the mist began to take shape. The wavering figure of a slender man formed.

"Get away from me! You're dead!"

The ghost silently raised an arm and pointed at Marcy.

"Out of my way!" she cried.

But the ghost moved toward her.

She backed up. Dave dodged and Marcy fell over his pillow and landed on her back.

Now the ghost was hovering over her. "Yo—"

"This is a trick. You're using a projection."

My heart sank at her skepticism. An unearthly wail came from nowhere and everywhere. The ghost—all pale and white—started to solidify and look a lot more like Alan. Its mouth distended as if its jaw had become unhinged, and it looked as though it might swallow Marcy. She crawled backwards. Then two holes appeared in the ghost's neck, and red blood dripped from the wounds.

"Help me!" Marcy cried.

Everyone backed away from her.

"We can't help you unless you tell us the truth," Jack said. "Did you kill Alan? Is that why he's after you?"

"No!" she screamed.

The ghost stuck a hand through her chest. I knew what that felt like. Her scream was pure terror. "Yes, yes! Help me! Protect me!"

Jack pulled out a cross and moved toward Alan's ghost, who wavered back into a less solid form and moved a little distance away from Marcy.

"Did you attack Samantha?" he asked Marcy.

"No!"

Alan's ghost thickened and menaced Jack.

Jack gripped the cross with both hands. "I—I don't think I can hold him off much longer."

"Okay. Okay. It was all self-defense." Marcy held her hands up in front of her face as if to ward off Alan's ghost.

"He's pressing me hard." Jack twisted the cross back and forth as if he were fighting a powerful force.

"He was threatening me just the way he is now. He was destroying my life. He threatened to take Sara away after I moved back here. I couldn't let him do that. He was cruel and uncaring to Sara. He didn't deserve her. Sara!"

Sara was crying softly.

"Let me go to her," Marcy said. "She needs me."

"Why Samantha?" Jack asked.

Marcy snorted. "She attacked me. I was just defending myself."

"How did she attack you?"

"I was righting a wrong and getting rid of someone who threatened Sara."

Sara sobbed.

Marcy tried to push around Jack. "Please let me go to her."

Alan's ghost howled.

Marcy pulled back. "That little bitch who claimed to be Alan's daughter. She would have hurt Sara. She would have stolen Sara's inheritance. I had to set things right."

Sara was suddenly silent.

"I had her in my sights when Samantha walked down the hill and nearly caught me. I lost my chance to get rid of the threat, but I made sure that Samantha would never get in my way again. These people don't have the right to ruin my plans, my life. I have the right to protect myself and Sara. Sara was stolen from me years ago, but now's our time. Now we can be together."

"Why did you damage this cottage?" Jack asked.

"Your sister is such a bitch. Sticking her nose in where it doesn't belong. This place should have been mine."

"Alan's ghost" surged toward Marcy again and I wondered if Marcy had pushed Doris a little too far. Jack looked at me. I nodded. We needed to end this, and I didn't think we were going to get anything more. There was no weapon to find and I didn't think Marcy would believe that Alan didn't know what she'd

303

stabbed him in the neck with. I also didn't think that any of this was evidence, but it might provide a chink in Marcy's armor that would help the cops build a case against her.

Somewhat anticlimactically, I said, "I think this brings our séance to a close. I thank the spirits who have joined us this night. Everyone is now free to go back to their own realms and homes. Thank you all for your participation."

Marcy looked at me as though I had a screw loose. Alan's ghost faded away. I knew she was back in Thor. Jack pocketed his crucifix. Gillian blew out the remainder of the candles and turned up the lights.

"You are all crazy," Marcy said. "Sara, come with me."

Sara shook her head.

"Please!" Marcy held out a hand.

Sara moved further away from her. Marcy's lips thinned, but she gave up and practically ran down the steps and out into the night. I heard sounds downstairs, and then Ricardo came up the stairs and joined us.

"Did you get it?"

Ricardo nodded. "All recorded."

Dave stood up. "You do a great séance, Cass."

"Glad you liked it."

"Invite me any time." He made his way downstairs and left.

Gillian went over to Sara, sat down next to her, and talked to her softly. Doris released Thor. She'd done an excellent job studying pictures and videos of Alan so that she could emulate him in wispy, ghostly form. She scared the pants off me, and I knew what was going on.

"Let's go downstairs and talk," I said.

Gillian went straight to the kitchen for some wine and beer and glasses. I thought something stiffer might be needed. With Marcy and Dave gone, our party consisted of myself, Jack and Gillian, Ricardo, and Sara, with Doris a silent and invisible party. I wondered where Mia was.

"I should be going, too," Sara said.

"How are you doing, Sara?" I asked.

"I'm not really sure." She dabbed at her eyes. "I don't think I really understand. Marcy. She's always been very kind and gentle with me. I had no idea she loved me like that. She never liked Alan, but I never would have believed that she'd kill him."

I looked over her head at Gillian who nodded and handed Sara a glass of wine.

"Sara, Mia Jamison is most probably your daughter, the one Marcy was talking about. I know this is a shock, and you should really have DNA tests done to confirm it, but we're as certain as we can be."

She was silent a moment and then looked at us with hopeful eyes. "Mia's my daughter?" Her eyes darted back and forth between me and Gillian. "No, that's not possible." Sara looked down at her glass. "Cass, my parents will be arriving very soon."

"Is that a good thing or a bad thing?" I asked.

"I don't know, but if I call you when they arrive, will you come over? Please?"

I only hesitated a moment, knowing she no longer would rely on Marcy. "Sure. Just give me a call."

Sara got up and gave me a hug. "Thanks."

"What are friends for. Please be careful. We don't know what Marcy may do."

"Thanks." Then she was gone.

I turned to Gillian. "I hope that was the right thing to do."

"We couldn't leave her hanging after talking about Alan's child in the séance. She's got a lot of stuff to process. Having a daughter will help her get through all the transitions," Gillian said.

"*If* they get along, and that's a big if. It could lead to a lot more heartbreak if they don't," Jack said.

Ricardo cleared his throat.

"Oh, sorry, Ricardo. How is Mia dealing with this?"

"It was more than she could handle. She's out in the car. She's confused. I'll take her home. She needs some time to process all this."

I nodded. "Good point. There's something else. Marcy mentioned trying to hurt Mia when she was talking about attacking Samantha. She said she had Mia 'in her sights.' That made me think of a gun. Can you keep Mia with you until we find out what the police are going to do?"

"I plan to."

My cell rang. "Hello? Oh, hi, Samantha. No…I… Yes, absolutely. Next time." I hung up.

"What does she need?" Ricardo asked.

"She called to complain that she wasn't invited to our séance."

Ricardo laughed. "That's my boss. Mia's waiting for me. I'm going to take off."

"See you later."

I called George. "Did you get the video I sent?" I held the phone away from my ear. I think everyone could hear George yelling at me. "Okay." I hung up and went to the door to let George in.

The first words out of his mouth were: "You are an idiot." Then he turned to the rest of the group. "We have surveillance on Mia and Sara and you, Cass. If Marcy makes a move on any of you, we'll have her."

"Sara's parents are expected any time now." I pointed out.

George ground his teeth. "You realize you provoked a possible murderer and only got a video that will probably not be admissible evidence."

Before I could say anything, the phone rang.

"Saved by the bell." I looked at the readout. "It's Sara." I answered. "Hello?"

"Cass?" The voice was barely a whisper, but I knew it was Sara's.

"Hey, Sara. Are they there so soon or is it something else?"

"They're here."

"Don't worry. I'm on my way."

"Thanks!" she said breathlessly.

I hung up. "Sara's parents are at her place already. I need to go provide moral support."

"Let me drive you," George said solemnly. "I'll be outside if you need me."

"Works for me." I looked at his face set in hard lines. "I think."

Chapter 22

George dropped me off in front of the house that had high peaked roofs and shake shingle siding in weathered gray. The overcast sky and low marine layer reflected my own concerned thoughts for Sara. The fine mist felt like tears on my cheeks.

"Sara!" I greeted her with an encouraging smile when she came to the door.

"Come in and meet my parents."

Her house was warm, so I took off my jacket and draped it over her hall bench.

She led me into her living room. Andrea Peterman was ensconced on the couch among the pink pillow cushions with a delicate saucer in her left hand and a bone china cup halfway to her lips. She was a tiny woman in a beige wool and silk suit with a string of perfect pearls around her neck. The family resemblance was obvious, but where Sara was robust and rounded, her mother was delicate and angular.

Bob Peterman, by contrast, was dark and square. He looked like a substantial man; he could have been built of bricks. There was nothing soft about him, but he set aside his cup and saucer and rose as I entered the room. Excellent manners.

Sara's mother set the cup and saucer down with slow, controlled movements.

Her father extended his hand. "We understand that

you're Sara's friend."

"That's right," I said, shaking his hand. "Cass Peake. I'm pleased to meet you both."

"We're glad to hear it. Sara needs friends." He looked at her meaningfully.

Sara cast her gaze downward.

"Come. Sit down near me." Andrea patted the couch cushion next to her.

I had a strong desire to sit somewhere else, but that wouldn't have helped Sara. I sat where I was told, and Andrea gave me three fingers, which I grasped briefly in a parody of a handshake.

"I hope the traffic wasn't bad," I said.

"Getting over the hill can be a bit of a trial during tourist season," Sara's mother said. "I can't imagine what Sara sees in this…quaint little town. We think she should move back down where her friends and family are. If there's a tsunami, surely this place will be wiped off the map."

There. It was out in the open. They wanted my help to persuade Sara to go home. Their weapons were fear and disdain.

"I'm sure it would take some time to close out Alan's business." I looked at Sara. "If Sara's planning to close the store. As for this being a quaint little town, that's what gives it its cachet, judging by the real estate prices." I smiled.

Andrea pursed her lips. Sara opened her mouth, but her mother cut her off. "Real estate prices notwithstanding, my daughter is not a shopkeeper. Of course, she'll come home."

"My little girl needs rest," Bob said. "We just want to see that she gets it." He smiled. "What she needs is a little pampering."

"Don't you think she'd be more comfortable in familiar surroundings?"

"What could be more familiar than her own room? She needs taking care of," Andrea said.

"We'll all come over to help her, bring her meals, and chat," I countered.

"We have servants who'll take care of her every need," Bob said.

"Yes, but—"

"You simply don't understand," said Andrea.

"I understand. I disagree," I said.

"I'm sorry you feel that way," Bob said stiffly.

Andrea picked up her teacup again, and I had the feeling I'd been dismissed. If there was ever going to be a time to get the truth, this was it.

"Excuse me," I said. "There's just one thing. Why did you give Holly up and put her in a foster home? Why didn't you release her for adoption? She would have been desirable as a healthy baby."

Andrea dropped her saucer, which broke neatly into two halves as it hit the edge of the coffee table.

"I beg your pardon?" Bob said.

"I understand that Mia Jamison is Sara and Alan's natural daughter—your grandchild. Since they married anyway, I wondered why you gave Sara's child up and lied to her?" I was only going to get one shot at this, so I decided to go for the gold. "Did you intentionally want to prevent her from being adopted?"

Bob stood. "I was mistaken. You are no friend of Sara's."

Again, I was being dismissed. I had an answer from Marcy, but I wanted to hear it from them. He was probably quite angry that I didn't have the good manners to take the hint and leave.

"It's because I'm Sara's friend that I've worked so hard to get to the bottom of this. You keep talking about her needs, her safety, her need for pampering, but where were you when she was pregnant? That's when she needed you. Sara will never be free or happy until she can put together all the pieces of her life."

Andrea said, "She can do that back home where she belongs."

"One of the pieces is her child." I looked at her. "She belongs here with her friends where she's made a life for herself."

Bob snorted. "She has no life here. At home she'll have everything she needs."

"Her child?" I asked.

Bob's eyes narrowed, and he pursed his lips so hard they turned white. "That 'child' isn't Sara's. Sara doesn't know her. Who knows how she was raised? What bad habits she has?"

"You do," I said. "You picked her foster family."

Sara took a deep breath. "Daddy—?"

"Sara, your mother and I will handle this."

Sara wilted. She looked down. Her shoulders drooped. Her spine curved as she slumped.

"You raised one child. Why not another?"

"For that reason," Andrea said. "We'd already raised one child. It was not easy."

"Okay, so then you didn't have to raise her. Sara and Alan would have."

Bob sighed. "Alan didn't want a child."

"You could have fooled me," I said. "He was only too happy to acknowledge her, support her."

"She was an adult by then. He told us he had no interest in raising a baby. He worked with us to place the baby."

He couldn't even call her by name. "So why did he marry Sara? More to the point, why didn't you try to prevent it?"

The Petermans exchanged a look. Then Andrea spoke. "He was blackmailing us."

"Blackmailing you?" Sara shook her head. "Not Alan."

"How do you think he could afford that store that never made any money? And the boat? And this house?"

"It was all a lie?" Sara said. "My whole life?" Sara's chin came up, and I liked the spark I saw in her eyes. "Why did you lie to me? Mother? Daddy?"

A little late maybe, but Sara was leaving home.

"Sara, don't speak to your mother that way."

Sara turned to her mother. "She's blonde, too, you know. She bleaches it out to platinum, but she's a natural blonde. She's fragile like you, Mother. She has your cheekbones, but she has my eyes although they're green instead of blue."

Startled, I thought about Mia's eyes and then Sara's. Sara was right. Mia's eyes were bright and round. I'd never noticed.

"Sara. Dearest."

"No, Mother. I don't know if Holly… Mia will even talk to me, but I want to try."

"Sara, dear, there's no need. Your daughter's a grown woman now. She doesn't need a mother." Sara's mother's voice rose to a shrill note.

"We all need a mother. I needed one who'd look

out for me, tell me the truth, stand by me no matter what, and help me learn to survive on my own."

At least her mother had the good grace to blush.

"Sara, everything we did, we did for you so that you could finally be happy. Alan could never have made you happy," her father said.

"How do you know what would make me happy? You've never asked me." Sara was a little slow to process, but I saw the horror spreading across her face. "Daddy?" She stood up. "What else did you do?"

Bob's face hardened, but her mother broke down. "We had a lovely talk with your old roommate. Your life was being ruined by that man. Marcy was happy to help with our little problem."

"I forbid this." Bob bellowed at them both. "Not another word until we've spoken to our lawyer."

I took two steps backward. They'd orchestrated Alan's murder. The adrenaline turned my blood to ice and I was profoundly grateful that George was outside. I didn't care how mad he was at me. Bob put a hand on Andrea's shoulder, and she sat up straighter and composed herself.

Sara looked back and forth between them. "You always told me that I had disrupted your lives. I always felt in the way. Why didn't you just leave me alone with my baby? All I wanted were parents who would love me, who would let me know that I was important to them. I intend to do that for my daughter—if she'll let me."

"Let's go ask her," I said, standing up.

Sara's smile was brilliant.

"Sara," her father said. "I forbid it."

"Goodbye, Daddy."

I drove Sara's car to Ricardo's apartment near Clouston College. Sara was shaking so badly that, had she driven, we'd have been killed. I caught sight of George in the review mirror as he tailed us.

"Sara," I said as I pulled into a visitor's spot and turned off the engine, "Before we go up, it occurs to me that those things in Alan's safe might be mementos of Mia's childhood. We know now that Alan was aware of her, so maybe he'd kept tabs on her for her whole life. Don't hate him for that. But you have her now."

She smiled. "Thanks, Cass. I feel as though I've missed so much."

"Look at it this way; you didn't have to deal with the terrible twos or the middle school years."

Sara gave a watery laugh.

"C'mon. Let's get you started on building new memories with your daughter." We walked up to the second floor, and I knocked on the door.

Ricardo answered but only opened the door a crack. Then he caught sight of Sara and opened the door.

"Hi, Ricardo. We've come to talk to you and Mia."

Before he could say anything, I heard running feet and someone wrenched the door from his hand.

"Come in."

"Sara's parents just confessed to putting her child in private fostering. Given that you've already had a DNA test with Alan, I suspect very strongly that you're that child although Sara should have a DNA test to make sure. You should know that they took her child away from Sara at birth and arranged for private foster care. They told Sara that you, Holly, her baby, had died at birth. They lied to her."

Sara edged around me and entered the room, walking toward Mia. "Your name is Holly. Did you know that? I picked out your name months before you were born." She walked closer to Mia, who hesitated. "I used to play classical music to you before you were born. I wanted you to be so smart."

"Ricardo, Mia only got half of the information off the Internet because only Alan's name was on the private fostering paperwork. They bought him off originally, Sara's parents. Sara never knew. But then Alan blackmailed them. It's why Alan always had so much money and did so well in a low-margin business like book sales," I said.

Sara started to talk again but had to clear her throat before continuing. "Mia, they drugged me. They told me you were born dead. They wouldn't let me see you. They had a funeral. They gave me your ashes to scatter."

The horror of Sara's last statement registered on Mia's face. "A-ashes? They gave you m-my ashes? That's so cruel." She stared at Sara as though she'd never seen her before. "Are you really my mom?"

"You're my baby. I'm sure of it. I don't need a test." Sara took the final step that closed the distance between them and put her arms around Mia. "My baby."

They both started crying.

"Baby, my baby," she repeated. "I never even saw you." Sara clung to her as if she'd never let her go.

Mia sobbed into Sara's shoulder. "I thought there was no way to find you since my f-father died."

"Sshh, Sweetheart. Everything will be okay now. You can come live with me. Would you like that?"

Mia cried harder.

"Wow," said Ricardo.

"Funny how that word sums it up," I said. "Will you guys be all right tonight? I've got to get home."

Sara gave me a sodden smile. "If Mia wants, she can move in right now." She turned to her. "Any room you want."

"Thanks. I'd like that." Mia smiled.

I handed Ricardo Sara's car keys and opened the door to leave. "Sara, what will you and Mia do now?"

"I don't know. We'll have to talk…like a family." She smiled. "Whatever we do, we'll make the decision together."

****

I walked out to the street. George pulled up. I got in.

George pulled away from the curb and drove to my house in silence.

When we got there, I said quietly, "Will you please come in?"

He still looked grim, but he turned off the engine and followed me in. Jack and Gillian were fixing food in the kitchen. Jack took one look at George and poured him two fingers of Glenfiddich.

"What happened?" Jack said.

"We dropped Sara off at Ricardo's. She and Mia are getting to know one another," I said.

Jack shook his head. "That's good, but it's not what I meant. At Sara's what happened?"

"Her parents are not exactly sympathetic people. They really should never have had a child much less a grandchild. Mia is pretty remarkable given the circumstances. What are you making?" I said.

"Didn't you just have tea or something with the parents?" Jack asked.

"Not really. I never got to eat anything." I eyed his sandwich.

With a sigh, Jack passed me his ham and cheese.

"Thanks!" I took a huge bite and closed my eyes. "Mmm."

"Lemonade?" Gillian handed me a glass. "Anything for you, George?"

"Any roast beef?"

Jack handed him a beer. "Sure."

I opened my eyes. "Sorry George, about the whole evening. We learned a lot."

"Hmph. No evidence." He took a bite out of his sandwich.

"I appreciated the protection," I said.

"It's my job." But George's voice was a bit less harsh, and the muscles around his mouth relaxed.

"When I first moved here, I thought Marcy was the only sane person in town. Everyone kept talking about ghosts except her."

Jack said, "She had the calm, no-nonsense certainty that one always associates with heroes. We naturally turned to her in crisis. She seemed to know what was going on."

"That's because she orchestrated most of it," George said.

"I still don't understand. Sorry, but these were her friends, people she'd been doing business with for years." I carried my plate and glass to the table. "Let's sit down if we're all going to eat. There are some leftover beans in the fridge."

Gillian got them out and microwaved them. George

sat next to me. I bumped his shoulder with mine.

He shook his head. "You are a major pain in the ass."

"I know, but you care about me, anyway."

He shook his head again, but he was smiling. "You might as well tell us what you found out."

I put my sandwich down, swallowed, and wiped my mouth with a napkin. "Alan couldn't tell Sara that Mia was their daughter because it would reveal his complicity in the scheme, not because he'd had an extramarital affair but because he'd colluded with her parents and then blackmailed them. And Brendan!"

"Yeah. Brendan doesn't realize how close he came to being framed for murder." George shook his head. "Brendan may be a scholar and a writer, but he should definitely give up on breaking and entering. Not his best skill set."

I smiled. "Poor guy. I think he enjoyed skulking around. Hey, it all turned out in the end. We got his web site up and running and they decided not to press charges against him. He's very repentant."

But George shook his head. "Howland is dead, Mia was in danger, you were frightened half to death, and Samantha was badly beaten. We know who the bad guys are but the evidence is a web of circumstance and hearsay."

I knew what he meant.

"She gets that look, too," Gillian said.

"Huh?" I said.

Gillian was staring at me. "You get that look that Jack gets."

"Genetics," George said.

"Don't tell me I look like my *sister*!"

But I was thinking. Something was still bothering me.

George's cell phone rang. "Excuse me." He walked out to the kitchen to get some privacy.

George walked back in a few minutes later. "You don't. I'm going to have to go in a few minutes."

"Another murder?" Jack asked.

"The same one. We asked Sara's parents to come in for an interview concerning their relationship with Alan since they were in town. They've lawyered up."

"They said that Marcy helped them with their little problem. I got the impression that they talked to her about getting rid of their blackmailer."

"Thanks for the information. We'll look for proof of blackmail." George walked to the door, and I followed him.

Neither Jack nor Gillian followed us out. We didn't say anything until we'd reached his car.

"George—"

He cut me off with a big hug. "It was great seeing you again. I didn't realize how much I'd missed you."

A big lump formed in my throat, and I couldn't speak.

"We live in the same town now." He patted me on the back and let go.

"What was that?" I said indignantly.

"What?"

"You patted me on the back."

"Yeah?"

"You dismissed me."

He laughed. "No, no. I would never dismiss you, Cass. I know better." Then he bent and kissed me on the end of my nose.

"That was romantic," I said sarcastically.

"I was going for sweet."

I grabbed him by the lapels. He didn't put up any resistance as I pulled him toward me and kissed him. A real kiss. I reached up and ran my fingers through his hair as we explored each other.

"I really have to go, and I can't look as though I've been making out in the back of a car." But he kissed me again and only reluctantly let me go.

I took an unsteady step backwards when he released me.

He grinned as he got in his car and drove away.

I stood in my driveway until his taillights disappeared. Then I turned and sniffed the ocean breeze. I'd been a fool all those years ago. This time I wasn't letting go.

I smiled as I walked slowly back to the house. I was growing to love evenings on the coast. Summer nights the fog is soft gray kitten fur. Summer nights I would enjoy walking with George on the beach.

Thor greeted me at the door and followed me silently as I walked around the house, bolting the doors and windows and turning on the exterior security lights.

Jack and Gillian were clearing up the dishes.

"Nice to see George again," Jack said.

"Mmm hmm."

They excused themselves and went to bed early. I suspected they were as tired as I was. They'd leave tomorrow, and I still felt guilty over keeping them so long, but I was so glad they'd been here. Plopping down on the couch, I let out my breath in a rush and then breathed in deeply. My head fell back against the couch cushions, and I shut my eyes. I felt a tentative paw on my leg, so I half-opened one eye.

Thor was slowly climbing into my lap.

I didn't want to move suddenly and scare him, so I waited until he was almost settled. Then I petted him and told him what a pretty boy he was. He purred, and I rolled him over on his back and stroked his belly. His purring grew louder, and his eyes started to close.

"Thanks, Thor, and when you've had enough of this, I think a little tuna juice is in order."

As Thor fell asleep, I reached over to the folder of notes for Alan's book that was sitting on the end table and thumbed through the pages, trying to figure out what was nagging at me.

I looked through all the pictures again, taking care to look at all the details. Then I started in on Alan's book notes. By the third page, I realized something I hadn't seen before. It was subtle, but Marcy must have been his main informant. There were notes on strange goings on at the bungalow. He'd made notes on the inside of the cottage and included information about Mary Ann that painted her in a favorable light as an innocent, but that ran counter to the information Doris had given us. I started to skim and stopped myself. I really needed to go over everything carefully.

I picked up a paper-clipped sheaf of typed pages of notes I hadn't looked at before because I had the handwritten notes and thought they were redundant. I unclipped them, turning each over slowly.

And there it was: a Xerox of a marriage certificate for Mary Ann and Donald Pierpont, Doris' father. The tumblers fell into place, and the key to both murders turned in the lock.

****

I was waiting for Jack and Gillian when they came down the next morning. I'd made fresh coffee. I had Alan's book notes in a pile in front of me on the table.

"You're up early." Jack yawned.

"And dressed," Gillian said.

"There were still a few things that bothered me. I had a nagging feeling about Alan's book. Why was he writing about Doris? Just seemed odd. Reading over his notes again, I realized that it was his relationship with Marcy that put him on his fatal path. He became obsessed with the stories she told him—from her grandmother's point of view—of the murders and the bungalow. As he researched, he realized that the story was cockeyed."

Jack poured some coffee and sat down.

"It's really the Snow White story. We had Mary Ann pegged as a mistress, but Alan had a copy of a marriage certificate in his file, showing that she actually married Doris' father, becoming Doris' stepmother. Wicked stepmother. She was jealous of Doris and also coveted the estate, which meant, if she was to inherit, Doris would have to go."

Gillian, who'd been leaning over Jack's shoulder, jumped when Doris popped in.

"Doris!" I said. "You nearly gave me a heart attack."

"Mary Ann was married to my father?"

I nodded. "Once married, she seduced Big Al and cajoled him into murdering you to get you out of the line of inheritance."

"Wait," Jack said. "We shouldn't tell her everything yet."

"Why not?" Doris asked.

"What if you go into the light?" Gillian asked.

"Isn't that what we want? For Doris to be happy? To move on?" I said.

"All I'm saying," Gillian said, "Is, are you both sure that's what you want?"

I thought for a moment. "We should get dressed and invite everyone Doris wants over. Then we can say goodbye, and I'll finish telling the story."

****

Mina, Dave, Ricardo, Mia, Jack, Gillian, and I were all gathered in my living room, sitting on the couch, various chairs and ottomans, and in the case of Ricardo and Mia, on the floor.

I called out, "Doris? Are you here?"

The air in the doorway to the kitchen shimmered.

I saw it out of the corner of my eye. "C'mon, Doris. Everyone you wanted is here. We want the opportunity to make sure we've solved this to your satisfaction and to say goodbye because we will all miss you when you go into the light."

Doris materialized, but she wasn't her usual spunky self. Opalescent tears rolled down her pale cheeks. "I don't want to go."

"Oh, I know. I don't want you to go," I said. "I wish I could hug you, Doris."

Doris vanished and Thoris jumped into my lap. I squeezed her until she squeaked. Then everyone else hugged, petted, and fussed over her. When Doris rematerialized, Thor indignantly stalked off to the kitchen to give himself a bath.

Doris stood straight in the middle of the group and looked at everyone. Then she said, "All right. I'm ready now."

"Okay," I said. "We have Alan's book notes here. We looked through them before, but now I think we have the pieces of the puzzle we need. Alan seems to have first gotten interested in Doris' story when Marcy told him her version of her grandmother Mary Ann Deluria's history. He figured out that the story was skewed in Mary Ann's favor, so when he started writing his book, he tried to correct the record. Marcy's motivation for murdering him wasn't entirely her love for Sara. It was less altruistic. She was very interested in suppressing the story of her grandmother's murder of Doris, which Alan was going to reveal in his book."

Mina nodded, and Ricardo put his arm around Mia.

"We had Mary Ann pegged as Doris' father's mistress, but they were married." I passed around the copy of the marriage certificate. "Doris stood in Mary Ann's way to inherit. She had to go. Mary Ann seduced Big Al and convinced him to get rid of his boss' daughter. No one realized that Lem had proposed to Doris, and they were shocked when Lem attacked Big Al, trying to save Doris."

Doris sobbed but stifled it quickly.

"After they bribed the police to find Doris and Lem and officially declare them dead, they called her father and made his murder look like suicide in grief over his daughter. Mary Ann inherited everything. Then Big Al found out she was pregnant, and he wasn't sure if it was his or his former boss'. He exploded in a jealous rage, frightening Mary Ann, who didn't really need him anymore, anyway."

"What happened to Big Al?" Jack asked.

"He seems to have faded into obscurity. I couldn't find anything more on him in Alan's notes or in any

Internet search. I don't have enough information on him to go into a genealogy site to go through census info or death records. If he moved, he may be harder to find."

Jack shrugged. "I suppose it doesn't matter, but I'd like to know if the law ever caught up to him."

"Alan clearly felt the police had been bribed, so my guess is no. Mary Ann coveted this bungalow even though Doris' mother Shelagh owned it outright. If she thought Doris' death on the beach in front of the cottage would drive Shelagh away, she was mistaken. Shelagh was pregnant with Doris' sister Francie, who would inherit the cottage. Francie couldn't inherit Don Pierpont's estate. Shelagh put the car in the garage and kept Doris' engagement ring. We found it where she left it. Mary Ann must have talked to a lawyer about settling the estate before leaving town. But leave it she did to escape Big Al. She raised her daughter on the story told from her point of view about how she'd been done out of much she should have had, including Shelagh's bungalow, which she was sure Shelagh had finagled away from Don, which explains why Marcy was so interested in it. Mary Ann always intended to come back."

"Do we know whether Marcy is Doris' niece or the granddaughter of Big Al Hanrahan?" Gillian asked.

"No idea," I said.

Dave broke his silence. "I know Shelagh's daughter Francie. I'm sure she knows the whole story, but she has dementia. It's part of why I paid the taxes on the place. I always hoped she'd come back. Her memories were pretty untrustworthy in general, so I didn't believe a lot of what she said until you moved in, Cass, and people started dying again. Her published stories were pretty wild, and she had a vivid imagination."

"We'll probably never know everything, but I'm changing the locks now that I know how many keys might still be out there. Every member of the writing group had a key."

The group lapsed into silence.

"I think that's it. It's all I have. Is that everything you wanted to know, Doris? Are you satisfied?"

Doris tensed, nodded, and squeezed her eyes shut, bracing for the unknown. Everyone held their breath.

Nothing happened.

Doris opened one eye. "I'm still here."

"Maybe you were expecting more information?" I ventured.

"I know how I died and now I know who did it and why." She stamped her foot. "I should be going to my reward!"

Leave it to Doris to be annoyed when she got her wish but not what she expected.

"Maybe it's because you didn't hang around as a ghost but were conjured up in a séance."

As Doris vanished, I yelled, "I'm glad you're still my roommate!"

"Hmph!" echoed around the living room.

****

I walked along the beach at twilight, a furry shadow at my heels. The air was already sharpening with the loss of the sun's light.

Jack and Gillian were safely at home. Sara and her daughter had found each other although neither had spoken to Sara's parents after their confession. Forgiveness would take a while. Dave's place was dark as deep space, and I suspected he'd forgotten all the excitement on the beach and was partying in the City as he'd said. Brendan had his books, Althea's collection, a new web site, and his father despite their relationship. And George… I'd just have to wait and see how that played out.

What, in the end, did Sara's parents gain from all their machinations? Everything they'd done was now undone, and they'd lost, perhaps forever, the opportunity to be part of their granddaughter's life. Perhaps that was too harsh. A judgment. You could never tell where forgiveness might lead.

And then there was Marcy. Her cold-bloodedness still shocked me. I'd trusted her. If it hadn't been for Doris…

As I approached the house, the shadow of a woman flickered at the window. I smiled. Doris was still watching out for me.

A word from the author...

I currently live in Cape May County in New Jersey after spending years in the San Francisco Bay Area with my Maine Coon cats Sierra and Ginger.

I attended Clarion Writers Workshop for Science Fiction and Fantasy at Michigan State University and sold a story I wrote there to Damon Knight for The Clarion Awards anthology.

I wrote technical manuals in Silicon Valley and also published several poems and science articles as well as a couple of chapters in *Research & Professional Resources in Children's Literature: Piecing a Patchwork Quilt*. I've also taught English in high school and community colleges.

Thank you for purchasing
this publication of The Wild Rose Press, Inc.

If you enjoyed the story, we would appreciate your
letting others know by leaving a review.

For other wonderful stories,
please visit our on-line bookstore at
www.thewildrosepress.com.

For questions or more information
contact us at
info@thewildrosepress.com.

The Wild Rose Press, Inc.
www.thewildrosepress.com

Stay current with The Wild Rose Press, Inc.

Like us on Facebook

https://www.facebook.com/TheWildRosePress

And Follow us on Twitter
https://twitter.com/WildRosePress